HALF
HUMAN

Pressman
House

By

Stan McMurtry

Pressman House

© Copyright 2023 Stan McMurtry

All rights reserved

ISBN: 978-1-915657-46-6
(Also available as an eBook ISBN 978-1-915657-47-3)

A CIP catalogue record for this book
is available from the British Library

MMXXIII

Published by
Pressman House Publishing Ltd.
Boston, Lincs, PE20 3BT
England +44 (0)1296 695 588
www.pressman-house.co.uk

For the McMurtrys, the Robinson's the Birches and Subly.

Publisher's note

Fergus Munroe was a well-known cartoonist
whose work appeared in the Daily Mail
newspaper from 1968 until 2002.
His death has never been fully explained but this
version of events which led up to his demise,
written by hand and printed here, was
discovered by his daughter, Karen, when she
was sorting out her father's belongings. The
police claim that Mr. Munroe's story
was concocted while the balance of his mind
was disturbed but Karen who witnessed some of
the events described in his manuscript swears
that every word is accurate and true. There are
no chapter headings.
This is exactly as it was found.

I have to get my story down on paper before it's too late. If I die no one will ever know the truth. There have been so many killings, so many innocents slaughtered and I have a strong premonition that I will be next. Oh God. If only the police would listen. Only a short time ago I was an optimistic and happy individual without a care in the world but no longer. Now I spend my days filled with dread. I'm scared, really scared. Not about heart attacks, dementia or any age-related ailment that might see me off. No, this thing that's turned me into a nervous wreck is evil, scarcely believable and has no rational explanation. I've never been a religious man and always remained sceptical about life after death, ghosts, faith healers, mediums and the like until well into middle age when my tunnel vision of the world changed dramatically. The curtains opened and I knew for certain that there is another existence running parallel to ours, a different dimension perhaps, or maybe it could be called a supernatural time warp. Who knows?

I am now sixty-four years old, but describing the events that took place nearly two decades ago is where I want to start the narrative. To explain how it all began. To tell the world the truth about all the deaths and how my life was turned completely up-side-down, plunging from dizzy sublime heights to the depths of despair. I will try here to recollect as best I can what happened from the beginning right up to the present day and I'll start with the sublime.

Back then I was a middle-aged man on the verge of a divorce with two grown-up children and living in a London flat that I'd rented from a friend. I was working for a national newspaper as its social and political cartoonist, commentating on whatever the day's news was and trying to prick the pomposity of the great and the good whilst hoping that I was doing it in an amusing way, although I recall that at the time being amusing was difficult because I was at a pretty low ebb, devastated that a twenty year old marriage had deteriorated into dullness and mediocrity, worried that my children would turn against me and financially strapped by the divorce settlement with its monthly maintenance payments. I was feeling quite sorry for myself, sitting most nights on my own with a tasteless ready cooked meal on my lap, watching rubbish on TV or writing gloomy self-obsessed poems about how badly life was treating me.

Then one day unexpectedly and completely out of the blue, fortune smiled down and my life turned around. I met Jenny.

Think of Romeo and Juliet, Anthony and Cleopatra, Napoleon and Josephine, romantic fairy tales and princesses kissing frogs. Our meeting was all of those things, and I was the lucky frog.

One of my colleagues on the paper was celebrating his fiftieth birthday at his large flat in Putney. He was our show-biz editor and consequently the place was packed with celebrities and fellow journalists all standing elbow to elbow in small tight groups whilst waiters struggled through the throng offering drinks and tiny squares of food on trays. A quartet of musicians crammed into one corner of the room battled manfully against the non-stop wall of human sound and I started to wish that I hadn't bothered to come. This was not my scene. It was altogether far too loud and crowded for a hermit like me. I decided to have just one more drink then scuttle back to my flat to feel sorry for myself again.

Standing on a slightly raised part of the floor where the covered up dishes of a buffet would be served later on in the evening, I got a full view of the gathering below. A blur of grey suits and bright dresses all trying to out-shout each other. I groaned and made a beeline for the door. The noise was deafening then a crash of glass and a roar of approval from the crowd made me glance back. An unfortunate waiter had dropped a tray of glasses and people were standing back to let the poor man clean up the mess.

I owe that man a lot because that's when I saw her. She was small with a cascade of light brown hair flowing down almost to her waist. Maybe it was the bright emerald green dress she was wearing but she dazzled anyway and would have stood out from the crowd whatever she had on as though picked out by a spotlight. I was transfixed. Everyone else in the room had mysteriously vanished and I could only see her. In my whole life I had never felt such an attraction. It held me rooted to the spot staring open mouthed and goggle-eyed like a fish out of water. It felt to me that I'd somehow wandered onto the set of 'South Pacific'.

Some enchanted evening
You may see a stranger
You may see a stranger
Across a crowded room ...

All at once an invisible line had been cast across the space between us and it was pulling at me, hooking me like a fish to her side. She was talking to a tall man with ginger hair who stood by her side then she turned and caught me staring at her. For a long moment she held my gaze before turning quickly away again with a slight tilt of the head and her nose in the air.

It was a rabbit in the headlights situation. I was usually fairly shy and unsure of myself, a child of strict parents who had taught me not to stare, but stare I did. I couldn't help myself. I expect my mouth was open and maybe I was even dribbling. I don't know. This was all new to me.

After a few seconds she glanced my way again, smiled briefly, then repeated that toss of the heard and tilt of the nose. The air somehow crackled. There was definitely some kind of frisson going on. At least there was on my part. I wanted to charge across the room, pushing other guests to one side so that I could speak to her.

> *... and somehow you know*
> *You know even then*
> *That somehow you'll meet her*
> *Again and again*

I decided a more subtle approach would be more acceptable so started winding my way through the crowd. There were lots of people there that I knew so accordingly I had to stop on my way to engage in party gossip for as short a time as was polite and acceptable until at last I was only a couple of yards away, my mind racing about how I could start a conversation with her and reasoning that it was probably not a good idea to begin with "Now look here. I think you're gorgeous and I want to discuss our future together," besides which she had her arm linked under the elbow of the tall ginger haired man who was probably her husband. She solved my dilemma.

"Hello," she said, turning to face me, "you're Fergus aren't you?"

"Yes," I said trying to look as though this was the first time I'd looked her way. "How do you know?"

"I asked our host," she smiled.

I smiled back. Things were looking up.

"I like your work," she said. "I always buy the Mail."

"I'm flattered," I said. "Are you in the newspaper business?"

"Gosh, no." She laughed. "I'm not that clever. I'm here with Keith." She turned to her ginger haired companion.

"Keith, this is Gus, the cartoonist."

"Hi," he said enthusiastically in a very Etonian upper class voice. "How nice to meet you. I'm quite a fan."

"Thanks."

"Keith's a writer, my cousin and my best mate," she said as I tried to stifle a sigh of relief. "… and I'm Jennifer." We shook hands.

"A would-be writer," Keith tutted. "Can't find an agent who's willing to take on an unknown. Beats me how anyone ever gets started, bit of a closed shop if you ask me."

"You'll get there one day," Jennifer said giving his arm a squeeze. He sighed manfully then went into great detail about the novel he'd written concerning the turbulent love life of a homosexual butler working at Buckingham Palace then without drawing breath, went onto the mess the present government was making of the economy and finally finishing his monologue with the despair he felt watching his once pure white hydrangeas turn slowly into a nasty shade of purple. I thought he was incredibly pompous and was glad when he turned his attention to the lack of waiters in our area and offered to go and get us some drinks.

"Thanks," I said. "Just a beer please."

"Jenny?"

"Yes please," she said and handed him her empty wine glass.

He disappeared into the crowd. I noticed she wasn't wearing a ring.

"Do you live in London, Jennifer?" I asked, suddenly at a loss for anything interesting to say.

"No, Suffolk. I'm down here helping Keith move into his new flat in Baron's Court."

"Ah. I thought I detected a slight accent."

"Is it that obvious?"

Close up she was even more beautiful than I had first thought. She had a way of looking down shyly then glancing up as she finished a sentence with the greenest eyes I'd ever seen. There was the slightest of gaps between her two front teeth and her face had the healthy glow of someone who spent a lot of time in the open air. I was smitten. A few yards away cousin Keith was edging his way slowly through the jostling guests clutching my bottle of beer and two glasses of wine, so I decided not to beat about the bush.

Then fly to her side
and make her your own
or all through your life
you may dream alone.

"Look," I said, "Your cousin's nearly here. I'm not normally this forward but I'd love to see you again. Will you have lunch with me tomorrow?" She looked up at me in surprise. "Gosh," she said laughing. "You must be the famous Speedy Gonzales." Keith was almost upon us. I didn't say anything I just stared at her willing her to make the right answer.

All too quickly he arrived. "Here we are folks," he said. "One bottle of beer and one glass of dry white." Jennifer took the drinks from him. "Thanks, Keith," she said. "Well done. You didn't spill a drop." She turned, put them down on a nearby table, fished in her tiny handbag, drew out a tissue, dabbed her nose then handed the bottle to me along with a small white card with her name and telephone number printed on it. And that's how it started. I was completely and utterly head over heels like a lovesick teenager. When we did meet for our first lunch date I was in such a state of nerves I couldn't eat. Until we met again I couldn't sleep. I felt that my innards were being stretched by piano wire. Until then I didn't know it was possible to fall in love so deeply or so completely. She was on my mind every second of the day. When we spoke on the phone I found myself kissing the receiver. 'For God's sake' I told myself. 'Pull yourself together!' but I couldn't. I was a lost man and it was painful.

We met several times during the next few days, mostly in restaurants or cafes and occasionally just for walks. I learnt that she was five years younger than me, was the oldest of six children and that she was divorced and had a son serving in the merchant navy. Apparently, cousin Keith would not have approved if he'd known that she was seeing a married man so I never got invited to the flat she was sharing with him. He thought she was visiting a girlfriend.

Then calamity! Two short weeks later as we were strolling along the riverside in Battersea Park she broke the news that I had been expecting but dreading. She'd finished helping her cousin in his new home and was going back to Suffolk. I felt wretched. It was like losing a limb. How could I cope with her being so distant? Suffolk seemed a million miles away.

"Aw, c'mon," she said seeing my downcast face. "You'll get by. I'll come down as often as possible by train and maybe we'll get together again."

"Maybe?"

"Well, how do I know? You might make it up with your wife."

"That's not going to happen, Jenny."

"Look," she said, putting her hand on my shoulder, "I have become very fond of you, Gus Munroe, but I'm not really comfortable you being married and all. I feel like I'm a marriage breaker. Do you understand?"

"You know I've applied for a divorce."

She nodded. "Let me know when it happens."

Two days later she was on the A12 heading for the flat she shared with a girlfriend on the outskirts of Ipswich. I felt abandoned and completely lost. I convinced myself that she was bound to meet someone else now that we were so far apart. How could she not with her looks? Men surely would be buzzing around her like the proverbial honeypot. I lasted without her for about ten days mooching around my flat trying hard to get her out of my mind, phoning her every day and enduring sleepless nights. What a wet wimp I truly was. Then on that tenth day I received a document through the post that made me get in the car and drive up to Suffolk. I booked into a beautiful old pub in the centre of a small village called Pin Mill on the banks of the river Orwell, then I rang Jennifer from my room. Her friend answered and I heard her call "Hey, Jen. It's some bloke for you."

"Who is it?"

"Says his name is Fergus."

"Oh, right. Hang on." A few seconds went by before she came on the line and said slightly breathlessly, "Hi Gus. An afternoon call. What's up?"

"I am."

"What?"

"Up," I said. "I'm here in Suffolk"

"Wow. Where are you?"

"A little place called Pin Mill."

"I know it. A lovely spot ... but why though?"

"Why else? I've come to see you. Can you come over?" There was a pause and she said,

"Oh, Meghan and I had arranged to go to the cinema … hang on a sec …" I heard a muffled conversation then she was back with "I'll be there in an hour. Where are you?"

"It's a pub called the Butt and Oyster."

"My favourite pub," she said. "Don't get drunk before I get there."

I unpacked my few belongings and sat beside the window. Pin Mill was truly a delightful place. Outside were old barges moored on the water, swans drifted up and down and a lone fisherman was sitting contentedly puffing at a pipe in small boat on the far bank. I went downstairs and booked a table for two in the tiny restaurant come bar before putting on my coat and going outside to wait. Forty-five minutes later Jenny was in my arms. She was wearing a black turtleneck sweater under a leather jacket, light blue jeans tucked into knee length leather boots and a huge excited smile on her face. She looked absolutely stunning.

"Well. This is an unexpected surprise," she said.

"I had to see you," I answered. "Got some news this morning that I want to share with you."

"You're pregnant," she said.
"Nope."
"You're having a sex change?"

"Nope."

"Give me a clue then!" She said digging me in the ribs.

"Well, you're cousin Keith doesn't have to worry about you hanging around with a married man any more." She stared up at me with a puzzled expression, then her eyes widened. "Your divorce came through?"

"You've got it. I'm now a bachelor again. Look out Girls. Fergus Munroe is on the loose." She took my hand and led me to a bench on the waterside. We sat down. "That's great news," she said, "but how do you feel? It was twenty years wasn't it?"

"Twenty one," I said. "Yes, it does feel a bit strange. Very sad really, the death of a marriage. My ex-wife is a lovely woman and I wish her well and hope we can still be good friends. She agrees that what we're doing is best. There was nothing left for us."

Jenny leant forward and kissed me gently on the lips. "She must be bonkers to let you go," she whispered. "Y'know Gus, I've missed you so much since I came back to Suffolk but I had to be sure you weren't just having a casual flirtation. You do understand, don't you?"

I nodded.

"I wasn't completely sure of my feelings but as soon as I saw you a few minutes ago I knew for certain that I'd fallen in love with you."

"I knew I had as soon as I saw you at that party."

She laughed and shook her head. "I never expected this to happen."

I put my arms around her. "Nor me," I said. "… but I'm so glad it did."

We kissed. Not in that desperate and hungry way often seen in films, but gently, softly and full of a joy and meaning that I'd never experienced before. My head was buzzing and when we stopped for breath, I found myself unable to speak. We just clung together looking into each other's eyes. Eventually Jenny broke the silence and said in a whisper, "Have you got a room?"

I leant forward and kissed her forehead, took her by the hand and we walked into the pub.

One month after the best weekend of my life Jenny left her home in Suffolk and moved in to my rented flat with me. We lived together for six glorious months before we tied the knot at the Chelsea registry office. There were eleven guests. My two children, Jenny's parents, her son, cousin Keith, my two sisters, her friend Meghan and my oldest pal Charles, who I'd been friends with since primary school accompanied by his wife,

Gail. I couldn't believe my luck. How could such an exquisite creature like Jennifer fall for someone the likes of me? I felt as though I'd become a character in a Mills & Boone novel or perhaps I'd died and had gone to heaven. We stayed in the flat for two more months until we could find a place of our own. I couldn't afford to buy anything lavish while I was still paying maintenance to my first wife plus college fees for my two children. Jenny had neither savings nor a job but eventually we found a very small detached cottage that was for sale in a small village called Monk's Green near Plaxtol in Kent. It was dilapidated and in need of a great deal of care and attention so was extremely cheap. The garden was a mess of tangled undergrowth and weeds. An old battered caravan peeped out from piles of corrugated iron sheets and baulks of rotten timber, bits of pipe and an old porcelain sink were just visible under a web of deadly nightshade which lay like a green duvet over everything.

The house itself was over four hundred years old with three tiny bedrooms, a bathroom, a living room with a rather impressive inglenook fireplace and a minute kitchen. The structure was sound but I guessed that most of the wooden doors, cabinets and shelves were only standing upright because the woodworm were all holding hands. The house faced directly on to a small lane but the rear of the building looked over open fields on the other side of which was about two or three hundred acres of dense woodland.

The village had a small shop at the end of the lane and a delightful pub at the other. Those two clinched the deal. We decided that this derelict wreck was absolutely beautiful and the ideal place for us.

The next few months were hard work for both of us but full of happiness. Once I'd completed my drawing for the next days' paper we set about the many tasks which were urgently needed to make the place habitable. Jenny was a keen gardener so while she struggled with the weeds I tackled the interior, pulling out all the old rotten woodwork, painting, hammering and patching, laying new electricity wiring, installing a new kitchen and often working late into the night. It was tiring, but working as a team to transform the crumbling ruin we'd bought into a comfortable home brought us even closer together.

Quite often we'd decide after a hard day's work to go down to the pub and have a few drinks with the locals before retiring then amazingly once we were in bed together the tiredness would disappear as if by magic and we'd make love.

Looking back I think that was the happiest period of my life. I was in a state of high euphoria most of the time and I think she was too. I wanted to touch her, hold her, be with her every moment of the day. She was like a magnet drawing me in. I would have done anything for her. Life was so good I was in constant dread that it wouldn't last, that the bubble of sheer rapture would burst and we'd end up like other couples I'd known, bored with each other, the relationship gone stale.

We bought a dog. A tiny West Highland terrier. He was a snowball on legs with two bits of coal for eyes who decided that the whole cottage was one big toilet built especially for him. So we named him Puta which was an affectionate abbreviation for Pain Up The Arse.

Gradually the cottage began to take shape and as it did we started to get a constant flow of visitors. Jenny's parents came down from Suffolk, my children took turns to arrive without warning usually clutching bottles of wine or bunches of flowers and Jenny's son, Marvin, would pop in when he was on leave from the merchant navy. We all got on well together so harmony reigned.

One night Jenny and I were sitting at the old trestle table in the saloon bar of the pub. Marvin, her son, had been with us for most of the afternoon, had joined us later for some pub grub together with just one drink then left to go back to his ship. It was late September and the lovely hot days of summer were rapidly changing into damp and chilly ones. For the first time that year the landlord had lit a fire in the big inglenook and the place had taken on a cheery glow. Two local men with ruddy faces wearing overalls and wellington boots were playing darts on the other side of the room. A young couple sat on stools at the bar and a man of about sixty sat clutching his pint at the end of our table. I knew his face well although we'd never spoken. He seemed to be part of the furniture of the pub, a permanent fixture always occupying the same end of the bench nearest the fireplace. At his feet lay something that looked like a rolled up rug but when the man leant down and put a crisp into one end it turned out to be a dog. After a while he shuffled along the bench towards us, cleared his throat and said, "S'cuse me, but are you the new people at Chart Cottage?" I said that we were

"How's it going?" he asked. "You're certainly doin' a find job in the garden. T'was a nightmare before."

I pointed at Jenny. "This is my wife, Jennifer. She's the head gardener."

"Hi," Jenny said. He held out his hand and shook hers. "Hello, my dear. My name's Ted. I hope you both like living in our village.

Nobody thought anyone was goin' to take that place on. T'was in such a state."

"It's been hard work but we're getting there," she said, then added, "… and we love living here."

"Had it been empty for long?" I asked.

"Oh for quite a long time. Old chap was the last one. Became a bit of a recluse. Had a son what lived in a caravan at the back. He was a bit simple, poor lad. Became a bit too much for his dad. He couldn't cope so the lad had to be taken into care."

"Have you lived here long, Ted?" Jenny asked.

"Ooh, about thirty years now. Came down from Reading when I left the army. I was in bomb disposal. I used to do odd jobs for folk around here. Carpentry, plumbing, mendin' fences. That kind of thing."

"We could've done with you in the cottage," I said. "My carpentry doesn't bear too close a look." He laughed. "Nor would mine now. Got too much rheumatism."

"Where do you live, Ted?"

"At the end of the lane next to McSweeneys."

"McSweeneys?"

"Aye. The shop. 'Aven't you been in yet?" He gave another crisp to the rug under the table then said, "Where d'you get your groceries and stuff?"

"Supermarket in Sevenoaks," Jenny replied.

"Ah," he said. "You keep doin' that an' we'll likely lose the shop."

"How come?" I glanced at Jenny

He gave a despairing gesture. "Well, they can't compete against the big boys. Can't sell their stuff as cheap. I've been trying to drum up support for them all around these parts an' it's starting to work. Folks don't want to lose the place it seems." He paused and shook his head. "Damned shame if it were to go. The McSweeneys have been part of the village nigh on fifty years."

"Well we don't want it to go either. I have to admit we haven't set foot in the place yet, but count us in. We'll use it as much as we can." I picked up his empty glass. "… and we want to support retired carpenters too. Can I get you another pint?"

*****

Next morning after breakfast, I decided to go and do my bit for McSweeneys. We needed some milk and a few other items so I strolled down the lane taking my time to admire the many charming cottages along the way. Most of them were a lot bigger than the one we lived in and I noticed the many Jaguars and Bentleys parked in the driveways. McSweeneys shop was part of a really ancient building that leant at an alarming angle over the pavement. It was the kind of place that you'd find a picture of on a box of chocolates. Lots of beams and crooked doors. There were hanging baskets on either side of the entrance with colourful plants just about clinging on before the onset of winter and half on and half off the narrow pavement was an old stone horse trough full of shrubs that I couldn't identify.

The shop itself was crammed with every conceivable product anyone would ever care to buy. Kettles and pots hung down from the ceiling, the floor was a clutter of boxes, sacks of vegetables and large metal containers filled with pieces of kindling wood ready for the colder weather. Along one wall was a large refrigerated unit containing milk, sliced meat and other edibles. The place had so much stock it would have been difficult to get more than six people in the shop at the same time.

Mrs McSweeney was a round ball of a woman, probably in her late sixties. She was about five foot tall and would have been the same height if she'd been lying down. She had rosy red cheeks and a frizz of white curly hair. She peered at me over a pair of rimless glasses. "Good morning," she said in a broad Scottish accent. "What can I get for ye?"

I was about to answer but she carried on. "Oh, you'll be the new man in Chart Cottage."

"Yes. That's me and you must be Mrs McSweeney."

"Uh huh," she said. "Welcome to the village."

"Thanks. We've been here a while now. Sorry we haven't been in till now."

"Aw. Don't worry. It's nice tae meet ye. How's it going? I hear you're doing wonders renovating the old place."

"Yes. It's hard work. We're doing most of it ourselves but its gradually becoming part of this century."

"Aye. Such a shame it was allowed to get into such a state. You were brave to take it on."

"I'm enjoying it. It's a challenge. Did you know the previous owner?"

She smiled. "Uh huh. His name was Gregory. He was a wee bit difficult to get to know. The old man kept himself to himself. Ye very rarely saw him. He'd stick a bit of paper through our letter box with a list of things he wanted. My husband Ted used to deliver whatever it was to his house together with the bill and the next time he called there'd be an envelope wi' the money in it at the back door."

"Someone told me he had a son," I said.

Mrs McSweeney gave a big sigh. "Aye. Poor laddie. He was fine up until he was a teenager. A bright wee fellow. But something happened. I don't know what but suddenly he became not quite right in the head. Went completely off the rails, turned into a half-wit dribbling and screaming and refusing to live in the house anymore. His father Gregory had tae buy an old caravan and the boy lived in it out in the back garden. I think in the end he was taken into care."

"That's so sad," I said.

She nodded. "Och, I'm sorry. What a gloomy story to be going on about. Can I get anything for you?"

I bought some eggs, a couple of newspapers and a few other bits and pieces then just as I was leaving she said, "Ye know you have a ghost?"

"A ghost?"

"Uh huh. A friendly ghost though. Doesn't do any harm. Way, way back the old man told my mother who used to run this place before me that he sometimes heard footsteps when he was alone in the house."

I laughed. "Well, thanks for cheering me up."

Her expression turned to a worried look. "Och," she said. "Don't take any notice of me. I'm a bit of a joker. There's no ghost. I'm winding you up. Just pulling your leg."

I smiled and held up my hand to reassure her that I wasn't worried. "Did you say your husband's name is Ted?"

"Aye," she said. "You bought him a pint last night."

Jenny was in the kitchen when I got back. She laughed when I told her that Ted had been drumming up customers for his own business. I described Mrs McSweeney and the shop then said in my best Scot's accent "… and did you know we've got a wee ghostie?"

Just as I said that there was a loud crash from behind us. We both jumped in alarm. A heavy china casserole dish had fallen from a high shelf on the other side of the room and smashed into pieces on the tiled floor. Strangely, it hadn't just toppled downwards. Instead it seemed to have swept quite a few feet from its resting place as though something was saying, "Yes, here I am!"

"Well, hello Ghostie," said Jenny.

I spent the rest of the morning working on next day's cartoon and in the afternoon Jenny travelled with me to drop it off at the office. Afterwards we did a bit of shopping near Fleet

Street, popped into a busy wine bar, had a delicious omelette washed down by a very nice glass of Chablis then drove slowly home stopping once at one of the many stalls selling vegetables by the side of the road. A delightful part of living in Kent, the Garden of England.

We decided not to do any more DIY jobs on the cottage with what was left of the day and instead snuggled down on the settee together with a giant sized pack of crisps and a couple of beers to watch TV.

I remember we were watching a detective series called, "The Sweeney", a very popular show at the time but I must have been either bored or tired because I nodded off. I don't know how long I'd been asleep before I was woken by Jenny shaking my knee and whispering, "Fergus, wake up … wake up, Fergus."

I blinked, rubbed my eyes and said, "What's the matter?" She leaned forward and switched the TV off. Puta was at the foot of the stairs growling. His hackles were raised and Jenny had her finger to her lips. "Listen," she said pointing to the ceiling. I listened but could hear nothing. I looked at her and shrugged. She held up her hand to stop me speaking and continued to stare upwards. A few seconds went by then I heard it. Something was moving upstairs in the corridor that led to the three small bedrooms.

This passageway stretched the whole length of the cottage, not a great distance but it went from one end to the other. What we heard was a dragging noise as if something heavy was being pulled along the wooden floor. Not a continuous sound. It paused occasionally for a moment or two then resumed until it had travelled the whole length of the corridor. Then it stopped. We waited, both staring upwards at the ceiling, scarcely able to breathe then Jenny whispered, "What the hell was that?"

"I don't know," I said and fairly sprinted through the kitchen, past Puta and up the narrow stairs to the corridor. It was empty but there was a strange musty smell that I couldn't identify. I walked slowly along peering into each of the bedrooms expecting at any moment to be confronted by a burglar who'd somehow entered the house. But there was nothing. The upstairs area was completely empty. All the windows were closed, there was no way anyone could have got in apart from up the stairs so whatever it was hadn't had time to leave the same way as it had entered. I looked closely at the wooden floor. There were no scratches on the polished boards or any sign of something being dragged along.

Back downstairs Jenny was standing on exactly the same spot. She had one hand to her mouth and looked scared. "What was it?" she said, still whispering.

"I don't know. There's nothing up there."

"Gus, I'm scared," she said.

I put my arms around her. "Oh, don't be," I said trying my best to be reassuring. "Old houses are always full of strange noises. It's probably the ancient timbers moving because we've put in central heating."

"Mrs McSweeney warned you we had a ghost."

"I know. But she said it was a friendly one."

"She said there were footsteps."

"Well, we didn't hear footsteps did we? It's like I said, just the old floorboards moving about a bit."

She looked up at me with frightened eyes. "Have we any brandy?"

"Yes. Good idea. Let's have a brandy." I looked up at the ceiling and yelled, "Hey, Mr Ghost. We're having a brandy. D'you want one?"

I had to coax Jenny into going to bed that night. She walked slowly along the corridor, clinging to my arm, peering anxiously into every bedroom and insisted that I stay with her until she was tucked up under the covers. For the very first time Puta was allowed upstairs and slept in his basket near the door.

Once in bed we didn't make love but huddled up close and it was a long time before either of us managed to get to sleep.

Three nights later we heard our friendly ghost again. An early warning that it was about to happen was given by Puta who leapt off the settee and rushed to the foot of the stairs growling loudly with the hairs on his back standing to attention.

This time the sound we heard was definitely footsteps together with the slow dragging noise a lame person might make pulling a useless limb across a wooden floor.

I went upstairs to check again but as before the whole upper floor was empty.

Two weeks after that a couple of friends turned up unexpectedly. They'd been on their way home from London and decided to get off the train and pay us a visit. Charles was my oldest pal. He was now a successful doctor with a thriving practice in Tonbridge a few miles away. His wife, Gail, was a very talented and much sought after portrait painter. We persuaded them to stay for supper but just as Jenny was dishing up steaming plates of pasta, Puta gave the alarm once again and we all sat frozen to our seats, staring up at the ceiling, listening to the laboured footsteps from above.

Our friends treated it as a huge joke making lots of oohs and aahs together with comments like "Look out, it's behind you!" and "D'you think it's got its head tucked underneath its arm?"

We laughed along with them for a while then Jenny suddenly snapped, "No, no, no! It's not funny. It's alright for you two, you don't have to live with it." Charles said, "Oops, sorry. You did say it was friendly though." "Friendly or not," Jenny sighed. "I'd rather it wasn't here. I find it very scary." Gail put her hand on Jenny's shoulder. "You're right Jen. I'm sorry. I wouldn't want it in my house either." Jenny shook her head and said, "I hate it. I think I want to move somewhere else." I stared at her. "After all the hard work we've put in doing this place up? You're kidding aren't you?" She looked at me, leant across the table and clutching my hand said, "Somewhere modern. A new build. A home which we don't have to share with an invisible bloody lodger."

"Yeah, who's not paying any rent," Charles chipped in. Jenny frowned at him so he shrugged his shoulders and added, "You could always call in an exorcist. The local vicar would know who to approach."

I was exasperated by the way the conversation was going. "Oy, listen you lot," I said. "Whatever it is up there, it's not doing any harm. It's probably just this old house moving about a bit … but even if it is a ghost, it's friendly. Nobody's getting hurt."

"Hmm," Jenny said. "Not so far."

"The previous owner lived here for years. It didn't spook him into leaving."

"It spooked his son. He went bonkers and had to live in a caravan outside."

"That was probably nothing to do with ghosts. The lad was obviously unwell anyway."

"Fergus is right," Charles said. "Whatever it is hasn't harmed anyone. I suggest you treat the whole thing in a lighthearted manner. Why don't you give it a name? What's a good name for a ghost?"

"Creepy," Gail suggested.

"Rodney," said Charles.

Jenny cheered up a little. "Gordon," she said.

Charles laughed. "Gordon the ghost. That's good. I like it."

"All agreed?" I asked.

"All agreed."

I looked up at the ceiling and bellowed, "Did you hear that, Gordon? Now be a good boy or we'll fetch the vicar!" Gordon didn't reply.

Instead there was a loud banging on the front door. We all jumped. Gail gave a little scream and dropped her glass. A faint voice from outside shouted, "Taxi." We all looked at each other and let our breaths go at the same time then laughed with relief.

Charles looked at his watch. "Sorry folks. My fault. It's our taxi. We'll just catch the ten thirty to Tonbridge. Time to go Gail and leave these two in peace."

"These three," she said.

They thanked us for supper and climbed into the cab. "Night, night Jenny," Charles called from the open window. "Night Fergus … Night Gordon!" Then they drove off down the lane.

Afterwards when we were stacking the dishwasher with crockery and glasses I asked Jenny if she had been serious about wanting to move. She nodded. "I'm sorry," she said coming up close to me and clasping her hands behind my neck. "I love this place. I really do. It's been such fun turning it into a proper home, but it does scare me. I find myself getting tensed up every evening waiting for the noise upstairs to happen. I can't relax, can't concentrate without keeping one ear cocked. Do you understand?"

I nodded and was about to reply but she carried on. "I'm not sleeping well either. Often when you're in dreamland, I'm wide-awake listing for the slightest creak, imagining that I can feel a presence in the room."

"I'm sorry, darling girl. I had no idea," I said.

"Don't hate me."

"How could I hate you?" I smiled. "I want you to be happy, so let's do a deal. I reckon that in about a month's time I'll be finished with all the renovations. The cottage will be done and dusted. It'll be a lot more sellable then and we should get much more money for it. I promise that we'll put it on the market as soon as I'm finished." I gave her a hug. "Deal?" She took a while to reply then said, "Promise?"

"I promise."

"Okay. Deal."

*****

Somehow I carried on with the work on the house but with a lot less enthusiasm. I'd been genuinely surprised when Jenny had said she wanted to move and also by finding just how scared she had been for such a long time before telling me. I have to admit I was bitterly disappointed. After all I'd put my heart and soul into making the old house into a place to be proud of. I could have lived with our ghost. It seemed harmless and I truly loved living in the place. However I couldn't force Jenny to love it like I did and I certainly didn't want it to spoil our relationship, so a move seemed to be the only solution.

Two weeks after making that promise I made a surprise discovery. I was working on the smallest of the bedrooms replacing planks of broken timber and insulating the roof with rolls of yellow fibre glass. The room was too small to accommodate a decent sized bed so my plan was to turn in into my own private study with a fold-up drawing board and lots of shelves to house sketch pads, boards and other art materials. Unnecessary of course if we were leaving but I was determined to follow through with my original design no matter what. I think I was also hoping that against all the odds Jenny might change her mind.

This small room had been wallpapered so many times over the past years that just by hacking it off seemed to make it into a much larger space. It wasn't just paper, there were also layers of thick plaster rammed into cracks and smeared on the walls which looked to have been applied with the finesse and skill of a blind and drunk chimpanzee. Once I'd stripped it all off I discovered underneath the chimp's handiwork a small area of wall where the sloping ceiling met the floor. Vertical planks had been built to cut off the unusable angle. I saw that if I removed them it would give me at least another two foot of extra room to store my materials. I took a heavy screwdriver, wedged it between the planks and started to lever them off the wooden beam behind. Surprisingly the middle plank was not nailed on at all, it was merely held in place by the ones on either side. I moved it away and took hold of the next one but as I was about to wrench it off the beam I noticed something in the dark recess. Crouching forward I peered into the hole I'd made. A bulky object covered in dust and bits of plaster lay in the small space I'd revealed. It looked like a wooden drawer. My heart started to beat faster with excitement. I reached forward to pick it up, tipping it slightly so that it could come through the gap. It was indeed a drawer. Flat like those often built into the top of antique writing desks. At one end was a brass metal handle and under the layer of dust I could see that sheets of paperwork lay under what looked like a child's doll. Placing the drawer gently on the floor I blew most of the dust away. The doll appeared to be made from an old sock. It had only one eye which was a brass button. Long yellow wool had been sewn to the head to serve as hair and a curve of red paint completed the rest of a smiling face. A torn lace handkerchief was tied like a shawl around the neck and small pieces of thin rope were stitched on to act as arms and legs.

I took the drawer over to the window to get a better light. Inside was a very battered notebook, lots of yellowed newspaper cuttings and the remains of a leather bound bible. It was in shreds, torn to bits and lying in a neat pile in one corner of the drawer. There was also the stub end of a candle and a tiny glass jar filled with what looked like dried ink. Very carefully I picked up the notebook and opened it to the front page. Judging from the handwriting it was obviously owned by a child of perhaps fourteen or fifteen. A laboriously neat hand written in the formal script style taught in schools at that time, every letter leaning a precise angle to the right. The spelling however was terrible and there were large blotches of ink scattered across each page where her pen had snagged on the paper. Tucked into the margins of each page were some very well drawn and charming pictures of dogs and other animals and between other pages were the sad remains of pressed flowers. I read the first page. It was the kind of narrative you'd expect find in a young girl's diary.

ELIZA CARWRIGHT'S DIARY
PRIVATE
DO NOT READ!

ME AND JOSH HAD ANOTHER TRIP IN THE WOOD.
NOBODY HAS FOUND OUR DEN THANK GOODNESS
AND IT IS NEARLY DONE. WE TOOK BRANCHES
FROM A FUR TREE WHICH WILL MAYKE A FINE
ROOF.

FATHER CAYM BACK FROM WORK IN A FARE
TEMPER. I HERD HIM SHOUTING AT MOTHER. I
HATE IT WHEN HE COMES HOME.

WHO WOULD WANT A BRUTHER LYKE JOSH? HE
HAS PULLED WON EYE OFF DAISY AND IT IS LOST.
MOTHER HAS NOT GOT ANOTHER LYKE IT.

BACK TO THE DEN AFTER I HAVE HELPT MOTHER
WITH THE WASHING.

I smiled to myself. What a find! So exciting to discover something owned so long ago by a previous occupant. I decided not to read any more but to wait till Jen returned from the shops so that we could enjoy reading it together so got on with the work in the bedroom. About an hour later however the phone rang. It was Jenny to say she'd bumped into an old friend and would I mind if she stayed on so that they could have lunch together? I said that was fine by me. She told me there was some ham and a salad in the fridge and that she loved me. Then hung up.

I couldn't wait any longer. Eaten up with curiosity I took the drawer downstairs, poured myself a beer and sat in my favourite armchair under a reading lamp. The newspaper cuttings were fragile and flimsy and threatened to fall apart in my hand so I was especially careful with them.

The first one I read was from a newspaper called "The Kent Bugle". This small excerpt had been encircled in a blue crayon.

A REPORT BY MR CEDRIC ARBUTHNOT

I think of myself as a man of broad mind and liberal values but I felt a profound sense of unease and revulsion when faced by the many grotesques on display when I visited Mr. P T Barnum's travelling fairground show which is now appearing on Morgan's Meadow near Plaxtol. A parade of physical, mental and behavioural rarities presented to a curious public ready to spend their hard earned money gawping at freaks of nature so deformed they deserve our pity, but instead suffer the laughter, derision and intense scrutiny of heartless audiences, complacent smug and consumed with a new found superiority which the poor creatures they mock and stare at have endowed them with.

I looked at the top of the page and saw that this edition was printed on Monday 20th July, 1846. It was interested to read that this show took place in Morgan's Meadow. Amazingly that meadow still exists. No land grabber has built houses on it. It remains a place of natural beauty, an area of about six hundred acres right opposite Mrs McSweeney's shop. A favourite place for locals to walk their dogs. It has public toilets, tennis courts, a children's play area and lots of benches along its pathways. A pretty stream winds its way through trees to one side which eventually ends up as part of the great river Stour and apparently from time to time the meadow is still used for outdoor concerts and sports' events. I picked up another clipping. It was an advert in huge bold type.

<u>COME TO THE GRAND OPENING OF:-</u>
MR P T BARNUM'S TRAVELLING FAIR
AT MORGAN'S MEADOW, PLAXTOL
ON SATURDAY 18TH JULY 1846
AT MIDDAY
"SEE THE EXTRAORDINARY CHIANG
AND ENG
SIAMESE TWINS!"
"MARVEL AT GENERAL TOM THUMB
ONLY
35 INCHES TALL!"

"MEET THE UNBELIEVABLE HAIRY
MARY
FROM BORNEO!"
… AND PREPARE YOURSELF TO BE
HORRIFIED
AND ASTOUNDED BY OUR NEWEST
AND
MOST FRIGHTENING EXHIBIT –
HALF MAN-HALF ANIMAL
THE THERIANTHROPE
BOOK NOW BEFORE IT'S TOO LATE.

I dug out my old encyclopaedia and looked up Therianthrope to learn that Therian is Greek for wild animal and Anthropes means man.

Back to Eliza's notebook. The next page had a drawing of long logs stacked against the trunk of a tree forming an Indian tepee. Green splodges had been painted on top of the construction which I assumed to be the branches of the fir she referred to earlier.

*OUR DEN IS FINISHED AND MOTHER SAYS SHE
WILL GIVE US AN OLD RUG THAT WE CAN USE TO
SIT ON AND SOME CUPS AND PLAYTS SO WE CAN
HAV PIKNIKS FATHER GAYV US TUPPENCE FOR
SWEETS. MAYBE HE IS NOT AS HORID AS I SED*

*TODAY IS BATH DAY. I LYKE IT BECOS AFTER
IT IS DONE WE ALL SMELL CLEAN AND FRESH*

AND THEN WE PUT ON CLEAN CLOTHES. FATHER
WHO IS THE SMELIEST AFTER HIS HARD WORK
GETS IN FIRST THEN MOTHER HEATS UP MORE
WATER AND HAS HER WASH THEN IT IS MY TURN
THEN JOSH
I AM GLAD HE IS LAST BECOS HE PEES IN THE
WATER THROO HIS BOYS THING FATHER CALLS IT
HIS TROUSER WORM – YUCK!

JOSH WANTS TO SLEEP IN THE DEN BUT
FATHER HAS FORBIDEN IT

BAD NEWS AT SCHOOL TODAY MISSES BULLIVANT
TOLD US THAT MARY PEARSON AND HER BROTHER
HAROLD HAV BOTH DYED OF DIPTHEERYA. SHE
SED THEY WER TAKEN TO HEAVEN BY ANGELS I
CRYED BECOS I LYKED MARY A LOT I DID NOT NO
HAROLD

IN 2 WEEKS TIME THERE IS GOING TO BE A
FAYRE AT THE MEADOW. MOTHER SAYS IF I
AM GOOD SHE WILL TAKE ME TO IT.
JOSH CANT GO BECAUSE HE IS TOO YOUNG
I SAW ALFIE TODAY HE GAVE ME AN APPLE

MORE BAD NEWS FATHER HAS STOPPED US GOING.
HE SED THER ARE MORE IMPORTINT THINGS TO
SPEND MONY ON THAN SPEND A HOLE SHILLING
JUST TO LOOK AT FREEKS OF NATCHUR.
I HATE HIM AGEN

The next few pages were full of drawings.
Given her probable age this young lady had been

quite a good artist. Her attention to detail was remarkable. She was particularly good at trees and buildings. One of them was of the front entrance to the school. It showed a high wall with an arched gate over which was engraved in stone the words "Morgan's School". Behind this was a low building with tall windows. Underneath the drawing Eliza had scribbled "MISSUS BULLIVANTS DOMAYN".

She'd also had several attempts to draw a young boy of maybe nine years old. Black tousled hair and dots for eyes. Eliza would have been a great cartoonist I thought.

The school by the way is now a swanky detached house only a hundred yards away from our cottage with a Ferrari parked outside.

WE WENT TO THE PEARSON CHILDRENS FUNERAL TODAY . IF THE ANGELS TOOK THEM AWAY WHAT WOS IN THOSE COFFINS?

IN THE AFTERNOON I SAW ALFIE AGEN HE WAS HELPING HIS FATHER WITH THE COWS HE'S NICE

This was followed by several more pages of drawings, lots of dust from disintegrating flowers and more about the boy called Alfie who apparently was another pupil from the school who she obviously had a bit of a crush on, her young brother Josh developing whooping cough

and her mother teaching her to knit.   Then a
rather sad entry.

FATHER HAS LOST HIS JOB AT THE TIMBER MILL.
THER WAS AN ACCIDENT AND HE HAS BEEN
BLAYMED. WHAT ARE WE TO DO? WE HAVE NO
SAVINGS. I HERD THEM SHOUTING DOWNSTAIRS
MOTHER WAS CRYING AND HE WAS CURSING
TERIBLE WORDS THEN HE SED I WOULD HAVE TO
LEEVE SCHOOL AND GET WORK. OH NO I DON'T
WANT TO WORK IN THE FACTORY IN PLAXTOL
PLEASE GOD DON'T LET THEM MAKE ME GO TO
THE FACTORY.

FATHER HAS PACKED A BAG AND HAS GONE TO
SEEK A JOB HE SAYS HE HAS HERD OF FARMWORK
DOWN NEER TONBRIDGE IT WILL TAYK A HOLE
DAY TO WALK THERE. MOTHER IS GOING TO THE
BIG HOUSE ON THE HILL TO SEE IF THEY WANT
WOSHING DONE OR ANYTHING.

JOSH IS VERY ILL
MISSUS BIRCH FROM ACROSS THE ROAD BANGED
ON OUR DOOR TODAY SHE SED SHE HAD HERD OF
OUR TRUBBLES AND HAD COOKED US A BIG MEAT
PIE ALSO OTHER PEEPLE HAV LEFT VEGITIBLES
AND APPLES ON OUR DOORSTEP.

THE DOCTOR CALLED AND BROT MEDICINE FOR
JOSH. I CANNOT GO INTO SEE HIM COS I MITE
CATCH IT.

I SAW ALFIE TODAY HE SED I HAVE LOVELY EYES

THEN LAFFED BECOS I WAS BLUSHING ALFIES
FATHER WHO WORKS ON A FARM HAS GOT A JOB
COLLECTING THE MONEY WHEN PEOPLE GO TO
THE FAYRE WHAT IS COMING AND ALFIE SED HE
WOOD ASK HIS FATHER TO LOOK THE OTHER WAY
IF ME AND MOTHER WANT TO GO IN. IS THAT
STEELING? I DONOT WANT TO GO TO JAIL SO I WILL
ASK MOTHER

At this point I got an urgent message from my stomach telling me I was hungry. I put the notebook down and went into the kitchen reluctant to tear myself away from this enthralling glimpse into the past and thinking how easy life is now compared with then. Eliza's poor father having to walk miles to find work, the children dying from diphtheria and the dreadful poverty and hardship. Looking around at my newly built kitchen with its electric cooker, the toaster, washing machine, dishwasher and centrally heated radiators I thought how lucky I was to be living in the twentieth century. I opened my shiny new fridge and took out the salad and ham Jenny had left there, poured myself another beer, put everything on a tray and carried it back to my nicely upholstered chair standing on a thick carpet a yard away from a new television set and wondered what that little girl would think if she could see her house now.

The next few pages of her diary spoke of her younger brother's health starting to improve and her mother at last finding a job up at the big house on the hill. I couldn't think where that building could be. There was certainly no house of that description nearby. It was probably miles away and the poor woman had to do what her husband had done. Walk.

A few pages on Eliza writes about pleading with her mother to take her to Barnum's fair, how it would cost nothing because Alfie's dad would let them through the gate and (devious little minx) father would never know because he was still in Tonbridge.

One whole page was taken up with her efforts at persuasion, promising her mother that she'd be a good girl, she'd study hard, help with the housework and never ever to miss Sunday school again. Eventually her mother buckles under the pressure and agrees so long as Eliza will keep to her promises and if Mrs Robinson, their near neighbour, will look after Josh while they are away.

TODAY WAS SO EXCITING. MISSUS ROBINSON TOOK JOSH TO HER HOUSE AND MOTHER AND I WALKED UP THE LANE TO MORGAN'S MEADOW. IT WAS VERY COLD AND A BIG DARK CLOUD WAS COMING TOWARDS US MOTHER LOOKED VERY PRETTY SHE HAD ON HER SUNDAY BEST AND THE

LITTIL VELVET WAYST COAT SHE MADE FROM
THE OLD CURTENS WE WER GIVEN. A LOT OF
PEEPLE WER GOING THE SAME WAY. I HOPED
NOBODY WOULD TELL FATHER THEY HAD SEEN
US THERE. WE GOT TO THE GATE AND ALFIE'S
FATHER PRETENDID TO TAKE MONEY FROM US
HE IS A NICE MAN JUST LIKE ALFIE.

WHEN WE GOT INTO THE MEADOW THERE WAS
LOTSOF TENTS ALL WITH DIFFERINT SHOWS
INSIDE. A MAN ON STILTS WARING A TOP HAT WAS
SHOUTING THROO A CONE SHAPED TUBE – COME
AND SEE HAIRY MARY FROM BORNEO AND SO
WE WENT IN. IT WAS VERY DISAPOYNTING
SURELY EVERYBODY COULD SEE THAT HAIRY
MARY WAS REELY JUST A MONKEY DRESSED
IN WOMEN'S CLOTHES. SHE HAD LONG ARMS
HUGE EARS AND A FALSE HUMAN NOSE WAS
STUK ON THE MIDDEL OF HER FACE. ALSO SHE
MADE MONKEY NOYSES – IT DID NOT FOOL ME
WON BIT.

CHANG AND ENG THE SYAMEES TWINS IN THE
NEXT TENT WERE GOOD BUT THEY LOOKED VERY
SAD. I DON'T THINK THEY WER REELY JOYNED
TOGETHER I THINK THEY WERE JUST SQUEEZED
INTO THE SAME SOOT. BEST OF ALL WOS GENERAL
TOM THUMB. HE IS AN ADULT BUT EVEN SMALLER
THAN ME HE SANG EVERYBODY A SONG IN A
HIGH VOICE AND DID A LITTLE DANCE WITH A
WALKING STICK WHAT WOS BIGGER THAN HE WOS
I LIKED HIM HE MADE ME LAUGH.
WHEN WE GOT OUT ALIFIE WAS STANDING
BY THE TENT WITH A TRAY OF GLASSES FILLED

WITH LEMONAYD. HE WINKED AT ME AND GAVE
US A GLASS EACH BUT DID NOT ASK US FOR ANY
MONEY I THINK I LOVE HIM XXX

This was punctuated by three or four big red hearts drawn in crayon and a sketch of a young lad wearing a flat cap and baggy trousers.

EVERYBODY HAD TO GO HOME ERLY.
THE WETHER ALL OF A SUDDIN TURNED
REELY NASTY. RAIN PORED FROM THE SKY
AND A GRATE WIND BLEW ONE OF THE TENTS
CLEEN OVER. MEN FROM THE FAIR WERE
TRYING TO FIX ROPES TO OTHER TENTS
AND THERE WOS A REEL COMOSHUN. THE
DAY WOS RUINED BUT A DIFERENT MAN AT
THE GATE SED WE COULD SEE THE REST OF
THE SHOW TOMORROW IF THE WETHER
WAS BETTER. WE GOT HOME SOAKED TO THE
SKIN MOTHER LIT A FIRE IN THE GRATE AND
WE CHANGED INTO DRY CLOTHES.

At this point in the notebook two of three pages had been ripped out and when Eliza resumed her narrative it came in short bursts. The writing had changed somehow and was no longer neat and tidy but hurried and sprawling as though she was agitated and no longer able to express herself properly.

I NEVER WANT TO GO TO THE FAIR AGEN.
IT WAS HORRID. WE SHOOD NOT HAVE GONE
BACK. HORRID HORRID HORRID! THE THING
ATACKED MOTHER. IT IS NOT HUMAN
I DON'T KNOW WHAT IT IS OH WHY DID THEY
LET THIS HAPPEN? IT IS VILE! WHAT IS IT?
PLEASE GOD GET RID OF THIS HORRID
CREECHURE.

The writing stopped and a newspaper cutting had been glued to the rest of the page.

PT BARNUM'S FAIR. A DANGER TO THE PUBLIC.
A FURTHER REPORT FROM MR CEDRIC ARBUTHNOT

It is my belief that Mr PT Barnum's menagerie of grotesques now on show at Morgan's Meadow should be closed down completely and forever. I have written previously about my distaste for such displays, relying as they do on the public's curiosity regarding unfortunate fellow humans who have the misfortune to have been born disabled or deformed. However one of Barnum's exhibits goes way beyond these descriptions. Manacled in what I can only describe as a flimsy and totally inadequate cage he has on display a creature that is truly neither man nor beast. Never have I witnessed such a repulsive and terrifying object. I use the term 'object' because surely it is not a species that has either kith or kin? It is not of human kind standing barely five foot high with short stumps for legs under a round flabby body with folds of pink blotchy skin hanging loosely from every part. It has the arms of an ape, long with massive hands adorned with sharp talon like claws and its whole frame is covered with sparse grey hair. Strangest of all is the head which is tiny. There does not appear to be a neck. The head rises between the shoulders like a growth with bulging eyes that are so far apart they appear to be on each side of the head. The mouth is devoid of lips and is a mere slit in the skin like a cut on a melon. When the thing moves around its small enclosure it makes a hoarse repetitive chittering noise, rather similar to the deep cooing of a pigeon.

I studied the creature for a considerable time looking for some kind of artifice or any accoutrements that might have been added to enhance its nightmarish appearance but could find none. This thing is real. God knows what begat a monstrous abomination such as this.

As I surveyed the hideous creature a woman and a young girl pushed their way to the front of the crowd. The creature who had been sitting still for a long time and whose only movement had been with its eyes, all at once came to life. It sat up and sniffed the air like a dog, then it turned and faced the woman, its eyes locked on hers. They stared at each other for several seconds, the low chittering noise suddenly increased in volume till it resembled the harsh cackling laugh of an Australian Kookaburra bird then the beast abruptly lunged forward, thrust a long hairy arm through the bars of its cage, grasped the woman by the throat and pulled her with great force towards itself so that her face collided painfully into the iron bars of its cage. She screamed as did the onlookers and I saw that this freak of nature had broken the manacles on its wrists and had thrust its other giant claw beneath the folds of the woman's skirt. The tent erupted into chaos. People were drawing back and stumbling into one another to get away. Instantly two hirelings of the fair appeared armed with wooden batons and laid about the creature until it released its hold and the poor woman slumped to the ground in a dead faint or unconscious from the collision with the bars of the cage. The child was in a dreadful state, wailing and trembling whilst cradling her mother's bruised head in her arms.

Eventually the crowd was ushered out of the tent. The woman was attended by a doctor and all was peaceful once again. A happy ending to the story but it could have been worse, much worse. The lady could have been killed. I had seen at first hand the remarkable strength of the beast and I shudder to think what might have happened had those two brave guards been unable to save the situation.

Therefore and not for the first time I call upon our new Prime Minister Earl John Russell to prevail and ban voyeuristic and undignified fairs such as these before the inevitable tragedy which lurks in the wings waiting to happen, happens.

****

Just then I heard the sound of car tyres scrunch across the gravel outside and Puta barking excitedly to be home. My Jenny was back. I put the notebook and cuttings into the drawer and carried it upstairs, knowing for sure that little Eliza's account of the past would make Jenny even more determined to move house. I put it back where I'd found it and replaced the wooden plank. Then I returned to the kitchen just before she came through the door like a breath of fresh air, her cheeks glowing and a huge smile on her face.

"Hi," she said, wrapping her arms around my neck. "I've come back to check how the worker is getting on."

I kissed the tip of her nose. "Good lunch?"

"Lovely," she said. "We went to the old barge pub on the river. You'd like it. Food's good, oh and Puta had his first swim."

"Wow that was brave. Must've been freezing."

"Not really brave. He was chasing a duck and fell in, but he did swim a long way for a little fellow."

"How long?"

"At least a yard and a half."

"Impressive."

She stretched up and kissed my chin. "I missed you."

"No you didn't. I bet you forgot all about me."

"Okay. Have it your own way." She took off her coat and hung it on the back of the door.

"Gail sends her love."

I held out the little sock doll I'd found in the recess. "Look what I found."

"Oh wow, that's amazing," she said taking it in her hands. "Where?"

"Under the floorboards upstairs," I lied, "… and this." I held out the small glass jar. "I think it's an inkwell."

"Isn't the doll sweet? Gosh, how old d'you think it is."

"Pretty ancient," I said.

"Some little child from way back." Jenny held it against her cheek. "I wonder why it was hidden." She gave the doll a kiss. "Welcome to the twentieth century," she said. "I christen you Nelson. He only had one eye."

"Oh, it's a boy is it with all that long hair?"

"Most definitely," she said then scooping up Puta in her arms she held the doll aloft and said, "I now have three men in my life."

"And one of them's had a sex change," I said.

"Wrong. Nelson had long hair. Don't argue, it's a boy."

She went upstairs and changed into her gardening clothes. Some grey dungarees over a thick roll-neck sweater. Her hair was tousled and she looked stunning. I resisted the urge to take her in my arms and said, "C'mon, I could do with some fresh air. I'll help you in the garden."

The sun was weak and a chill wind blew white fluffy clouds across the clear blue sky. Jen didn't trust me anywhere near her flower beds so put me to work digging a large area of weedy ground which she intended to make into a vegetable patch. It turned out to be a good day for finding things. First Eliza's notebook, then from the garden I dug up a treasure trove of old Victorian bottles, the wheels of an old pram, a few bones, several tin cans and an ancient stone sink.

Much later we snuggled up on the settee with a bottle of wine and watched an old movie on TV.

That night as we lay in bed Jenny said, "I think there's someone up there watching us."

"Up where?" I said.

"You know. A guardian angel."

"Sorry. I'm not following you.

She tutted and was silent for a while then said, "Until you came along I wasn't really living. Now I feel complete. I'm so happy I could burst. I think someone up there is organising it all.

I turned to her. "I feel the same."

"Don't let's change, Fergus. Let's always stay this way."

I kissed her. "I won't if you don't."

She pulled me to her and I felt her breast rub against my arm, her soft lips against mine and I was immediately aroused. I glanced up at the ceiling. "I hope your guardian angels aren't watching," I said.

Gently and softly we made love. It was always heaven with Jenny. Our bodies moulded together physically and spiritually and it seemed to me that instead of two people we became one. I wanted to absorb her and become part of her, to be joined to her for the rest of my life. Maybe she was right. There was someone up there organising things. A heavenly lonely hearts' club bureau getting people together, matching couples up.

Afterwards Jenny fell into a deep sleep. She'd had a glass of wine with her friend Gail at lunch time and more with me when we were watching television so it was not surprising. I however didn't feel tired, I felt exhilarated. I lay there with my beautiful wife's head on my shoulder staring into the semi darkness and wondering how it was possible that I could be so lucky. I had a great job, some money in the bank, good friends and this exciting, wonderful, ecstatic love life. I pitied every other man in the world. I had it all.

I was so absorbed by my good fortune that at first I didn't hear the noise. Jenny was breathing gently close to my left ear and my mind was elsewhere. It was a soft thump which seemed to come from the passageway beyond the bedroom door. At first I thought I had imagined it. I held my breath and listened … nothing … then it came again. This time the creak of a floorboard and a dragging sound as though something was being pulled along the ground. I'd heard this noise before but only when we were downstairs. This was the first time I'd heard it from the bedroom. Gently I eased Jenny's head back on to the pillow and as quietly as I could got out of bed and felt my way in the darkness across the room, heart thumping hard.

I lifted the latch and eased the door open. The corridor was empty. One of the bedroom doors further along was open and the moonlight coming through from outside was enough for me to see the whole length of the corridor to the stairs at the far end ... total silence ... a few seconds went by then another soft thump followed by the scrape of something heavy. I felt the hairs rise on the back of my neck. Whatever it was was coming along the corridor towards me. Foolishly I felt the urge to cover myself up, to put my pants on. I felt exposed. Instead I stood there naked staring into the dimly lit passage. For a long time there was nothing. It was as though it was waiting. Then it came again, the noise very slowly getting nearer and nearer. I wanted badly to turn, go back into the bedroom and shut the door but I stood my ground, scared stiff and determined not to move. I waited frozen to the spot until this invisible thing was directly in front of me. Its presence was almost tangible. I felt sure that if I reached out I would be able to feel it, to touch a face or an arm but instead I could only stand unable to breathe with the cold trickle of fear consuming my whole body.

There was complete silence. Apart from abject terror the only thing I was aware of was a smell. It reminded me of the odour that comes from cold fat left to congeal in a frying pan.

For a long time I waited for something to happen but nothing did. Gradually and slowly the smell disappeared and so too did the certainty that something was standing in front of me. It had somehow evaporated. I was just staring into an empty corridor. Ahead lay a turbulent night with confused dreams.

*****

For the whole of the next day it was not possible to get back into Eliza's notebook. It was raining for most of the time and Jenny insisted on helping me to decorate what was to become my study. I wanted to share the story with her and would have liked to tell her about the events of last night but I didn't want to make her any more nervous than she already was, so I thought I would save it for another more appropriate time. I hid the old drawer and its contents in the loft above the bedroom and the pair of us got to work with polyfila and paint turning the shabby room into a bright space that when finished seemed to have doubled in size.

By mid afternoon we'd finished all the painting and decided that as it had stopped raining we'd venture out for some fresh air. Puta was eager for a walk, so we donned coats and wellies, clipped the lead on to his collar and set off. A few yards down the lane there was a stile on the other side of which was an ancient right of way which led across a ten acre field to the woodland beyond. The sun had decided to come out and the trees in their autumn plumage of reds, browns and yellows glistened spectacularly after the rainfall. I love spring when the trees put on their new coats of green but I love them even more in autumn when their plumage is in its last flush of death and they put on a defiant display of magnificent colour before falling to the ground. Just as we entered the wood we bumped into Ted McSweeney coming the other way. He was dressed in his customary flat cap, a mackintosh two sizes too big for him and brown corduroy trousers tucked into well-worn wellington boots.

"Good afternoon, Ted," I called. He stopped and stared at us, taking a few seconds to recollect who we were then he grinned broadly and said, "Well I never, Gus and Jenny. You gave me quite a start."

"Sorry, I didn't mean to startle you."

"No matter, no matter," he said waving his arms. "Just don't often see folks walkin' durin' the week. Mostly they come at weekends. Been decorating have you?"

"Yes. How d'you know?"

"You've got a big dob of white paint on yer face an' it's in your hair an' all."

Jenny turned to me, "Have I?"

"Suits you," I said then, "no dog today, Ted?"

He turned and looked back into the wood.

"He's here somewhere. Probably still 'oping to catch a badger."

"Badger?"

"Yeah. Further up there's a badger's sett. Silly bugger stands for ages staring down the hole. Dunno what he'd do if one of 'em popped its head out."

I laughed. "Probably be terrified," I said. "By the way, nice shop you've got."

"Yeah. The Missus said you'd been in. 'Ope you'll make a habit of it."

"Of course. Like you said in the pub, we wouldn't want to lose it."

He grinned. "Gotta drum up trade when I can," then he put two grubby fingers to his mouth and gave a long whistle. We waited then heard something crashing through the undergrowth. The rug bounded out from some bushes covered in bits of straw and grass. I could now tell which end was which. Puta was sniffing at one extremity where a short stub of a tail I hadn't noticed before was wagging ferociously. "What, no badger?" Ted said. "You're bloody useless." We laughed. "Anyway, nice to see you both," he said touching his cap. "Enjoy your walk." He gave another short whistle, climbed over the stile and walked into the field.

"He's a nice old boy isn't he," Jenny said.

"A real village character," I agreed.

We walked further into the wood. Each side of the path was deep with ferns now starting to go brown. The trees here were mainly silver birch but as we progressed they became bigger. Huge conifers, oak trees and chestnuts loomed over larch and ash and below them were large areas of wilting nettles and rotting logs.

Soon we rounded a bend and there to one side was the badger's sett that Ted had mentioned. It covered an area of about four square metres and had at least three entrance holes. In front of each were fresh scrapings of earth, twigs and grass thrown out by the house proud animals doing the daily clean of their burrows.

"In an hour or so this place will be a hive of activity," I said. "I'm told that if you were to bring a red light here when it gets dark, they'd come out and ignore you completely." "How vulgar," Jenny said. "I don't want to live near a red light district." I punched her lightly on the shoulder. "Idiot," I said. We walked on and after a while came out of the wood and found ourselves on the perimeter of Morgan's Meadow. A narrow planked bridge took us over a small stream. Straight ahead was the children's play area. It was completely deserted. Water still dripped from the swings next to a roundabout which sat like a small island in a gigantic puddle.

I tried to imagine what it must have been like when PT Barnum set up his fair here. Tents and bustling crowds, ladies with long dresses and moustachioed men wearing bowler hats or caps. Vendors selling sweets, hot potatoes, chestnuts or ice cream. How nice it would be to have a time machine and experience it all for real. We seemed to have the whole meadow to ourselves, there was not another soul to be seen. Across the way we could see our little cottage partially hidden by a bank of trees. It looked so tiny compared with its neighbours further down the lane. I loved the house, we'd put so much effort and so many hours into renovating the place I hated the idea of having to leave it. I looked across at Jenny. She was staring at the house too. I wondered what was going on in her mind. I didn't ask. She gave a little shake of the head, glanced back at me, smiled and walked on.

The next morning I got a phone call from my editor's secretary to tell me that he wanted to see me. Jen was lunching again with a friend which was quite convenient for me because apart from seeing my editor there was something else I wanted to do in town and I had to do it alone.

Back then my newspaper's offices were in Tudor Street which runs parallel to what was the hub of British journalism, Fleet Street. I managed to find a parking space a few yards from our main entrance, entered the building and climbed into the rather scary and rickety cage which the management called a lift and went up to the third level. The editorial floor was a vast space housing the many different departments of a busy newspaper. Sports, show business, news, pictures, the foreign desk, features and many more groups of contributors all in their separate enclaves beavering away to produce the next day's paper.

At that time in the early afternoon however it was fairly quiet. Later on in the evening it would be buzzing with noisy activity. Journalists crouching over their typewriters, secretaries bustling to and fro, telephones ringing, news editors waving sheathes of newsprint ... organised pandemonium. I looked at my watch, it was one twenty five. A lot of journos would be in the pubs refreshing themselves before getting down to the serious business of stringing words together for the next day's edition.

I had a brief chat with a couple of old colleagues then went into the editor's office.

Carla, his secretary, was doing what she always seemed to be doing for most of the day, gazing at herself in a hand held mirror, applying dark Dusty Springfield mascara onto her eyelashes. It was like painting the Forth bridge, a work constantly in progress. She didn't look up from the job in hand. "Hi Gus," she said. "Go in, he's expecting you."

Howard Kirby was sitting behind his vast desk squinting at some papers in his left hand whilst the other held between nicotine stained fingers the ever present cigarette. A big overflowing ashtray sat beside an old chipped mug full of cold tea with a cigarette butt floating in it. Howard was about forty five years old, portly with a thick jungle of curly grey hair. He was not a man who smiled a lot. "Ah, the Country boy," he said. "So glad you had a moment or two to drag yourself away from your turnips."

We shook hands and he bellowed, "Carla, drop the war-paint and see if you can find my bloody glasses will you?"

"They're probably on top of your head," came the bored reply.

She was right. He cursed loudly and slipped his spectacles down into place on his nose. "At least you have some uses," he groaned.

"Indispensable," she replied.

It turned out that the paper was going to do a tribute feature on one of the royals and Kirby wanted me to do a drawing to go with the article. Accompanying this would be reproductions of several cartoons featuring that royal which I'd drawn over the past few years.

I know what you're thinking," he said after he'd shown me the proposed layout. "All this could've been arranged by phone. Well it doesn't hurt country bumpkins like you to get their arses into work occasionally. Other poor buggers like me have to."

"Howard, I miss you more each day."

"Okay. You can fuck off now."

He was right. It was a good idea to show my face now and then but on this occasion I had another reason for being in town.

Almost at the end of the Northern Line on London's underground network there is a place called Colindale. It was here forty years ago that a vast and rather ugly mausoleum of a building stood. This was the home of the British newspaper archive. Since the eighteenth century editors had been legally obliged to send copies of every edition published in the UK to be stored for future generations of readers and researchers. Now of course it has all been digitalised and has been moved to an ultra modern abode in Boston Spa, Yorkshire.

I decided it would be quicker to jump on the tube rather than face all the inevitable traffic jams on the road. Little did I know, country bumpkin that I am. It took well over an hour standing pinned to the wall of the carriage by a crush of commuters before I was spewed out on to the platform at Colindale station thanking God that I now lived in the countryside and only had to endure this torture once in a while.

I remember that it was raining when I left the underground and by the time I got to the archive building I was soaked to the skin and cursing myself that I hadn't come by car.

As soon as I entered I was hit by the smell of old newspapers. They give out a unique aroma of their own, a kind of mustiness which reminded me of the smell I experienced when I was a child on visits to my grandmother's house. Age and decay. I told the receptionist what I wanted and she led me along a passageway lined from floor to ceiling with movable shelf units packed with leather bound volumes of newspapers, some of which were over three hundred years old.

To my left was a room in which a group of women were ironing creases from papers and magazines before they were put into the leather covers. Men trundled by pushing trolleys piled high with the collected words of long dead journalists and as we wandered along the seemingly endless lines of print my escort who told me her name was Joyce gave me a detailed history of the place and politely answered all my questions. Everywhere I looked the floor was covered in tiny bits of yellowed paper. I asked her what they were. "Ah," she said. "We call it Colindale dandruff. A lot of the collection is very old. Newspapers get quite brittle as time goes by and as they're being constantly handled by researchers bits inevitably fall off. It probably wouldn't happen if we had a stable air conditioned environment."

We entered a large room furnished with rows of antiquated brown desks in front of which several people were seated scanning old newspapers, making notes, lifting each page with gloved hands delicately and carefully yet still managing to shed more Colindale dandruff. Joyce sat me at an empty desk and asked me to wait.

After about ten minutes an elderly man appeared pushing a trolley on which were three heavy green leather bound volumes covering the years I had requested. 1840-1846. He handed me a pair of white gloves, gave me a short lecture on how to handle each page with care and respect then with a curt nod of the head he trundled off down one of the dark rabbit warrens and disappeared. I opened the book for 1844-1846.

There were quite a few adverts for PT Barnum's show and lots of similar reviews similar to that of Cedrick Arbuthnot who's cutting I'd found in Eliza's hidden drawer. There were long articles about the California gold rush and a war in Mexico but I could find nothing I didn't already know about the fair at Morgan's Meadow. The second volume was the same. Apparently a man called Adolph Sax introduced the saxophone to the world about that time. 'Good old Adolph,' I thought. 'What would jazz be without him?' The earliest tome proved the most interesting to me. the headline and most of the front page of a paper called "The Morning Post" was devoted to the treaty of Waitangi which resulted in New Zealand becoming a British Colony but tucked away on page four I found the following:-

A MEDICAL ABOMINATION!
SCIENCE INTERFERING WITH NATURE

Earlier this week at a research building on the outskirts of Leipzig two of Germany's leading scientists were apprehended by the Polizei. Professor Siegfried Lutz and Fritz Leiberman were found to have been conducting foul and illegal experiments in their laboratory which flew in the face of God and humanity.

Both men have admitted that the reason for their research was to create a new species, one that was half human and half animal, the purpose of which apparently was to impart human reason and thinking into our fellow creatures on earth. Several grotesque foetuses were found in the laboratory. All dead thanks be to God, but one hideously deformed abomination was discovered in a cage barely breathing with a conglomeration of wires and tubes attached to its body. It was immediately put out of its misery by one of the officers.

The alarm was raised by a member of the public when another of these despicable creations which had escaped from the confines of its cage was seen scaling a wall outside the premises. The German Chancellor in a statement said there was no need for public concern, and that he was confident this unnatural creation would be caught within days and despatched in the same way as the first of its kind. The trial of the two scientists will begin next week. Meanwhile the Polizie are diligently searching an area on the outskirts of Leipzig. We are told that although this creature is thought to be harmless, the German public are being asked not to approach it if seen but to report the sighting to the authorities.

I spent the next hour or two searching for news that the creature had been found but couldn't find any such report. What a find. I could not believe my luck. I was sure that this creature was the one described in little Eliza's collection of cuttings and that somehow PT Barnum had captured it and brought it to England and made it the main attraction of his travelling fair. After thanking Joyce, the helpful receptionist, I made my way home, feeling jubilant about my discovery.

It was nine o'clock at night by the time I got back to the cottage. Jenny was watching TV. She switched it off. "Ah," she said, "here's that man who said he'd be home early."

"Sorry, darling. The meeting went on for a long time then I had a drink with a couple of journos," I lied.

"C'mon. Who is she? I'll kill her."

"Oh, very well, if you must know it was Fifi de la Bom bom. She's a French stripper and contortionist, very discreet and quite cheap."

"Oh, that's alright then." She laughed. "Have you eaten?"

"Only crisps."

"Good. I thought I'd wait for you. I'm glad you're back. I get a bit scared on my own."

"Ah, Jen. I'm sorry but I'm sure there's nothing to harm you. Gordon the ghost hasn't been bothering you has he?"

"No, you're right," she shook her head. "I'm just being silly. C'mon, I've made some spag bol."

We cracked open a bottle of red wine and had a slap up meal in our tiny kitchen. I was dying to tell her all about little Eliza and my discovery as the newspaper archive. It would have been great to share it but I kept quiet. Instead I listened as she told me about having lunch with her friend, Natalie.

The next morning I phoned the editor with a few cartoon ideas for the following day's paper. Margaret Thatcher was Prime Minister back then and the Brixton riots were in fully swing. I always preferred making people laugh with my contributions but given the news this one had to be a serious comment. He liked one of the ideas especially and said he'd call back once he'd got it cleared by the paper's resident lawyer. While I was waiting it seemed a good time to have another look at Eliza's notebook. Jenny had only just left to take the dog for a walk so I guessed it would be a good hour before she returned. Once I'd retrieved the old drawer from the loft I sat on the bed and got back to Eliza's narrative. It didn't make for good reading. I shuddered at the terror this poor little girl endured and tried to put into her own words.

*THE THING WHAT I SAW AT THE FAIR HAS
ESKAPED. THE THING WHAT ATTACKED MY
MOTHER. ALL THE VILLAGE IS TALKING ABOUT IT.
MOST PEOPLE DON'T KNOW WHAT IT IS BUT THE
ONES WHAT HAVE SEEN IT ARE SCARED BECOS
THEY NO WHAT IT LOOKS LIKE. THE PEELERS
HAVE BEEN HERE NOCKING ON OUR DOOR ASKED
US TO BE VIJILENT AND TO KEEP OUR EYES OPEN
FOR IT AND TO LOCK ALL OUR DOORS AND ALL
THAT STUFF. MOTHER IS THE WURST. SHE CANNOT*

SLEEP BECOS OF THE WORRY. THE VICAR AT CHURCH ON SUNDAY SED A SPESHUL PRAYER TO KEEP US SAFE HE SED THE LORD WILL PROTEKT US. FATHER HAS COME HOME HE HAS A LITTLE BIT OF MONEY AND MAYBE A GARDINING JOB AT THE BIG HOUSE. HE HAS FIXT ANUTHER HEVY BOLT ON THE DOOR.

This was followed by several pages relating the good news that Eliza's brother Josh was fully restored to health, that their mother insisted on walking them to school each day even though it was only a few yards down the lane and how both children had been banned from visiting their den in the wood. Alfie had sent her a letter which he'd delivered by hand at school. A whole page was devoted to a drawing of a heart pierced with an arrow. Glued to the bottom of this page was another newspaper clipping.

MURDER MOST FOUL

Today sixty eight year old Arthur James Burrows a farm worker was arrested and taken into custody by the constabulary after the mutilated and partly clothed body of his wife Edna Mary Burrows was discovered in the outside washroom of the cottage they shared near Morgan's Meadow, Plaxtol in the county of Kent. The headless corpse of a dog believed to be the family pet was found in undergrowth nearby.

Neighbours were shocked to hear the news of the death most of whom spoke warmly of the couple describing them as friendly, gentle and devoted to one another.

This was followed by a terrifying and disturbing entry in Eliza's spidery hand.

I DO NOT BELEEVE THAT MR BURROWS COULD DO SUCH A THING. THEY WAS SUCH A NICE MAN AND LADY. I USED TO DO SHOPPING FOR THEM AND SUM TIMES THEY WOOD GIVE ME A PENNY. I NO HE DID NOT DO IT BECOS OF WHAT HAPPENED TO US.

I DO NOT NO HOW TO RITE THE NEXT THING. IT IS THE MOST HORIBLE THING WHAT HAS EVER HAPPENED. I CANT STOP CRYING. THEY HAVE BEEN NOW AND TAKEN IT AWAY. THANK GOODNESS OUR FATHER CAME HOME SUDDEN LIKE. HE IS WITH MOTHER NOW. OH PLEESE GOD DONT LET THINGS LIKE THIS HAPPEN AGAIN. PLEASE PLEASE GOD. LOOK AFTER US. I WILL PRAY TO YOU EVRY DAY.
TODAY WHEN SCHOOL WAS OVER OUR MOTHER WAS NOT WAYTING AT THE GATE LIKE WHAT WAS USUAL. JOSH AND ME WAYTED BUT THEN WALKED HOME BY OURSELVES. WHEN WE GOT TO OUR HOUSE THE DOOR WAS WIDE OPEN, THERE WERE BITS OF WOOD ON THE GROUND. BITS FROM THE DOOR. FATHER'S NEW BOLT WAS SNAPPED IN TOO PIECES. I COULD HEAR SCREEMING AND NOISES COMING FROM UPSTAIRS. I TOLD JOSH TO STAY IN

THE KICHEN AND I RUSHED UP TO SEE WHAT THE
NOISE WAS ABOUT. IT WAS HORRIBLE TO SEE ...
MOTHER WAS ON THE FLOOR IN THE BEDROOM
AND THE THING FROM THE FAIR WAS ON TOP OF
HER ... THE THING WHAT ATTACKED HER WHEN
WE WENT TO THE FAIR. MY POOR MOTHER'S DRESS
WAS ALL RUCKED UP AROUND HER WAIST AND
THE CREACHERS BIG CLAWED HAND WAS
PINNING HER TO THE FLOOR. I SCREEMED REAL
LOUD AND THE THING GOT OFF MY MOTHER AND
STOOD UP ON ITS LITTLE STUMPY LEGS. IT HAD A
TROUSER WORM LIKE WHAT JOSH HAS GOT BUT IT
WAS HUGE AND STUK OUT FROM ITS BODY LIKE A
BRANCH ON A TREE EXCEPT IT WAS WET AND
SHINY. I MUST HAVE SCREEMED AGEN BECAUSE
IT ALL OF A SUDDEN JUMPED LIKE A JACK-IN-THE-
BOX AND PUT ITS CLAWS ROUND MY NECK. I FELL
BACKWARDS AND NOCKED OVER MOTHER'S
SIDEBOARD. THE CREECHER WAS ON TOP OF ME
AND WAS TEARING MY CLOTHES.THE SMELL WAS
TERIBLE AND I WAS SO FRIGHTENED. THEN I SAW
MOTHER HAD GOT UP AND WAS BEHIND THE
THING. ALL AT ONCE ITS HORRIBLE MOUTH
OPENED AND A GREAT SHREEK CAME FORTH. IT
FELL OFF ME AND ROLLED ON ITS BACK.
MOTHER'S DRESS MAKING SISSORS WERE SUNK
DEEP INTO ONE OF ITS EYES. SHE PULLED ME UP
AND HUGGED ME TO HER. I COULD HEAR JOSH
CRYING DOWNSTAIRS. THEN FATHER APPEARED
HE WAS YELLING SWEAR WORDS AND STARTED
STAMPING ON THE CREECHER WITH HIS BIG
BOOTS. I HERD A LOWD CRACK AND SAW THAT
WON OF THE CREECHERS LEGS WAS AT A FUNNY
ANGLE.

For a while I couldn't read any more. It was just too harrowing. What an ordeal for someone so young. I sat for a long time trying to imagine the scene that had taken place here in my own home. Probably in this very room. It was impossible to get a clear picture in my head what this repulsive man-made monster actually looked like. What devastating effect it had on the family or why the two German scientists so long ago had spent their time trying to create a creature on a par with Mary Shelley's Frankenstein. I went downstairs and made a cup of tea, carried it back up to the bedroom, took a deep breath and continued reading.

I COULD NOT STOP TREMBLING AND WANTED REAL BAD TO RUN AWAY FROM THE HOUSE AND RID MYSELF OF WHAT I HAD SEEN. MOTHER WAS IN A TERRIBLE STAYT SCREAMING AND CRYING. SHE TOOK THE TUB FROM THE WALL AND FILLED IT WITH WATER THEN GOT IN AND SCRUBBED AND SCRUBBED HERSELF FOR A LONG TIME TILL SHE MUST HAV BEEN SORE. THE WATER WAS COLD TOO. FATHER WAS DOING HIS BEST TO CALM HER BUT IT WAS A FULL 2 HOURS BEFORE SHE GOT DRESSED AGAIN. I PUT MY ARMS ROUND HER AND WE SAT TOGETHER SHIVERING AND CRYING. JOSH WAS CRYING TOO BUT ONLY BECOS WE WERE HE DID NOT NO ABOUT THE THING UPSTAIRS. THEN FATHER LEFT THE HOUSE AND WAS GONE FOR A

*LONG TIME AND WHEN HE GOT BACK IT WAS
IN A FINE CARRAGE PULLED BY HORSES THER
WERE THREE MEN WITH HIM AND WON OF THEM
WAS MISTER PT BARNUM HIMSELF. HE WAS
WARING A TOP HAT AND VERY GRAND CLOTHES
AND THE OTHER 2 WORE FLAT CAPS AND SCRUFFY
GARMINTS AND SPOKE VERY LITTIL. FATHER
TOOK THEM UPSTAIRS AND WHEN THEY CAME
DOWN AGEN I WAS TOLD TO GO OUT IN THE
GARDEN WITH JOSH. WE DID AS WE WAS TOLD BUT
I TIP-TOED BACK IN AND WATCHED THROUGH A
CRACK IN THE DOOR. I HERD MISTER BARNUM SAY
THAT THIS MUST NOT GO ANY FURTHER AND ON
NO ACCOUNT SHOULD THE PEELERS BE TOLD
BECOS IT WOULD COS A SCANDLE AND RUIN HIS
BISINESS. HE OFFERED MY FATHER SOME MONEY
BUT FATHER SED NO AND THAT HE WANTED
MUCH MORE OR HE WOULD TELL THE POLICE
WHAT HAD HAPPINED AND THE NEWSPAPERS
TOO. THER WAS A LOT OF MUMBLING WHAT I
COULD NOT HEER THEN THEY SHOOK HANDS.
AFTER THAT THE TOO OTHER MEN WENT UP TO
THE BEDROOM THEN CAME DOWN CARRYING THE
THING RAPPED IN A SHEET. THEY PUT IT IN THE
CARRAGE AND ALL THREE DROVE AWAY. I RAN
INTO THE ROOM AND SED THAT WE SHOULD TELL
THE POLICE AND THAT I THAWT IT WOS THE
THING WHAT KILLED MISSUS BURROWES UP THE
ROAD AND THAT IF WE DID NOT TELL THEM
POOR MISTER BURROWES WOULD HANG FOR
SOMETHING HE DID NOT DO BUT FATHER
SCOLDED ME FOR LISTENING TO WHAT HAD BEEN
SED AND HAS FORBIDDAN ME FOR EVER TALKING
ABOUT IT. IF THEY HANG MISTER BURROWES I WILL*

NEVER SPEAK TO MY FATHER AGEN. NOT EVER.
ALSO I WILL NEVER GO INTO THAT BEDROOM EGEN.

The phone rang. It was my editor to say that the newspaper's lawyer had given one of my ideas approval and that I could get on with the drawing. Reluctantly I put everything back into Eliza's drawer, hid it away again and got down to work. It was difficult to concentrate. My mind kept replaying Eliza's story. How could a child of her age ever get over a trauma such as she described and have to keep all that she'd seen secret? It must have stayed with her for the rest of her life. No wonder she had felt the need to write it all down, to get it off her chest and by putting it on paper hoped that it would do what her poor mother had tried to do – somehow scrub the experience away.

Three hours later I was on the road heading for London to delivery my drawing. The traffic was particularly heavy that evening and it took me much longer than usual to get there. Then later as I was leaving the editor's office I bumped into two feature writers that I knew who were on their way to a wine bar directly across the road from our building. In those days there was no breathalyser or stringent checks on drivers who'd been drinking so I accepted their offer to join them. Somehow another two hours slipped by before I stumbled back into my car and drove slowly home without killing anyone. It was raining hard and by the time I reached home it was nearly ten o'clock.

This time I wasn't greeted by a happy joking wife pretending to be cross at my being late home. Jenny was curled up on the settee clutching her knees to her chest. She looked terrified.

"Oh God, Gus," she whispered. "Where have you been?"

"Sorry, Jenny. I …" She didn't wait for an explanation.

"It's been again."

"What?"

"The bloody thing! That horrible thing! Gordon … banging about upstairs." She got up and clung to me, her arms wrapped tight around my waist. "Gus. We can't live here anymore. I want to leave!"

I stroked the back of her head. "Calm yourself, sweetheart," I soothed. "Tell me what happened."

She looked up at me and screamed angrily. "Do you hear me? I want to leave … get away … anywhere, but not here!"

Gently I pushed her back down on to the settee. "Whoa," I said, "hang on a sec." I hurried to the kitchen, poured her a brandy then went back and sat beside her. "Okay," I said. "Take this and tell me what happened."

She glanced up at the ceiling then took a nervous sip from the glass. "We'll move back to London," she said speaking not to me but more to herself. "Yes. That's it. We'll move back."

I waited.

"Please don't leave me on my own again," she pleaded. "Oh God. I was so scared." Her shoulders started to shake and she was trembling violently. I stroked her arm then she said in a whisper, "I'd been out in the garden, then come in to watch the six o'clock news. I'd only just sat down when Puta started to growl. He was on the settee with me then he got to his feet. The hackles on his neck were standing up like a ... like a wire brush. I tried to calm him but I couldn't ... then suddenly he gave a loud yap, leapt to the ground and rushed up the stairs barking his head off. I followed him but when I got half way up ..." Jenny stopped and took several loud breaths.

"Go on," I said.

"When I got half way up I heard Puta give a really loud scream of pain ... then he came flying towards me ... it was as though he'd been kicked like a football. He hadn't just jumped. The poor dog crashed into me almost knocking me backwards down the stairs then he scrambled to his feet, rushed down to the kitchen and lay whimpering in his basket." She took a large gulp of brandy then continued. "I went down to see if he was alright but he wouldn't let me anywhere near him. I've never seen a dog so frightened."

"Oh my God, Jenny," I said. "I'm so sorry I wasn't here." I looked across the room. Puta was lying against the far wall. His head was erect and he was staring at the staircase leading up from the kitchen. Jenny said, "then I heard it … the noise … the scraping. Much louder than before …" She looked up at me, fear written on her face. "Gus, I think I saw it."

"You saw it?"

She nodded. "I went back up. I didn't want to. I forced myself to go up. Weirdly the noise stopped as soon as I reached the landing. It felt … I felt as though that something had stopped whatever it was doing and was watching me. Oh God. It was so scary. I stood for ages staring into the empty corridor. There was not a sound … then I saw something move. At the far end there was a shaft of light coming from the street light outside our bedroom. Something passed through it … something small, hunched over … it was … it was so quick I couldn't pick out any details, but Gus … it went into our room, I saw something go into our room."

"I'll just go up and have a look," I said and went upstairs cursing myself for having those drinks at the wine bar. As expected there was nothing to see. When I returned to the living room Jenny said, "Please don't leave me on my own again, Gus. Not at night anyway."

I started to apologise again but she interrupted with "I spent most of the evening at the front gate, too scared to come back inside, then it started to rain so I had to."

"Aw, Jen. If only I'd known. I'm so sorry."

She stood up, folded her arms and looked down at me. "I want to move, Gus. I can't stay here."

"Okay," I said. I'll call an estate agent tomorrow. I promise."

'I'd like to stay with my mum and dad till we find a new place."

I was horrified, "Aw, no! Our marriage has just got started. We can't be parted so soon. I don't want to live anywhere without you."

She cupped my face with her hands and kissed my forehead. "I don't want not to be with you either, Gus. Maybe we could rent somewhere while we find a buyer for here."

This was not what I wanted but what could I do? Jenny was so unhappy I had no other option. I shrugged my shoulders. "Sweetheart. I'd live in a ditch as long as I'd got you. I'll sort something out in the morning."

"Thanks, Gus." She sat down again and put her arm around my shoulder. "I know what this place means to you after all your hard work but we'll be just as happy somewhere else. I promise you."

That night she absolutely refused to sleep in our bedroom so we snuggled up on the sofa under a pile of blankets. It was a bit cramped, even more so when Puta decided to join us and lay at our feet gently snoring.

The next day was Friday. I had three clear days before I had to do another drawing. With a heavy heart I phoned two local estate agents and arranged a time for them to come and view the cottage. Then I called a London agent and made some enquiries about rented accommodation.

Gloom upon gloom. After breakfast Jenny dropped the bombshell I'd been half expecting. She was going to spend a few days with her parents in Suffolk and they were coming to collect her that afternoon. She didn't want to be apart from me but needed to get away from Gordon for a while. It was no use, she'd made up her mind so I reluctantly agreed to go along with her wishes. She went upstairs to pack and I got on with fixing some shelves to the walls of the study. At midday there was a knock on the door. Two wet and bedraggled people stood on the doorstep. Rain was hammering down on their umbrellas, one of them held out a bottle of red wine. "Good morning, sir," he said. "We are in the area promoting our excellent pinot noir and wondered if you'd like a sample."

He looked me up and down, taking in my torn jeans and ragged jumper, both covered with paint, and enquired, "Is the master of the house at home?"

"No zurr. He baint," I said. "So oill ave ter do the sampling. You'd best come in."

They squelched into the house. "Welcome to our humble abode," I said, helping my in laws out of their wet overcoats. "It's been a long time."

Tom and Katie Merridew were a delightful couple. Both in their seventies, slightly overweight but with healthy, happy faces and broad Suffolk accents. Tom was dark, almost swarthy with thick black eyebrows while she obviously once had the striking good looks of her daughter.

"Wow! What a transformation," Katie said staring around at our clean new living room. "Who's a clever boy?"

"Hey," came Jenny's voice from the stairs. "Don't give him all the credit. I helped too." She swept excitedly into the room with Puta at her heels. "Mum, Dad, oh so lovely to see you." She flung her arms wide and they stood for a joyous moment or two in a group hug.

"I'll put the kettle on," I said.

"Kettle?" Tom groaned waggling the bottle.

"Oh, right. I'll get some glasses."

"Hang on, you boozers," Katie said waving her arms. "First I want a tour of the premises."

We were pleased to show off our efforts on the cottage. It had been quite a long time since their last visit and they were genuinely impressed with the improvements we'd made.

"How do you find time to do all this and keep a job going at the same time?" Tom asked as he traipsed upstairs.

"I do most of it at weekends," I said "… and every spare moment I get."

"Take note," Katie said, nudging her husband with her elbow. He scowled at me. "Now look what you've done. I'm going to get nagged all the way home."

They peered into my newly painted study and then the spare room. "We haven't got round to buying a spare bed," Jenny said. "… but when we do it'll be lovely to have you to stay over."

I looked at her in surprise. It was obvious that she hadn't told her parents the reason she wanted to stay with them awhile.

"Can't wait," Katie said, then "but I think you should fix a radiator in the hallway. It's freezing."

Downstairs we cracked open the bottle and Tom proposed a toast to happiness in our newly re-modernised house. Jenny glanced across at me and for a moment I thought she was about to tell them she wanted to move but she gave me a quick reassuring smile and instead looked out of the window and said, "Hey, it's stopped raining. Let me show you the garden."

The two women walked out. Tom chose to stay indoors. We chatted aimlessly for a while then he asked "Is everything alright, Gus?"

"What d'you mean?"

"Everything okay between you and Jenny?"

"Oh? Yes, we're fine."

"Only I wondered why …"

"She misses you." I broke in. "She just wants a few days with her Mum and Dad. We're fine, honestly, still nuts about each other."

"That's a relief," he said. "Hope you don't mind me asking. We were a bit worried when we got her call. It seemed a bit urgent."

"It was a sudden decision. I've been busy lately. There's not much she can do in the garden. Maybe she's a bit bored. A break will do her good," I lied. He nodded then clinked my glass with his. "Well, don't worry. We'll look after her."

An hour later I watched them climb into their car with the love of my life clutching a bag of her belongings. She promised to phone every day, told me she loved me and then she was gone, leaving me feeling as though someone had just chopped off one of my limbs.

Back in the empty house I poured myself another glass of Tom's wine and sat for a long time staring at the wall and wondering if I'd handled things right. Should I have told Jen about Eliza's notebook? Was I being too protective? Had I been a completely thoughtless bastard for leaving her on her own knowing how nervous she was about Gordon's spasmodic visits? I remembered how scared I'd been on my last encounter. I shook my head not able to answer all the questions running through my brain, topped up my glass and went upstairs to my secret hiding place. This time I was able to read more of Eliza's narrative in the comfort of my armchair in the living room.

TODAY IS MY FOURTEENTH BIRTHDAY. JOSH HAS GIVEN ME A SKIPPING ROPE WHAT HE MADE, IT HAS RAFIA HANDLES. I THINK FATHEER HAS FORGOTTEN.

*I HAVE NOT WRITTEN HERE FOR MONTHS AND
MONTHS BECAUSE SO MANY HORRIBLE THINGS
HAVE HAPPENED. WHY HAS GOD NOT HELPED
US? WHAT HAVE WE DONE WRONG? I PRAY TO HIM
EVERY DAY BUT HE DOES NOT HEER.*

*MR BURROWES WAS FOUND GUILTY AND HAS
BEEN HANGED. I BEGGED FATHER TO TELL ABOUT
THE THING WHAT ESCAPED BUT HE HIT ME WITH
HIS FIST AND SED THAT HE WOULD SEND ME TO
MY MAKER IF I SPOKE ABOUT IT ANY MORE. I HATE
HIM FOR WHAT HE HAS DONE. HE IS STILL
WORKING AT THE BIG HOUSE AS A
GARDINER AND SOMETIMES DOES NOT COME
HOMETILL LATE AND IS MANY TIMES DRUNK.*

*MOTHER IS NOT WELL SO I HELP WITH THE
COOKING. I BEGGED HER TO GO TO SEE DOCTOR
PETTIGREW BECAUSE SHE WAS SICK IN THE
MORNINGS, BUT SHE WOULD NOT.
THE RENT MAN CAME TO OUR HOUSE AND
FATHER SED HE HAD NO MONEY AND COULD HE
PAY NEXT MONTH. HE IS TELLING FIBS BECAUSE I
NO HE GOT LOTS OF MONEY FROM PT BARNUM.
TWO MONTHS PAST AND LATE AT NIGHT I HERD
MY PARENTS HAVING A TERRIBLE ROW. FATHER
WAS SCREAMING AT MOTHER SO LOUD LITTLE
JOSH WOKE UP AND STARTED TO CRY HE WAS SO
SCARED. I LET HIM CLIMB INTO MY BED AND WE
CUDDLED. FATHER WAS SHOUTING "ITS NOT MY
CHILD AND WELL YOU KNOW IT" I COULD HEAR
MY MOTHER CRYING THEN MY FATHER SAID WHO
IS THE OTHER MAN WHAT SHE HAD BEEN WITH
AND THERE WERE LOTS OF SCARY NOISES LIKE HE*

*WAS THROWING OUR FURNITURE ABOUT. THEN I
HEARD HIM HITTING MY MOTHER AND HER
CRYING AND CRYING. I WENT DOWNSTAIRS.
MOTHER WAS ON THE FLOOR AND MY FATHER
WAS GOING TO HIT HER WITH A CHAIR I WENT
TO STOP HIM BUT HE PUNCHED ME HARD IN THE
FACE AND I MUST HAVE BEEN KNOCKED
UNCONSHUS.*

*WHEN I WOKE UP MY MOTHER WAS CUDDLING ME.
SHE HAD BRUISES ALL OVER HER FACE AND WAS
WIPING BLOOD FROM MY FACE WITH A CLOTH.
SHE SAID IT WAS SAFE NOW BECAUSE FATHER
HAD GONE TO THE PUB AND THAT I SHOULD GO
BACK TO BED. I DID AND SED A PRAYER ASKING
GOT TO STRIKE MY FATHER DEAD. PLEEEEEEEESE!*

At the bottom of this page there was a drawing of a coffin with the word 'Father' on the lid. After reading about the rotten birthday the poor child endured I was starting to wish her bastard of a father dead too. I turned to the next page.

*MISS BULLIVANT SAYS THAT MY SUMS IS DISMAL
AND THAT I AM FALLING BEHIND. SHE HAS
MOVED ME TO THE FRONT ROW OF THE CLASS SO
SHE CAN KEEP AN EYE ON ME. I DO NOT LIKE IT
BECOSE I AM HAVING TO SIT NEXT TO GEORGE
CROSBY WHO SMELLS SOMETHING TERRIBLE AND
HAS A SQUINT IN ONE EYE I MUST TRY HARDER
AT MY SUMS SO I CAN MOVE BACK AND AWAY
FROM GEORGE.*

*ARTHUR PERKINS BROUGHT A RAT TO SCHOOL
AND IT RAN ACROSS THE FLOOR. MISS BULLIVANT
SCREAMED AND BANGED ARTHUR'S EAR. HE
TOOK IT HOME.*

*MOTHER HAS GIVEN ME A LITTLE GLASS JAR
WHAT CONTAINS SUM BLOOD. THIS IS THE BLOOD
WHAT SHE TOOK FROM THE THING WHAT
ATTACKED US. SHE WAS TOLD BY
HER MOTHER GRANNY GERTRUDE THAT TO KEEP
THE BLOOD OF AN ATTAKER WILL MAKE SURE
THAT IT WILL NEVER ATTAK AGEN. HOW CAN IT
ATTAK AGEN? IT IS DEAD. I HAVE PUT THE HORID
THING IN MY SECRET PLACE.*

*MY MOTHER AND FATHER ARE HAVING MORE
ROWS MOTHER DOES NOT LOOK AT ALL WELL SHE
HAS STOPPED BEING SICK IN THE MORNING BUT
SHE IS PAIL AND HAS TO SIT DOWN A LOT. ALSO
SHE IS GETTING FAT.*

*THE RENT MAN CALLED AGAIN. MY FATHER
MADE US ALL STAY QUIET SO HE WOULD THINK
THERE WAS NOBODY AT HOME. HE KNOCKED FOR
A VERY LONG TIME THEN WENT AWAY.*

*I THINK GEORGE CROSBY HAS GOT FLEES. HE IS
FOREVER SCRATCHING HIS HEAD.*

When I turned to the next page a cloud of
dusty remains of real flowers that long ago had
been pressed within the notebook cascaded to the
floor. Taking up half the page at the top was a

drawing in black crayon of a Christian cross standing on a bank of flowers. On the horizontal of the cross were the words "my lovely mother".

I CANNOT BEAR IT. OH GOD. WHY HAVE YOU ALLOWED THIS? WHY HAVE YOU TAKEN MY POOR MOTHER WHO HAS NEVER DONE NO WRONG. WHY DID YOU NOT TAKE MY FATHER INSTEAD? WHAT IS TO BECOME OF US NOW? I CANNOT STOP CRYING. I WANT TO DIE TOO SO I CAN BE WITH HER IN HEAVEN. WHY GOD, WHY? SHE WAS SUCH A LOVELY MOTHER. I LOVED HER VERY MUCH AND YOU ARE CRUEL FOR TAKING HER AWAY FROM US. WHEN WE CAME OUT FROM SCHOOL MRS BIRCH FROM ALONG THE LANE WAS WAITING AT THE GATE. SHE SED THAT SHE HAD COME INSTEAD OF OUR MOTHER AND THAT WE WERE TO GO WITH HER TO HER HOUSE. WHEN WE GOT THERE SHE GAVE US LEMONADE AND BISKITS THEN TOLD US TO BE VERY BRAVE SOLDIERS BECAUSE GOD IN HIS WISDOM HAD TAKEN OUR MOTHER AWAY TO HEAVEN.

WHY DO ADULTS TELL LIES TO CHILDREN? MRS BIRCH TOLD US THAT MOTHER HAD TAKEN A LITTLE NAP IN THE AFTERNOON AND JUST NEVER WOKE UP AND THAT GOD HAD TAKEN HER TO BE WITH THE ANGELS BUT NEXT DAY I FOUND A NEWSPAPER TUCKED UNDER THE FIREPLACE WHAT OUR FATHER MUST'VE HIDDEN.

Glued under the above was a cutting from the Morning Post.

TRAGEDY AT MORGAN'S MEADOW

Yesterday a young couple walking with their dog through Morgan's Meadow near Plaxtol in Kent were shocked when they came upon a woman who had climbed to the top of the broken water fountain next to the bandstand. She was obviously in great distress and was praying loudly. The couple rushed forward to offer help but as they advanced the woman gave a great cry and leapt forward impaling herself on the spiked railings below. The two witnesses to this tragedy, a Mr and Mrs Wilkinson from nearby Claygate Cross, said it appeared that the woman had deliberately jumped on to the railings. The deceased, Hilda Winifred Cartwright of 23 Morgan's Lane, Monk's Green near Plaxtol in Kent was apparently with child and leaves a husband, Frank Wilmott Cartwright, and two children. A note of farewell was found at her dwelling place. An inquest is expected to say that the woman was of unsound mind.

I was beginning to wish that I hadn't found Eliza's notebook. It was fascinating but so depressing. If you were poor in the mid nineteenth century life was so grim. Trouble and grief seemed to be followed by yet more trouble and grief. Misery, cruelty and hunger were what one woke up to every day. Eliza's story would live with me a long time. Worse was to come. I read on ...

89

*MOTHER HAS BEEN BUREID TODAY AND FATHER
AND 2 NAYBORS WERE THERE. AND THE VICAR.
JOSH STAYED AT MISSUS BIRCH'S COTTAGE.
EVERYBODY WAS CRYING EXCEPT MY FATHER.
HE NEVER SED ANYTHING. NOT A WORD. I
PRAYED AND PRAYED FOR GOD TO LOOK AFTER
MY MOTHER BUT I DO NOT THINK HE LISTENS TO
CHILDREN. WHEN WE LEFT ALFIE WAS STANDING
BY THE GATE. HE GAVE ME SOME WILD FLOWERS
WHAT HE HAD PICKED.*

*WHEN WE GOT BACK TO THE HOUSE MY FATHER
SAID TO STAY THERE WHILE HE PICKED UP JOSH.
I MADE A CUP OF TEA AND WAITED A LONG LONG
TIME. IN THE END I WENT ALONG THE LANE TO
MRS BIRCH'S COTTAGE BUT SHE SAID FATHER HAD
COME FOR JOSH HOURS AGO. THEN WHEN I WENT
BACK I FOUND THIS NOTE ON THE MANTLEPIECE
WHAT I HAD NOT SEEN BEFORE.*

A scruffy bit of paper was glued here with barely legible writing.

*ELIZA. ME AN JOSH IS LEAVIN. YOU ARE A BIG
GIRL NOW. GET WORK AT THE FACTORY. GOOD
LUCK. PA.*

I swore loudly and punched the notebook with my fist. The bastard! How could he do that to his daughter? I wanted him to be alive and nearby so I could strangle the selfish, unfeeling and inhumane shit with my bare hands.

*I DO NOT NO WHAT TO DO I HAVE NO MONEY TO
BUY FOOD. I AM WORRIED ABOUT MY BROTHER
JOSH. WHAT WILL HAPPEN TO HIM WILL MY
FATHER LOOK AFTER HIM PROPER? I HAVE NOT
CRYED I DO NOT NO WHAT WILL BECOME OF ME.*

*MISSUSS BIRCH KNOCKED ON THE DOOR TO SEE IF
MY FATHER HAD COME HOME YET AND I SHOWED
HER THE LETTER. SHE GAVE ME A BIG HUG AND
TOOK ME HOME WITH HER. I STAYED AT HER
HOUSE AND SHE GAVE ME SOME SOUP. MISTER
BIRCH IS VERY NICE.*

*THE NEXT DAY I SAW THE RENT MAN. HE WAS
VERY CROSS AND WANTED TO KNOW WHERE MY
FATHER HAD GONE TO. I SED I DID NOT NO. I DID
NOT GO TO SCHOOL. I SAW ALFIE AND TOLD HIM
WHAT HAD HAPPENED.*

*I HAVE BEEN AT MISTER AND MISSUS BIRCH'S
HOUSE FOR SEVEN DAYS. I HEARD MR BIRCH SAY
THAT I MIGHT HAVE TO GO AND LIVE AT A PLACE
CALLED AN ORFINAGE. I DON'T NO WHAT THAT
IS.*

*ALFIE CAME TO THE COTTAGE AND WE WENT FOR
A WALK. HE TOLD ME THAT HE HAD SPOKEN TO
HIS MOTHER AND FATHER AND THEY SED THAT IF
I STOPPED SCHOOL AND HELP AT THE FARM
WHERE THEY WORK I COULD STAY AT THERE
HOUSE BECAUSE THEY HAVE A ROOM WHAT IS
EMPTY. I SED YES PLEASE. I DON'T WANT TO GO TO
THE ORFINAGE. I WANT TO LIVE IN THE SAME
HOUSE AS ALFIE.*

At last. A bit of cheer amongst all the gloom. Eliza was going to live with her Alfie. I hoped that for the rest of her life she was happy. She deserved it. There were lots more hearts drawn around this page, then it was back to gloom. Folded between the next two pages was her mother's suicide note.

FRANK. FORGIVE ME. I CANNOT BEAR TO LIVE ANY LONGER CARRYING THIS BURDEN. I GO NOW TO KILL SATAN'S CHILD. PLEASE LOOK AFTER ELIZA AND JOSH. I WAS NEVER UNTRUE TO YOU. YOUR WIFE. HILDA.

Then came the last words in the notebook.

TOMORROW I AM GOING TO LIVE AT ALFIE'S HOUSE. MISSUS BIRCH HAS GIVEN ME A PAIR OF BOOTS THAT HER DAWTER WORE WHEN SHE WAS A LITTLE GIRL. ALSO SOME CLOTHES.
I AM GLAD I WILL NEVER SEE MISS BULLIVANT AGAIN. SHE IS ALWAYS SO CROSS AT SCHOOL. I WENT BACK TO MY HOUSE AND HAD TO CLIMB THROUGH A WINDOW BECAUSE THEY HAD NAILED WOOD ACROSS THE DOOR. I HATE MY HOUSE NOW AND STILL FEEL FRIGHTENED TO GO PAST THAT ROOM UPSTAIRS.
I AM PUTTING DAISY INTO MY HIDEY HOLE. I THINK ALFIE WOULD LAFF AT ME FOR HAVING A DOLL. ALSO IF I AM GOING TO WORK ON THE FARM WHAT HIS FATHER WORKS ON THERE WILL BE NO USE FOR WRITING SO I WILL PUT THIS BOOK INTO

THE HIDEY HOLE TOO. MAYBE SOMEONE WILL
FIND IT ONE DAY AND READ IT.
ELIZA CARTWRIGHT 14

At around eight o'clock that night Jenny rang. She'd only been away a few hours but it seemed to me like a month.

"Hi Gus. We've just got in. Traffic was terrible on the A12."

I felt a sudden lump in my throat just listening to her voice knowing she was now nearly a hundred miles away and not here where she belonged. "I'm glad you got there safely," I said.

"You okay?"

"I'm fine. Missing you."

There was a pause then, "I'm missing you too. I'm sorry Gus."

"Yeah. Me too. Estate agents coming tomorrow I think."

Another long pause. "What're you doing?"

"Getting drunk on your dad's wine."

She laughed. "Coincidence. We're all sitting here clutching gin and tonics."

I heard her mother and father shout "Hi Gus!"

"Hi, you two," I shouted back.

"Any sign of Gordon?" Jenny asked.

"Not so far. Maybe he's decided to have a holiday and has gone up to Ipswich with you."

She gave a great sigh. "Oh, don't."

"They've sent lots of brochures from London. Properties for rent."

"Gus. I didn't want this to happen."

"Nor me."

"Don't hate me."

"How could I ever hate you? … and don't hate yourself. As long as we stick together over this we'll be alright."

"Are you able to work with all this worry?"

"I've decided to take a few days off. You know, agents coming, maybe people turning up to see the cottage."

"Oh, yeah." She said. "I bet you're off to some tropical island with a blonde you've picked up."

"I wish."

We chatted on for a little longer, promised to speak again next day then hung up.

I sat for a while thinking about how things could have been if Gordon hadn't made his presence felt. This little haven we'd built for ourselves would have been perfect. Sometimes it seemed that just when things are going right, life has a perverse way of kicking you in the teeth. I made a decision. I picked up the old drawer with its newspaper cuttings and notebook and carried it upstairs to the bedroom where I had found it, then I put it back into Eliza's hidey hole and screwed the plank that covered the space firmly back into place. It seemed to me that her writings were part of the history of the cottage and that it was only right that they should remain in it forever or until discovered again by a future occupier. I papered over the section of the wall then went to bed. It had been an exhausting day. Gordon must have been tired too because there wasn't a sound from him, or maybe I was just too tired to notice.

The next morning, one after another, the estate agents arrived. I followed them around the cottage with a great grey cloud floating over my head. They loved the cottage as I knew they would, made notes in their little pads, took measurements and photographs, muttered 'How cute' and 'So delightfully quaint', promised me an almost instant sale then scuttled back to their plush offices in Sevenoaks.

I needed cheering up. I rang my friend Charles.

"Hey," he said. "I was just thinking about you. What're you up to?"

"How about I tell you over a pint at my local?" I said.

"Sounds a good idea. I'll see you in there in about half an hour … mine's a pint of Guinness."

I was first to get to the pub. There was quite a crowd there, nobody I knew but propping up the bar was Ted McSweeney. He was wearing the same old brown coat he always wore together with the wellies and the flat cap which had all seen better days. The rug lay at his feet. "Well, well," he grunted. "Ain't seen you a while. How's things going?"

"Mustn't grumble," I said. "How are you?"

"Oh, business a bit slack but not too bad." He emptied his glass and put it on the bar. "Really good pint that," he said then picked up the glass again and held it up to the light. "Yes," he sighed, "a really good pint."

"Want another?" I said getting the hint.

"Oh, are you sure? That'd be very nice. Thanks kindly."

I ordered two pints of bitter.

"Where do you buy all your groceries?" Ted asked.

I held up my hands, "Oy, stop right there. You've given me your sales pitch already."

"Oh, sorry. Course I 'ave." He lit a cigarette and puffed at it for a while then said, "Lot's a comin' an goin' at your cottage.

'Hello,' I thought. 'The village jungle drums had obviously been at work.

"Thinkin' of selling?" he asked.

There was little point in lying to him. Photos of the cottage would be in the estate agents' windows within the next couple of days and would also feature in newspaper adverts.

"Afraid so," I said. "We don't want to leave but ... well, it's private ... family business."

"Shame. After all your 'ard work."

I nodded. "We'll miss you and the rest of the neighbours."

Ted took a massive swig as his new pint, wiped his mouth on his sleeve and said "Where you off to then?"

"Not sure yet."

"Trouble with the missus? Saw her leavin' yesterday morn."

I was about to tell him to mind his own bloody business when I felt a hand on my shoulder. Charles stood there with a big smile on his face. "I see you've started without me. Where's my Guinness?" he demanded. I smothered a sigh of relief, turned and shook his hand. "Charlie this is Ted McSweeney. He lives in the village."

They shook hands. "How do," said Ted.

I ordered a Guinness and another pint for myself. Ted stared pointedly at his empty glass but I ignored him.

"'Scuse us," I said picking up the drinks. We've got business to discuss." I took them to a vacant table on the other side of the room.

"Thank God you came. It was like being rescued by the cavalry," I said when we were seated.

"Looks like a harmless old boy," Charles said.

"Harmless but the village gossip. It seems my every move is being watched."

"Okay, what's this all about?" he said taking a sip from his glass.

"Eh? What d'you mean?"

He shrugged his shoulders. "I can't remember how long it's been since you last suggested a pint and a chat. Something's in the wind."

"Jen's left me," I said.

He looked shocked. "What? ... for good?"

"No, thank God. Nothing that bad. Gordon, our bloody ghost has been stomping up and down the corridor again. It's spooking her badly. She's gone to live with her mum and dad for a while."

"But you're still okay together?"

"Oh yes. I'm missing her already and vice versa."

"Well that's a relief. What're you going to do?"

"She's had enough," I said. "Wants to move. I'm scared that if I refuse to sell up I'll lose her."

"Shame," he said, repeating Ted's words. "After all your hard work."

He sat for a while with his chin cupped in his hands, then "Tricky one," he muttered to himself. "Can't see a way out of this." He put his hand on my arm. "Dammit, Gus. You two can't split up. You were made for each other."

I nodded.

"What about an exorcist? D'you remember we spoke about it a while back?"

I laughed. "Nah. They're only in films."

"No, you're wrong. I'm sure I read somewhere that they're often successful. Why don't you ask the local vicar? He'll find the right person for you or at least give you some advice."

I shrugged my shoulders. "Maybe I'll give it a go."

"Well do it before you flog the cottage."

"Is that your final prognosis, doctor?"

"You could always get a second opinion."

"Okay," I said, "but I'm pretty sure all I'll get is a lot of mumbo jumbo, weird incantations and a big bill at the end of it."

"What would you rather do? Take a chance and spend a few quid or move house?

Besides which if you do it through the church it'll most likely be free."

"Gosh. Free mumbo jumbo."

He punched my shoulder. "Give it a try."

"What if it doesn't work?"

He made a hopeless gesture with his arms. "Think about it. If you want to stay married, my old pal, you'll just have to bite the bullet, pull up your roots and find another place. It's not the end of the world is it?"

I sighed. "Yes, I suppose you're right."

He stood up. "Right," he said. "Consultation over. Where should I send my bill?"

"You earn enough money. I'll have it on the NHS."

"Skinflint," he said, picking up the empty glasses. "Same again?"

I watched him walk over to the bar and smiled to myself when I saw Ted sidle over and engage him in conversation. Three drinks were poured then Charles brought two of them back to our table.

I laughed. "I see you got hooked. Did Ted ask you where you bought your groceries?"

"Yep. I told him I live in Outer Mongolia."

"Well done. That would've shut him up."

"He asked me if that was anywhere near Sevenoaks."

We decided to have lunch in the pub and while Charles was working his way through a massive plate of sausage and mash he told me of his plans to buy a house in Crete, enthusiastically showing me photos of a tiny ruin that he intended to renovate.

"Looks fabulous," I said. "But before you buy check it doesn't have any noisy Greek ghosts."

The next morning I came down to find my doormat completely covered with expensive looking brochures sent by the estate agents, bulging with glossy photographs of properties ranging from pokey little houses not much bigger than rabbit hutches yet still well above my price range to vast mansions that would take me six life times to pay for. I piled them on to the kitchen table and promised myself that I'd read them later. Then I made myself a light breakfast, pumped up the tyres on my bike and cycled off through the village heading in the direction of Plaxtol. It was a beautiful morning. The woods on either side of the road had shed most of their leaves which now lay like a red carpet beneath the black trunks. I saw a deer foraging between the leaves and rabbits skittered across the empty road. I hadn't cycled for quite a while so after only a short distance my legs started to ache and my lungs were protesting about all the hard work as I pedalled up the hilly road. Then, just as I was promising myself to do more exercise, I rounded a bend and found what I was looking for. A massive, slightly dilapidated Victorian building standing well back from the road, surrounded by pine trees at the end of a short drive full of potholes. An old car sat abandoned knee deep in weeds to one side and the long wooden gate which led into the property hung from just one hinge and had to be lifted to one side to gain entry. On the gate in faded letters were the words 'The Vicarage'. I parked my bike against the old car and made my way through the potholes and banged on the huge front door. A cacophony of barking immediately started off from far away in the bowels of the building. Deep throaty barks coming from what sounded like very big animals getting closer until I heard them crash against the other side of the door growling and clawing at the woodwork. I stepped back sure that I was about to be eaten alive, then after what seemed a long time the barking was joined by a human voice. "Come away with you … will ye stop making all this fuss. Down! Down!"

The door opened a crack then a tawny coloured Great Dane barged its way through the gap, reared up, put its massive paws on my shoulders and pushed me backwards from the step to land painfully on the stony ground where I lay pinned whilst the Hound of the Baskervilles gave my face a thorough wash with its tongue. Then another Great Dane appeared. Black this time and determined to help with the cleaning.

"Ah. Sorry about that," the voice said. "They're a little bit boisterous."

'Understatement of the year,' I thought.

A very small woman with long wispy grey hair and wearing a blue pinafore appeared in my line of vision. She grabbed the ravening hounds by their collars and yanked them away. "Don't mind them. It's their way of welcoming strangers," she said. "Are ye hurt?" I shook my head and scrambled to my feet. The dogs whined and tugged at her arms desperate to check if there was a bit of my face that they'd missed. My rescuer was small but obviously strong because her two pets were chest high against her tiny frame. She was possibly in her seventies with scrawny arms and the complexion of a prune. "The vicar's expecting ye," she said. "Ye'll find him in the garden, so ye will. Just go round the side of the house." I nodded and dabbed at my face with a handkerchief and wondered how he could he be expecting me? I hadn't said I was coming. The two dogs were dragged reluctantly back into the house and the door was slammed shut.

I did as I was told and made my way around the house to the back garden. At the far end of a rather scruffy lawn I could see a man bent over a pile of leaves. As I got nearer he turned and waved a hand in greeting. He was tall with a mop of thick white hair sweeping across his forehead and was probably about the same age as the Irish lady I'd just met. He was wearing a pair of faded dungarees tucking into green wellingtons. There was no sign of a dog collar.

"Ah, Mr Bricknal," he said. "You're a lot younger than I expected." There was just a trace of an Irish accent but nowhere near as strong as the lady with the dogs. Before I had a chance to reply he added, "But you're a welcome sight. This garden is getting too much for me on my own."

"I'm sorry," I said. I think you've got the wrong person."

"Eh?"

"I'm not Mr Bricknal."

"You're not? Then why aren't you?" He smiled.

"Sorry to disappoint you. My name is Fergus. Fergus Monroe."

"So you're not my gardener? What a pity. Well now, what can I do for you, Mr Munroe?"

104

He took off a glove and held out his hand. We shook. "I assume you are the vicar," I said.

"That I am," he replied. "… and if you bothered to come to church you'd know that. My name is Peter Reilly."

"I'm sorry," I said, "I'm a lapsed church goer."

He tutted and shook his head. "Ah, you're not on yer own. Sometimes on a Sunday I think I'm just talking to myself."

I shrugged my shoulders and apologised yet again.

I was about to tell him why I'd come but he held up his hand to stop me and glanced down at his watch.

"Time for some refreshment," he said. "Come up to the house for a drink of somethin' nice and ye can tell me what you're here for."

"Oh, right." I followed him across the lawn. He threw his gloves on top of a barrowload of leaves and opened the back door. The clamour of dogs barking started up again and I edged closer to his back so he'd be first to meet the onslaught. They charged towards us but he stretched out his arms like Moses parting the waves and bellowed, "Shut up, you noisy buggers! Go lie down!" The dogs seemed to shrink in size, screeched to a halt then slunk off and went back into the kitchen.

"That's impressive," I said.

"Come on, we'll sit in the front room. It's more peaceful in there," Peter said leading the way into a large room. I gazed around. It was exactly what I'd expected a vicarage front room to look like. Heavy curtains covering high dusty windows, big comfy settees, massive heavy side tables with damask overlays, lots of old photos, a roll top desk, a piano. I was disappointed not see an aspidestra.

"Sit yourself down, Fergus," he said pointing to a big floral patterned armchair. "Now what would you like to drink?"

"A cup of tea would be nice," I answered.

"Ah, a lapsed churchgoer and a teetotaller. What a dreadful combination," he muttered to himself, then, "will ye not join me in a beer? I've been working hard all morning."

"A beer would be even better. I've had a long cycle ride."

He left the room and I could hear him talking to someone in the hallway. Then he reappeared, plonked himself down on a chair opposite mine and seconds later the old Irish lady appeared carrying a tray with four bottles of beer on it. "This is my sister, Rosemary, Mr Munroe," Peter said. "Rosemary, this is Fergus, who's here on false pretences. I'm afraid he's not the gardener."

"Ah," she said to no one in particular, "I didn't think he had the makings of a gardener, too posh, so he is."

"Do you hear that, Fergus? You're too posh for working in a garden," Peter said grinning widely.

"My wife's the gardener in our house," I said.

"Typical!" Rosemary muttered to herself, then "and what'll I do with yer man, Bricknal if he decides to show up?"

"Send him in here with a beer for himself." She shuffled off out of the room.

The Reverend Peter Reilly leaned forward and flipped the caps of the bottles. "Please excuse my sister," he said. "She's not had the best of health and can be a bit abrupt at times." He handed me a bottle. "Cheers," he said clinking his against mine, then he sank back in the chair. "Right. Let's be having it Fergus. How can I help you?"

I was a little hesitant at first but I told him the whole story starting from how I met Jenny right through to finding Eliza's notebook, the ghostly experiences and Jenny eventually leaving to live temporarily with her parents. He listened attentively, only interrupting occasionally to ask a question and when I'd come to the end of my talk he sat for a long time, saying nothing, his chin cupped in one hand and staring out of the window. At last he said, "Tis a strange story right enough and a sad one too. So you're hoping that I can get rid of the demon or whatever it is … perform an exorcism?"

"Or if you know another way," I said.

"It's the only way I know of getting rid of unwanted spirits. A few years have gone by since I did one but I'll give it a go."

"Have you had any successes?"

"Oh, aye. Way, way back," he said, nodding his head vigorously. "I seem to remember the last one worked but I was driving the evil out of a person, not a house. It's called a possession."

"I just want a normal home and my wife back," I said.

"I'll do my best," Peter smiled and opened the other two bottles.

"When can you do it?"

"How would tomorrow afternoon suit you?"

*****

That night I rang Jenny and told her what I'd arranged. There was a long silence before she spoke, then she said, "Do you really believe all that piffle?"

"I just thought it was worth a try. The vicar seems fairly confident it'll work."

She sighed. "I'll always be worried it might come back."

"Remember that the house is now on the market," I said.

"I know. It must be awful for you. Has anyone turned up to see it?"

"Not so far," I said, trying to keep the relief out of my voice.

"And what about Gordon? Have you heard from him?"

"Not a peek. He might have left already."

"I doubt it."

"Strange that," I said. "When you left it seems he left too." There was another long pause, then she whispered, "Oh Gus, I miss you."

"I miss you too," I said. "How are your Mum and Dad coping having their daughter back?"

"Oh they're fine. A bit worried about us I think. Gus, I'm sorry I'm such a wimp. Please forgive me. I shouldn't have left you on your own."

"It's quite understandable. You're no wimp."

"I want to be cuddled up with you in bed. I'm back in the room I had as a child. Same single bed, same hard mattress … and Puta misses you too. He's not the same dog without us being together."

I felt my throat close up and for a moment I couldn't speak. "We should be together, Jen," I managed to say. "Come home to me as soon as you feel able to and I promise that if the exorcism doesn't work we won't wait for a buyer, we'll move out straight away.

*****

At two o'clock the next afternoon the old car that I'd seen at the vicarage and assumed had been abandoned turned up outside the cottage in a cloud of billowing smoke which nearly blanked out the whole village. There was a loud crashing of gears as it was reversed into our small parking space then the Reverend Peter Reilly leapt out to greet me. He was carrying a large canvas bag. "Here we are," he said, a big smile on his face. "What a fine morning." He turned and faced the cottage. "Ah, so this is where you live. What a change you've made of it. I used to know the fellow who lived here before you."

"Oh yes. I'd like to hear about him. What was he like?"

"Ah. Poor fellow had more bad luck in life than anyone deserves. It wasn't fair, just one rotten thing after another."

I led him into the cottage. "How come?" I said. "Grab a seat and tell me about it."

He held up his hand. "First things first," he said. "T'was a long hot drive from the vicarage."

I went into the kitchen and took two beers from the fridge. That long hot drive must have taken at least five minutes.

"Ah," he smiled as he took his bottle. "This'll pep up the old exorcism muscles. They do get a bit rusty if not used for a while."

"Okay, what about the boy? Your wife told me he was a bit simple."

Peter perched himself on the arm of the settee. "The girl was the first of his troubles."

"Girl?"

"Yes. Gregory had two children. A boy and a girl. The girl was the oldest by about two years. Her name was Winifred. A rather plain child. I think she had learning difficulties. Very shy and hard to get a peep out of. She was only fifteen when it happened."

"What?"

"She went and got herself pregnant. It was the talk of the village. Everyone was surprised. She'd never been seen with a boyfriend. Like I said, she was no beauty so speculation was rife about who the father was and inevitably suspicion pointed at poor Gregory. He called me in to question the girl but she wouldn't tell me or anyone else who was responsible for her condition."

"So what happened?"

"Well, about six months into her confinement she disappeared. I think her da sent her to live with his sister up in Nottingham. Least ways that's what I was told."

"Poor kid," I said. "… but what happened to the boy?"

"Well, that was a real mystery. Nobody really knows." He took a sip of beer than stared wistfully at the bubbles rising in the glass.

"Little Felix was what everyone called him and although he'd grown into a beanstalk of a lad the word 'little' stuck with him right until he left."

"Go on."

"Like I said, no one really knows for certain. Felix was very bright at school. He was a regular church goer along with his sister and their da. Never saw much of the mother. Her name was Marion and she kept herself to herself. I don't think I clapped eyes on her once but I got to know her family quite well. A nice man, nice son, bit of a dull girl but very respectful and popular in the village. The da's name was Gregory. Big fellow who used to sell logs for a living together with various odd jobs around the area. I think little Felix had ambitions to be a vet. He was passionate about animals. They had two dogs, a cat and a long-eared rabbit called Hutch, a sweet little chap who used to nibble the …"

"But Felix. What happened to Felix?" I interrupted.

"Ah, sorry. I digress." He emptied his glass, wiped his mouth and said, "To tell the truth there was a bit of a scandal. People in the village are a tad reluctant to speak of it. One night the lad had to be rushed into hospital. Apparently he was hysterical, talking complete gibberish and was in great pain."

I waited for him to continue but he just sat there shaking his head and staring down at the carpet.

"Go on," I said at last.

"Turns out he'd been raped," Peter said, almost in a whisper.

"Raped?" Peter nodded. "The hospital discovered internal injuries which pointed conclusively to male rape."

"Was it the father?"

"Well, that was what was first suggested. That he'd raped both his children. There were all sorts of clinical examinations. Poor Gregory went to hell and back what with all the recriminations and gossip but it turned out that he was completely innocent and the police put it down to an intruder who must somehow have got into the little caravan at the back of the house.

"Did they ever find the rapist?"

"No. Sadly not. Case unsolved as far as the police were concerned."

"But why was the boy living in the caravan?"

"Like I said, nobody really knows. He'd stopped sleeping in the house a month or two earlier. Absolutely refused to spend another night in the place so his da bought a second hand caravan, cleaned it up and that's where the boy stayed."

"Big mistake," I said. "Caravans are pretty easy to break into."

"That's for sure. After that the boy was never the same again, went completely doolally. Had to be taken into care.

"What a sad story."

"I'm afraid it got even sadder after that." Peter sighed. "As if Gregory hadn't had enough grief to contend with, about two months' after the rape the ma suddenly and without any nasty symptoms ups and dies. I don't know from what but I was asked to do the funeral. The weird thing about that was Gregory didn't turn up. Not to his wife's own funeral. I'd never experienced such a thing and of course that got the gossip mongers going again. Weeks went by. He stopped coming to church and was rarely seen in the village. He became a complete recluse. I felt so sorry for the poor fellah so I decided to pop down here to try my best to console him. When Gregory opened the door I was shocked. He was like a different man from the one I knew. He'd lost a huge amount of weight, his cheeks were sunken and his eyes had lost all their sparkle. I don't think he'd had a shave for days and what's more I think he'd neglected to have a bath for a good while too. T'was a sad sight to see. He had always been such a big cheerful man and was now shrunk down to half the size, poor fellow." Peter went quiet for a while, reliving the moment.

"Go on," I said.

"Well, I gave him my condolences about his loss and asked if there was anything I could do to help." Peter stood up and walked over to the window shaking his head from side to side. He seemed reluctant to continue. I waited and watched him as he drummed his fingers on the window sill as though he was making some big internal decision until eventually he turned to face me. "I find it difficult to relate what happened next," he said.

"Take your time."

He shrugged. "You'll excuse the language I hope. It wasn't very pleasant."

"Don't worry about that. Please go on. I'm fascinated."

"I thought he was going to hit me," Peter said. "Gregory's face went red with anger and he yelled loud enough to deafen the whole county."

"Yes, there is something you can do, he screamed. You can fuck off! You won't do a ha'porth of good with your pious God claptrap. There is no fucking God. Least ways, he never showed his face in this house. But Satan. He's a regular visitor. Can't keep him away. So do me a favour and fuck off and don't come back! Then he slammed the door in my face. I've never seen a man so angry. I don't know why. I was only there to help."

"Gordon?" I said.

"Eh?"

"It's Gordon," I repeated. "The reason you're here. He scared the hell out of me and my wife and must have done the same thing to this man Gregory and his children."

"I take it you're referring to your ghost."

"I am. It all fits. Whatever it is that's still lurking in this house must have frightened Gregory's son out of his wits and is succeeding doing the same with us."

Peter cupped his chin in his hand. "Well the sooner we can persuade him to move along the better," he said. "So let's get on with it." He walked over to the doorway where he'd left his bag, fished out his ceremonial cassock together with a long white silk drape and put it on. All at once he was transformed from a rosy cheeked elderly man with a slight drink problem into a traditional country vicar. I felt my confidence rise. If anyone could do the job this man in his fine raiment could certainly do so.

"I think it best if we do the ceremony in your hallway upstairs where you say most of the activity takes place," he said. He gestured with his hand. "Lead on Macduff." We went upstairs and stood in the narrow corridor leading to our three small bedrooms.

"So this is where your unseen tenant does his patrolling is it?" Peter said. "I can think of prettier walks to go on."

"Yes," I agreed. "I don't think he's an outdoor type."

Peter opened all the bedroom doors then the windows looking out on to the street beyond. "I know this'll sound strange or maybe a bit barmy but if we are to ask Gordon to leave he's got to have a way out." He held out a small leather bound book. "This," he said, "is a world famous exorcism manual by a gentleman called Vincentius von Berg. Quite a celebrity in his day for driving out evil spirits." From a hidden pocket in his cassock he produced a small golden coloured tube perforated at one end rather like a pepper pot. It dangled from a loop of gold chain.

"And this …" he continued, "is an amulet. It's been the property of my church for nigh on a hundred and fifty years, so it has. It's supposed to invoke angels and archangels to intervene."

My heart sank. 'Here comes the mumbo jumbo' I thought.

"If you want to watch I must have complete silence. There must be no interruptions so I suggest you sit at the top of the stairs."

I did as I was told and perched myself on the top step.

"Okay, quiet now. I'll start the ritual." He smiled and winked at me. "D'ye know any Latin?"

"Afraid not."

"Ah well, you won't understand a word of this. Here's a weird fact. Latin tends to be more effective against the devil. Apparently he doesn't like the language of the church."

I nearly laughed but kept a straight face and just nodded.

"Okay. Here we go. Hush now." He pushed his spectacles to the end of his nose, peered down at the book and started to read. He was right. I didn't understand a word of it. He read clearly and without hesitation for about twenty minutes. From time to time swinging his amulet towards the open door of one of the bedrooms as though enticing someone or something to leave. This was accompanied by lots of gestures with his book hand, his arm making great sweeping arcs like a golfer practicing his swing. By now his face had reddened considerably and perspiration was running down his forehead. I was concerned that at any moment he might collapse from exhaustion but at last he stopped his oration and closed the book with a final flourish. "And don't come back," he yelled.

After all his ranting the silence that followed seemed intense. I waited then asked tentatively, "Is that it?"

"That's it."

"Has it gone?"

"There's no guarantee," he said. "You'll have to wait and see. If he sends you a postcard from Cornwall you'll know he's moved on."

I laughed. "Mother of God," he exclaimed. "That was hot work." He started to struggle out of his heavy cassock. "Why they make these bloody things out of such thick materials I'll never know." He threw it over his arm. "There ye go, Fergus. You've witnessed an exorcism and the unfrocking of a vicar all on the same day. Aren't you the lucky one?"

"I feel very privileged," I said. "Come on downstairs. You've earned yourself another beer."

"Ah. You're a good man. I have a thirst on me, that's for sure."

Back in the living room Peter busied himself packing all his regalia back into its bag while I poured the first of three beers. Much later when he was leaving he refused absolutely any payment for his spirit rejecting efforts but accepted my promise of a donation to church funds, then he was off swaying tipsily to his car before, with a cheery wave, a great belch of smoke and a crunching of gears he disappeared down the lane.

I stood watching long after he'd gone. Smiling to myself, glad of the experience and of his warm company then walked back into the house. A small shiny object lying on the kitchen floor caught my eye. It was a brass button. I felt a cold prickle run up my spine and for a few moments I couldn't breathe. A few feet away lay the remains of little Eliza's doll. It had been torn to shreds.

*****

The following morning there was a phone call from the estate agency in Sevenoaks. They had two couples eager to view the cottage. Reluctantly I agreed to seeing the first pair at ten o'clock and the second an hour later. I scurried around tidying the place up then went upstairs and spent a long time opening up Eliza's hidey hole again. Tearing off the new wallpaper, prizing the plank from the wall I placed the ragged pieces that used to be a doll on top of Eliza's notebook in the old drawer. I couldn't bring myself to just throw the shattered remains away. This was where it had been found and this was where it belonged.

Before closing the hole again I sat back on my heels and stared at the sad remnants wondering what evil force could have caused such damage. This thing I shared a house with was no longer just an invisible, harmless ethereal spirit. It could tear, rip and violate with the same savagery as an angry dog. There under the notebook and newspaper cuttings I could see the shredded remains of Eliza's bible and at that moment I knew for certain that it had been destroyed by the same creature. The bible when the thing was alive and terrorising Eliza's family and the doll now nearly one hundred and thirty years after its death.

I felt a shiver run up my spine. All at once I wanted to be rid of this feeling of dread. To hell with the cottage. I'd sell the damned place, move on with Jenny, start afresh. I screwed the plank back into place, did a hasty job of repairing the wallpaper and went back downstairs to wait for my first customers.

First up accompanied by an agent was a young couple barely out of their teens. He was tall and extremely thin with long black hair which reached to his shoulders and a stubble of a beard. His girlfriend looked as though she ate for both of them. Short and tubby wearing a mini skirt which only just covered her backside and a tattoo of a butterfly on her neck. Surprisingly they both spoke in privately educated upper class English. "We absolutely love it," he said to the agent ignoring me completely. "Is he willing to consider an offer?"

The agent, a slip of a girl herself, said "Well, why don't you ask him?"

He turned to me as though he'd only just spotted me for the first time. "Well?" he asked.

I shook my head. "Fraid not. I'm asking a fair price."

He turned to his girlfriend, eyebrows raised. She said, "Don't worry, Simon. I'm sure daddy will stump up." Simon nodded, pointed at me and said to the agent, "Tell him we'll think about it."

And that was it. He opened the back door and all three trooped out. I hoped daddy would stump up. Simon deserved Gordon. Deserved to have the shit scared out of him.

Later on a very fat middle aged man arrived red faced and sweaty with his pale wife and the same girl agent. He wandered quickly from room to room muttering to himself, "Too small, too small," and "Good God, no!" then stomped out, his poor silent wife in tow with a final, "What a waste of time," he muttered as he left, there were no hellos, no goodbyes. Just a permanent frown and a looming heart attack.

How was it I thought that beautiful Kent had so many bad mannered people living in it?

I made myself a cup of tea, slumped down in my armchair and switched on the TV. I don't often watch day time television but I was bored and needed some distraction. An old film starring Sophia Loren and Frank Sinatra was half way through. I settled back comfortably, kicked my shoes off and put my feet up on a padded stool. Peace reigned.

There was a knock on the door. I groaned. What now? Not another bloody estate agent. Muttering more curses to myself, I walked through into the kitchen and threw open the back door.

Jenny stood on the doorstep clutching her large suitcase in one hand and Puta's lead in the other.

"Surprise, surprise," she said with a big grin on her face.

"Jenny!" I rushed forward and took her in my arms.

"Wh…. What happened? I don't understand."

"Sorry," she said. "I couldn't stay away any longer. You're not cross are you?"

"Cross?" I said. "I'm ecstatic. Oh, heck, Jen. I've missed you so much. Welcome home."

"I've missed you too, Gus."

I kissed her and hugged her tightly, lifting her off the ground and swinging her around. "What a surprise. Boy, am I glad to see you."

Bending down I picked up Puta who was going berserk and trying to climb up my leg. "And welcome back to you too," I hooted. "We're a family again."

With Jenny back at home it felt like we were on honeymoon again. Nervously at first but over a period of time she relaxed and became her old self once more. There was no sign of Gordon and we started to believe that the exorcism had worked. We went on long walks, cooked together, went to the pub, laughed a lot and made love frequently. More people came to view the cottage but there were no offers to buy. A recession had hit global markets and housing prices had slumped dramatically.

My seventy five year old mother travelled down from the Midlands and spent Christmas with us. As always she and Jen got on very well. We threw a party for her. Our tiny living room was packed with old friends and colleagues from London plus a few neighbours from the village. Later, my son and daughter made a flying visit and so too did Jenny's son, Marvin. Even later still I was awarded Cartoonist of the Year by the Press Association, given a rise by my paper and it seemed that the sun was permanently shining down on us. Happiness prevailed and all was well with the world. We had climbed to the peak of marital bliss. Things could not have been better. With luck we could stay on that high plateau because the only other direction was down. Which of course could not possibly happen. Or so we thought.

One evening early in February I took Puta for his nightly walk along the lane so that he could do his business before bed time. There was never much traffic at that time of night so I let him off the lead. It was intensely cold. There was a full moon and a sharp frost had turned the hedges and fields white. The pungent smell of foxes wafted around in a chill wind which always drove Puta into a state of frenzy. He loved to chase foxes. Brave as hell when he spotted one but quick to back off if one stopped to call his bluff. On this occasion a large male fox ran across the path right in front of us, dived through the hedge and into the wood beyond with Puta in hot pursuit. The hedge was thick with brambles and too dense for me to climb through so I waited impatiently for him to return, calling his name and cursing myself for letting him off the lead. He had gone for probably only ten minutes but which with the extreme cold seemed more like an hour. I'd almost given up on him when at last he reappeared covered in mud and twigs, wagging his tail and looking puzzled why I was swearing, no longer in a good mood and was dragging him back to the cottage. I cleaned him up as best I could and told him to get in his basket. Jenny had gone to bed so not wanting to wake her by putting my frozen body next to hers I sat by the dwindling fire with a hot cup of tea and waited for my teeth to stop chattering and to get some feeling back into my toes.

I must have nodded off. I woke up feeling cold again. The fire had gone out completely and I was shocked to see that it was nearly two o'clock in the morning. Puta lay, paws twitching, in his basket probably dreaming of another fox chase and I needed to be snuggled up with my wife under a warm duvet.

I crept up the stairs and went into the bathroom to clean my teeth. Just as I was dabbing my face with a towel I became aware of a soft moaning noise. At first I thought it was the dog downstairs but then realised it was coming from our bedroom next door. I walked into the hallway and stood by the closed door. Then it came again. A low moan followed by quickening gasps. I thought at first that Jenny was in pain but quickly realised that it was the opposite. Not pain but sexual pleasure. Quietly I opened the door. Moonlight was filtering through the curtains and I could see her clearly. She was lying on her back, her mouth wide open with an expression of ecstasy on her face. Her body was moving rhythmically under the duvet while her groans got louder and more frequent until at last with a piercing scream her back arched upwards and she reached orgasm, shuddered and lay down again, her face glistening with sweat.

I closed the door again and stood in the darkness of the hallway, feeling completely stunned. I'd never heard or seen Jenny pleasuring herself before, didn't think she had the need. We made love often and I had assumed that her sexual needs were being satisfied. I suddenly felt inadequate. I'd always thought out love making was perfect but it had never reached the intensity of the scene I'd just witnessed. Our unions were passionate right enough but much quieter. I felt incredibly depressed and absolutely demasculated. It was as if I'd just watched my wife being unfaithful with a much better lover than me.

I crept back into the room, climbed under the duvet and lay well over on my side of the bed. It was a long time before I was able to sleep.

For the next two weeks I didn't attempt to make love to Jenny. We snuggled up together to watch TV, kissed goodnight when we went to bed but that's about as intimate as it got.

My son, Andrew, phoned to say that he'd fallen out with his girlfriend, she'd chucked him out and could he stay with us for a couple of days? Of course I said yes. I never had to persuade Jenny. Everybody was always welcome as far as she was concerned. The two days stretched into five. It was a pleasure to have him to stay. He had an easy going rapport with Jen. They'd go for walks together when I was working then in the evenings we'd either go to the pub or he would cook us a meal. Since he was a child he'd always had a fascination for food. Not just the eating of it but the preparation. His mother was a good cook and it was from her that he got his enthusiasm. We played golf together. A humiliating experience. I had always considered myself a reasonable player but Andrew who hadn't touched a club for years proceeded to completely annihilate me, smashing the ball fifty yards past my feeble drives, chipping on to the green, taking only one or two putts then walking off with a mock yawn and a "Ho hum. What an easy game."

"Arrogant upstart," I snarled. "Have you no respect for the elderly?"

"Fraid not," he laughed. "Loser buys the beers.

We sat in the clubhouse with full pints, facing a long glass window looking out on the course and watched as golfers ended their rounds on the last green.

"Nice to see you so happy," Andy said.

"Happy? I'm devastated."

"No, not about the game. I meant you and Jenny. You're great together."

I smiled, pleased that we'd got his approval. "Thanks Andy. Yes, we get along fine."

"She's a very nice woman."

I nodded enthusiastically.

"I was all prepared to hate her at first. Bit of a shock when you left Mum."

"I'm sorry. It must have been."

He nodded. "Selfishly I guess part of it is the inconvenience. Most children take it for granted that their parents will be together for the duration, no matter what … then boom! It happens and you realise, probably for the first time, that they have feelings too. You know. Boredom, dissatisfaction, new needs, desires."

"What d'you mean, inconvenience?"

"Well, Mum lives in London, you live here. Sis and I still want to see you both. Much more convenient when you lived in the same house." He smiled at me, "… and that's what I meant about being selfish. Sorry."

"Understandable, not selfish," I said.

We sat silently for a while. Outside on the eighteenth green a very overweight man in a pair of vivid yellow and green plus fours sank his final putt and turned to shake his opponent's hand with the same glee as if he had just won the Masters at Augusta.

"Jen told me about your ghost," Andrew said.

"I thought she would. We call him Gordon. He seems to have gone quiet lately."

"I don't believe all that crap," he said.

"Oh, it's real enough. You'd believe it if you heard it."

"Yeah, yeah. And do you still think there's a man with a beard called Santa Claus?"

"It scared Jenny enough for her to escape to her parents for a week."

He rolled his eyes up to the ceiling in exasperation. "Dad," he said, "She's a woman. Women are totally irrational."

I looked at him to see if he was joking. He wasn't.

"No wonder your girlfriend chucked you out," I said.

"Yeah, and I'm glad she did. It's a relief to be rid of her. Good riddance!"

I laughed. "The last time you spoke to me about her she was the woman of your dreams."

He groaned. "Yeah, that was before I got to know her properly. Maggie is a fantasist. She's convinced the Loch Ness monster exists, believes in horoscopes, won't leave the house if Taurus is on the cusp of Jupiter or whatever it says in the paper that day. She's completely loopy. No wonder some blokes turn to homosexuality."

"She was sane before she met you," I said.

He thought about it for a while then said, "Nah. She's always been bonkers."

"Well, Jenny won't thank you for putting her in the same category."

"Dad, this conversation is strictly between ourselves."

I got up and walked over to the bar to get us another drink. There were several golfers waiting to be served, all swapping stories about their exploits on the course so it was a while before I got to the front of the queue. Then, just as I was about to order, the phone behind the barman rang. He turned and picked it up.

"Hang on, madam," he said. "I'll ask." He swung round and called out, "Is there anyone here called Munroe, Fergus Munroe?"

"That's me," I said. He handed me the phone. "There's a call for you."

It was Jenny. "Hi sweetheart," I said. "Is there anything wrong?"

"No. Everything's fine. Andrew's girlfriend Maggie phoned. Wants to talk to him. Sounded a bit urgent. Will you ask him to call her?"

"Okay. We're just having one more drink then we'll be coming home."

"No rush," she said, "see you later," then she hung up.

There was a public telephone near the entrance to the members' bar. Andrew practically sprinted to it. I followed and made my way to the toilets. As I passed I heard him say, "Maggie, darling. Oh Jesus it's so good to hear from you. Yeah, I've missed you too. Oh my gorgeous girl, how are you?"

I gave him a thumbs up and walked into the gents.

Early next morning he had packed his bag and was off back to London in his beat-up Volkswagen, pausing only to give us a swift thankyou and goodbye. Jenny promised that next time he visited us we'd have a proper bed for him to sleep on and not just a mattress.

"Great," he replied, "… and who knows? There might be two of us."

We waved as his car disappeared down the lane.

"That was nice," Jenny said. "He's a sweet boy."

"Takes after his dad."

"Funny. I didn't notice he had a big head."

I laughed and put my arms around her. "I love him but it's nice to be on our own again."

She tapped me on the nose with her finger. "Now, now. No hanky panky. Haven't you got work to do, my man?" I sighed. She was right. Today was my first day back on the paper. We returned to the cottage, had a light breakfast then I took that day's newspapers up to my study, switched on the radio for the latest news and scanned the papers, jotting down events that were taking place at home and around the world. It was November 1982. The Thames Barrier designed to protect Greater London from high tides and storm surges had at last been largely completed. Great! A good object to have a go at.

It was 1.30 pm before I'd roughed out about four ideas and faxed them through to the paper. Then as always there was the interminable wait for the editor to finish his conferences /lunch/managerial meetings and all the other appointments editors have to deal with before having a moment or two to cast an eye on his cartoonist's contribution. After a two hour wait I got a call to tell me that my Thames Barrier idea had been accepted. Four hours later I was on my way to London to deliver the drawing and two hours after that I was back at home sitting in the kitchen enjoying a delicious fish pie that Jenny had prepared along with a bottle of crisp Chablis that had been left as a thank you present by my son. Jen had dressed up for the occasion, wearing one of my favourite of her dresses with a low cut top under a white blouse. She'd washed her hair, tied it in a ponytail and looked absolutely stunning.

We had moved into the living room and were sitting together on the settee sipping at the remnants of the Chablis before I asked her, "What's the occasion?"

"Occasion?"

"Yes. You look dressed to kill. Are we off to the Ritz?"

She smiled shyly. "I just thought I'd make an effort."

"You look fabulous … and look at me, a complete tramp."

She fell silent for a while then shook her head. "To tell the truth, Gus, I'm worried that you've gone off me."

"Wha ....?"

"I expect it's because most of the time you see me in a pair of scruffy jeans wearing no makeup with my hair in a mess. It's quite understandable."

"What's understandable? You'd look great in an old sack. I could never go off you."

She put her glass down and put her hand on my knee.

"We don't cuddle any more. You sleep as far away from me as possible. There must be something wrong."

I took both of her hands in mine. "Oh, you daft woman. I felt inhibited having my son sleeping in the next room. I adore you. I could never stop loving you, you are my life."

"Are you sure?"

"How can I prove it to you?"

She gave me a mischievous smile. "Well there is one way that springs to mind."

I stood up and looked down at her beautiful face, marvelling at the greenest eyes I'd ever seen. "Darling Jenny, I said. "Don't ever doubt me."

*****

135

I find it extremely difficult to write about what happened next. I still find it scarcely credible even after all these years and the memory of it haunts me to this day. The fire had started to dwindle in the hearth so we decided to go upstairs to the bedroom. We undressed and fell on to the bed in a passionate embrace. Jenny had an amazing body, slim and long legged with firm rounded breasts and I? Well, I was just me, Mr Average, nothing remarkable apart from being the most fortunate man alive. I remember switching the bedside lights off and admiring the pale glow of her skin from the light cast by the street lamp outside, her long blonde hair cascading across the pillow and her hands on either side of my waist pulling me to her. I remember the absurd feeling that somehow I was taking the lead part in a film or a romantic novel. We'd made love many times before but this time was totally different, altogether special as though a whole lot of new ingredients had been thrown into the mix and I was a small boy let loose in a sweet shop. I was in awe, hardly able to fully comprehend my good luck as I lay between her legs and felt her warm stomach against mine, her whole body arching upwards to receive me.

As I said earlier, I still find what happened next unbelievable although I know for certain that it did. It is definitely not a false memory or a bad dream or a hallucination. I remember Jenny groaning softly as I entered her body then feeling a sharp pain on either side of my waist. It was as though I'd been clamped in a giant vice. All at once I was lifted from her and thrown across the room, crashing painfully against a chest of drawers on the far wall. I lay there for a moment or two completely dazed and wondering what the hell had happened. Blood was dripping onto my chest from a wound just above my eyebrow. The room seemed to be spinning around and I felt totally confused. I remember crawling across the floor, picking up a pair of underpants I'd shed only minutes before and holding them against a cut on my head then as the dizziness subsided standing up and staggering towards the bed. Jenny was lying on her back. Her eyes were wide open staring fixedly at the ceiling. They appeared to be glazed over as if she was in a trance. She was groaning softly and her long legs were raised and crossed at the ankles as though they were encircling another body. Horrified, I glanced down at her genitals. The lips of her vagina were moving as though something or someone was penetrating that part of her body. Her moans were getting louder and I watched helplessly, too astounded to move for what seemed an eternity until her head tilted back, her mouth opened wide and she groaned loudly as she reached orgasm. I sat down heavily on the side of the bed. Slowly she put her legs down and after a minute or so her glazed eyes returned to normal. She blinked then looked across at me. "Wow!" she breathed. "That was amazing!"

I didn't know what to say so I said nothing.

"You must've been saving that one up. Oh my God. Is the top of my head still there?"

I tried to put on a smile. Jenny propped herself up on her elbows and leant forwards to give me a kiss then her eyes widened in alarm and she sat up quickly. "Gus," she gasped, "your head. What've you done?"

"There was no way I could tell her what I'd just witnessed so I just mumbled lamely. "Don't worry. It's just a scratch. I hit my bead on the bedrail."

She jumped out of bed and rushed into the bathroom reappearing seconds later with a wet towel. "This is what happens when a girl marries a sex god," she laughed. "He gets a sore head and she gets a sore you know what!! I allowed her to fuss over me for a while as she dabbed my head with the towel, smeared ointment on and placed a plaster over the wound. Later when she was satisfied with her handiwork she lifted the bedclothes and ushered me back into bed.

"C'mon Romeo," she said. "I want to snuggle up to my patient."

I waited till she was asleep then crept out of bed and went into the bathroom. In the large mirror over the bath I saw that to the left and right of my body, just below the ribcage, there were red welts. Five identical punctures on each side rather like the claw marks of an animal.

*****

That was the turning point for me. Now I wanted to move. To get away from this place with its malevolent but unseen occupant. Last night had terrified me. I wanted to move as quickly as possible so the next morning I was on the phone to the estate agents hoping that they might have an interested customer. No such luck. I was told that the market was at a standstill but they'd let me know if and when anyone wanted to view. I put the phone down feeling completely despondent. Try as I might I couldn't get my brain into the right mode for work. I kept reliving the terror of the night before trying to convince myself that it had been a bad dream or that I'd had some kind of funny turn and imagined it all, but the claw marks on my sides were evidence enough that it was real. I tried to scan the newspapers so that I could get on with the day's work but at each attempt the words became a blur and instead I relived the scene again. It was hopeless. I just couldn't concentrate. Late that afternoon I gave up trying and phoned the office to say I was ill and would be back as soon as possible. In contrast Jenny's mood on that day was totally opposite to mine. She was radiant. Happier than I'd seen her for some time. Her cheeks had a rosy bloom and she skipped around the kitchen like a teenager, singing along with whatever pop song was on the radio. I was kissed, cuddled and fussed over. For most of that day I was no longer Gus, my new name was "lover man" which given the circumstances depressed me even further. Up until then I'd assumed that I was Jenny's "lover man" but now I'd been usurped in that department by an invisible, hostile rival that I could not fight, challenge or understand. Once again I kept my distance and I gave her the same lie that I'd given the office. A stomach bug. So I was plied with aspirin and a foul tasting pink medicine which she'd stored in the cupboard long ago in case of this kind of emergency. Forcing the medicine down I sat on the settee propped up by what seemed like every cushion in the house with a hot water bottle on my lap and watched rubbish on day time TV.

After an hour or two of this torture I couldn't stand it any longer and suggested a walk with the dog.

She protested but was outvoted two to one by me and Puta who somehow had sensed a walk and was now bouncing around the room making little whimpering noises of joy.

It as a cold blustery day and we headed down the lane leaning into the wind, both of us wearing raincoats, scarves and wellington boots. I probably looked like the Michelin man's older brother but Jenny as always looked amazing with her long hair blowing out from under a jaunty multi-coloured beret, her small pert face almost swamped by the high collar of her coat.

We climbed over the stile and splashed through the many puddles towards the wood. Relieved to be sheltered from the wind once we reached the trees, I let Puta off the lead and he scampered off to see how many trees he could water before we went home.

It was dark in the wood. I remember feeling as though we'd entered an empty church. Apart from the constant drip, drip of water falling from the overhead branches the place was completely silent. No bird calls, no traffic noises, no sounds at all to disturb the peace. Consequently when we did speak it was in hushed tones as if we had indeed walked into a holy place.

Jenny was first. "How are you feeling now?" she asked.

"I'm fine. Must've eaten something bad. It'll go.

She grinned at me. "More like you over exerted yourself last night."

I changed the subject rapidly. "No luck yet from the estate agents, I'm afraid."

"There's no hurry."

"I think there is. I want to move. Start again."

Jenny stopped walking and turned to face me. "Hang on," she said. "You're the one who's always wanted to stay."

I nodded. "Yeah, I know but I've changed my mind. It's time to go."

She looked at me quizzically. "Is it Gordon you're worried about?"

"It's more about how he's worried you. Remember standing outside the cottage in the rain because you were too scared to go inside?"

Jenny laughed. "That was then," she said dismissively. "I think Gordon's packed his bags and gone. We haven't heard anything from him for ages."

I had a great urge to show her the scars on my body but decided against it.

"Besides which," she continued, "think about all the work we've done on the place. Now it's nearly finished I want to enjoy it. It would be crazy to move."

"Yes, but …" I started.

"Gus, don't be such a wimp." She turned and walked further down the path which was Jenny speak for "end of conversation".

I was at a loss what to do. I couldn't bring myself to tell her what had happened the previous night. She wouldn't have believed me, would've said I was imagining things, that I'd gone barmy and in truth I was starting to believe that I was. Maybe that knock on the head had caused me to think I'd seen things that I hadn't. Even the claw marks might have a rational explanation. It all seemed too preposterous to be real.

Things were to get worse. That night Jenny was extremely amorous and obviously wanted me to make love to her, but for me it was impossible. I couldn't get what happened in our bed only hours ago out of my mind and was terrified that it might happen again. Negative thoughts filled my brain and there was no way that I could get aroused despite her efforts. I was Mr Flaccid and was forced to continue the lie that my non-existent stomach was to blame. Her disappointment was obvious but Jenny being Jenny just smiled sympathetically, told me not worry, turned over and was soon asleep.

This was to happen on several subsequent nights and I had to pretend that my medical problem was getting worse. I even lied that I had an appointment with the local doctor, drove into town for an hour, bought some syrup of figs at the pharmacy in the High Street and told Jenny that this was what had been prescribed. Looking back on that period of our lives together I think that I had blinded myself to anything negative. I was so smitten with love and happiness I viewed everything through rose coloured spectacles. Every day had seemed to get better and better. Sunshine all the day, our path strewn with flowers, our relationship strengthening. The world was our oyster and indeed it had been right up to that fateful night when abruptly and unaccountably everything went into reverse.

Although we had abstained from sex for several weeks we had at least shown a modicum of affection and gradually the horror of that terrible night, although still vivid in my memory, faded so I decided to give up the pretence of being ill and try to reignite our love life. Stupidly, I thought she'd be pleased, so I was shocked when she brushed me away, turning her back and saying she was tired and needed to sleep. I didn't know it then, but this was the start of a slow decline in affection. Gradually, over the following weeks, the cuddles became less frequent until eventually they and the kisses just didn't happen at all and were replaced with shouts of "Oh for God's sake, stop pawing me!" I couldn't believe what was happening to us. "Why are you being like this?" I asked. "You used to enjoy our love making."

"That was then. Life moves on," was her reply.

"Is that it? Are we to become strangers to each other?"

"Get used to it!"

This rejection was not confined only to the bedroom. If I tried to kiss her she'd quickly move away and even a peck on the cheek seemed to be out of bounds. I was totally confused and bewildered.

It seemed we had been driving happily towards an unseen cliff and were suddenly in free-fall. Jenny stopped laughing. That free spirited, joyous woman I had loved began to wear a perpetual frown. She started to use foul language, became irritable, argumentative and quick to take offence at any unintentional slight.

What upset me most was this change didn't happen gradually. Within the space of four weeks my beautiful wife became Dr Jeckle who's turned onto Mr Hyde. I was distraught. Nothing I could say made her recognise the transformation she'd gone through and the sad deterioration it was making to our life style and relationship. She absolutely refused to see a doctor or to admit there was anything wrong.

We stopped going to the boring pub with all its ghastly and ignorant people. Guests were no longer welcome to our cottage. A new bed that we'd ordered to replace the mattress in the spare room was cancelled. "Why should we want people to stay? Eating our food, drinking our booze, dirtying our sheets."

The weekly phone calls to her parents stopped and if they rang she refused to speak to them, forcing me to say she was out or was taking a nap. They apparently had become tedious old bores.

My children were unwanted (fucking needy upstarts). My poor mother became that stupid old cow and I was labelled a mummy's boy for continuing to contact her.

The only person allowed to venture over the threshold was Jenny's son, Marvin. I was very fond of him and was glad of his company but even he became aware of the sudden change in his mother and soon scuttled back to his home in Suffolk.

I had been absent from work for just over a month when I got a phone call from my editor. One of his secretaries who lived nearby had seen me leaving the pharmacy in town and had reported that I looked fit and healthy.

"When the hell was I going to get back to work?" he roared.

"I've been ill," I replied. "Thanks for your sympathy."

"I've got a paper to run, Gus. Not a nursing home."

"I'll be back next week."

"Halleluiah!" He said and hung up.

I wondered how I was going to keep that promise. I'd been so preoccupied by events at home that I'd hardly glanced at a newspaper or tuned into the news for weeks. Somehow the things I had loved doing for most of my adult life, creating ideas and drawing had been neglected, forgotten about and put on the back shelf. I never thought that possible. I was at my wits end then just as I thought things couldn't get any worse – they did. Jenny started being sick in the mornings and her stomach began to swell.

Part of me still held on to the hope that it was a phantom pregnancy but a conversation I'd had with Peter Reilly a long time ago kept coming back to me and a growing suspicion had been buzzing around in my brain ever since.

I phoned the estate agency that had sold me the cottage and asked if they could tell me where the previous owner, Gregory, had moved to. I lied about a parcel for him having been delivered and that I wanted to forward it to him. It took them a couple of days to get back to me but eventually they called with a telephone number.

A woman answered when I phoned. She had a gruff almost masculine voice and was obviously a heavy smoker judging by the many times our conversation was punctuated by long rattling bouts of coughing. I guessed correctly that this was Gregory's sister and told her that I had bought her brother's cottage and wanted to have a word with him so would it be possible to have his address.

"He aint here no more," she said.

"Oh. Where is he?"

"He's dead. Two months ago."

"I'm sorry to hear that."

"I reckon it was that bleedin' cottage what killed him. All of the carryings on sucked the life right out of him."

"That's what I wanted to talk about."

"You 'aving problems too? Weird hauntings?"

"A few."

"Well get out. Sell the place. Scarper before the same 'appens to you."

"Is Gregory's daughter still living with you?"

"Winifred? Who told you she was here?"

"The local vicar," I lied.

"Well that surprises me but yeah, she's still here. Had nowhere else to go when 'er dad died. What d'you want with her?"

"Just a chat. A few things I want to clear up."

"You won't get much out of Winifred. She 'ardly talks at all. She's not the brightest knife in the box."

"Could I pay her a visit?"

I waited while she had a violent coughing fit followed by a lot of gasping for breath then the click of a lighter as she lit up again.

"It won't do you no good," she wheezed at last.

"It's worth a try," I said.

"Well, okay, but don't say I didn't warn you. When d'you want to come up?"

"Tomorrow?"

"Right. But don't expect nothin' posh. We don't live in a palace." She gave me an address in a town called Mapperley in Nottinghamshire then hung up.

The next morning I told Jenny that I had to go to the office then boarded a train to London, changed to another train and headed north. It was a long journey and I was glad I'd remembered to bring a book. A taxi took me from the station to a small bungalow on the outskirts of Mapperley.

Gregory's sister introduced herself as Grace. She was a thin strip of a woman with long grey hair tied in a bun on the top of her head over a gaunt grey face with heavy rimmed spectacles perched on a thin, bony nose. She wore a baggy blue cardigan over a floral dress which went down to her ankles under which were a pair of lime green trainers. When she opened the door a thick cloud of tobacco smoke escaped into the fresh air and I was ushered in to the fog.

"Where 'ave you been?" she asked as we walked down the hallway.

"Been?"

"Yeah, from the Mail. You 'aven't been in it for a while. Somebody told me what you did so I started getting the paper."

"Oh, right. Er … I've been having some time off. Had a tummy bug."

"D'you want a cup of tea?"

"That would be nice."

We entered the living room. Sitting on an armchair on the far side was a young woman who I guessed would be in her early twenties. She was extremely obese with short cropped hair surrounding a round featureless face. She didn't glance up when I walked in. Her eyes stayed fixed on the flickering screen of the television. A plate of biscuits were on her lap and smudges of chocolate surrounded her mouth.

"Winifred, this is Mr Munroe. He's come to see you," Grace said very loudly as though her niece was deaf.

Winifred slipped another biscuit into her mouth but did not respond.

"I told you," Grace said to me. "Like getting shit out of a rocking horse." She wandered off to make the tea.

I sat down on the settee opposite. "Hello Winifred," I said. "I live in the cottage you used to be in with your dad and brother."

She didn't stir.

"Do you remember living there?"

Again there was no response. I was ignored completely. The only sound I got from her was a gulp as another biscuit went down her throat. I tried again. "We've been decorating the place. Your old bed room is a different colour now."

Grace came in with the tea. A cigarette hung from the corner of her mouth at the end of which a long tube of ash threatened to fall into my cup. I took the cup just in time and the ash joined its predecessors on the floor.

"You're wasting your time," she said. "I get about two words a day if I'm lucky and they're usually 'I'm hungry'."

"What a shame," I said. "I didn't think things were as bad as this."

"Maybe I can answer any questions. What do you want to know?"

"I was going to ask about the hauntings at my cottage. What Greg heard or saw. What Felix and Winifred might have seen. Looks like I'm going to be unlucky."

"Footsteps," Grace said. "Mainly footsteps. But I reckon young Felix saw more than that. We never did find out but it sent him loopy. Poor bugger's in a care home now. He's even worse than this one." She pointed at Winifred. "Broke my brother's heart it did."

"Where's the child now?"

"What child."

"Somebody in the village told me Winifred was pregnant when she left."

This brought on another violent spell of coughing then Grace said, "I didn't think anyone knew about that."

"Village gossip, I'm afraid."

She nodded. "Yeah and they were right. Shameful it was, a girl of her age. She didn't know what she was doin' and got took advantage of. I'd kill the bastard what did it if I knew who it was."

"But what of the baby?"

Grace looked uncomfortable. She stubbed out her cigarette and waved her hand dismissively. "We … we lost it. Miscarriage … Winifred 'ad a miscarriage."

"Knitting needle," Winifred said.

We both turned and stared at the girl in astonishment that she'd spoken at last.

"Shut up, Winnie!" Grace snapped.

"Knitting needle," Winifred said again, still staring vacantly at the TV screen.

"Will you be quiet," Grace hollered.

"Hang on," I said. "You were complaining that she never spoke and now she has …"

"She doesn't know what she's talking about," Grace snapped.

There was a long silence. Grace lit up another cigarette and fidgeted with her cup.

I turned to her and looked straight into her eyes. "Did you abort the baby?"

She shook her head. "No, of course I didn't."

I continued to stare at her and waited. A long silence ensued then at last she said, "Oh, alright then. It 'ad to go. The whole thing was shameful an' besides which how would the poor little thing survive with a mother like 'er. She wouldn't have been able to cope with a baby. Feedin' and so on, takin' care of the kid. It was what Greg wanted me to do, what she was sent up here for."

I was trying hard to block out the thought of an abortion with a knitting needle so said nothing. Then Grace spluttered, "And it was a bloody good job that I did what I did. It was deformed. Horrible with limbs all distorted and hairy. I'm glad I did it. Poor thing would've had a terrible life."

Everything suddenly fitted into place. I put down my cup and stood up. "I'm going now, Grace. Thanks. You've sorted out something that's been troubling me for a while."

She clutched my arm. "You won't say nothing will you? I don't want to go to jail."

"Don't worry. I won't say a thing. Thanks for the tea. Goodbye and goodbye to you too Winifred."

Grace stayed where she was and I walked out into the clean fresh air.

The next day I rang my friend Charles and asked if we could meet for a drink and a chat. He suggested a pub equidistant between our homes. "Gail will be glad to see you both again," he said. "It's been a long time."

"Sorry, Charlie. Do you mind if it's just you and me? I need to have a man to man."

"How intriguing," he said. "What's going on? Don't tell me you've been playing away."

"Good God, no. I'll explain all at the pub."

The Fox and Feathers is a beautiful seventeenth century inn on the river Thames in a small village called Cantley, a few miles south of London. It has a thatched roof, inglenook fireplaces and a blue stone flagged floor. Charles told me that it was usually packed but on this occasion quite late in the afternoon there were only a few drinkers and the staff were busy laying out the tables in readiness for the evening diners who'd be arriving in droves after six thirty. I led the way to a table in the snug, the only other occupant being the pub cat who was fast asleep on a chair by the fire.

We waited until we'd been served two foaming pints of bitter then Charles said, "OK. Let's be having it. What's up?"

"It's hard to know where to start," I said.

"At the beginning is a good idea."

I nodded, took a deep breath and said, "Jenny's pregnant." He nearly choked on his beer. "What? That's wonderful news. How old is Jenny."

"Forty three."

He shook his head. "She's left it late but she's strong and healthy. I'm sure she'll be alright."

I bit my lip but said nothing.

"Wow. You're going to be a daddy again. How d'you feel about it?"

"I'm not the daddy."

He stared at me and the smile left his face. "Oh no! I can't believe it … Jenny? Are you sure?"

I nodded. "I had a vasectomy straight after my first wife gave birth to Andrew."

He gave a low whistle. "You're definitely shooting blanks?"

"Positive."

"But you and Jenny … I still can't believe it. Who is the father? Do you know?"

I shrugged and shook my head.

Charles sat back and folded his arms across his chest. "C'mon Gus, out with it. You have your suspicions."

I took a long swig at my beer. "OK. Sit back and prepare yourself to assume I'm going loopy." I told him about being thrown from the bed by an unseen force, about Jenny apparently being in a trance, that I had seen her private parts move as though she was being penetrated. How much sexual pleasure she'd derived from the encounter and how she had assumed it was me who had given her such bliss.

He put his glass down with a thump and stared at me with a pitying expression. "Gordon," he said.

"Yep."

"You suspect Gordon of impregnating your wife?"

"Yep."

"Gordon the ghost?"

I nodded and told him about my meeting with Grace. "Don't you see?" I implored him. "The same thing happened to her niece Winifred when she lived in the cottage.

He stared at me then shook his head. "Okay then Gus," he sighed. "I do think you've gone loopy. In fact to give you an official medical diagnosis, you're nuts, completely barking and should be confined in a padded cell. It's obvious what happened. You fell out of bed and hit your head. You must have been concussed. Babies are made from human sperm, not plasma from the undead. Jesus, what're you thinking? This girl Winifred got humped by some randy schoolboy behind the bicycle sheds. It's obvious."

"Well you explain it then. You're a doctor. How come Jenny's swelling up like a balloon? How come her whole personality is changing? Suddenly she hates her own parents, is vile about my children and my mother. People she adored only a month ago. Then to cap it all she won't let me anywhere near her. I can't even get a kiss on the cheek."

"She's having a phantom pregnancy," Charles said as if this was an explanation any fool should know about.

"Phantom pregnancy?"

"Yes, a very common occurrence. Jenny is madly in love with you. The pair of you have the most sublime relationship. You have everything except for one thing – a child. A living, breathing symbol of your love. She longs for that one thing you don't' share. So her body starts to transform. Her breasts begin to take on changes exactly like those of a pregnant woman. I have had patients who've started to lactate, to produce milk. At the same time the stomach starts to swell. They are absolutely convinced that they are genuinely pregnant and bitterly disappointed when they find that they are not. Gus, believe me, it happens all the time."

"But what about the peculiar behaviour? She's not my Jenny."

"Behaviour changes too. Take my word for it. Eventually it will all go away and things will return to normal. Would you like me to examine her?"

I shook my head. "I've begged her to see a doctor but she's adamant that she doesn't need one – even you."

Charles clinked his glass on mine. "I'm afraid then, Gus, my dear friend, you'll just have to put up with it. Be patient and the old Jenny will reappear. I guarantee it."

The next few months were difficult. I tried hard to work but was well aware that my ideas were nowhere near their usual standard. It was mortifying to watch my wife getting bigger. Always at the back of my head was the thought that perhaps it wasn't a phantom pregnancy, that in fact she had been unfaithful. It made me shudder to think of her in the arms of someone else and I tried desperately to put the thought out of my mind but it was impossible. The suspicion lay like a heavy weight on my shoulders each and every day till eventually I couldn't stand it any longer and asked her outright if she had taken another lover. She was furious that I could suggest such a thing, said that she was perfectly aware that I'd had a vasectomy and dismissed my question with "For God's sake, Gus. Vasectomies can go wrong and yours obviously has. Get used to it, we're having your child and instead of accusing me of being a slut you should be pleased."

If she was right I would indeed be pleased but I never have believed in miracles.

By the June of the following year Jenny was huge. I'd never seen a pregnant woman grow to such proportions. She had to lean backwards to support the weight and consequently tired very quickly. We were now sleeping in separate bedrooms as she took up the whole of our double bed. Gordon hadn't bothered us for months so that was one less thing to worry about. It was obvious by this time that it was not a phantom pregnancy. The child inside her was kicking so hard that her stomach moved and undulated like the surface of a choppy sea. She was still adamant with her refusal to see a doctor but had agreed to take advantage of Mrs McSweeney's midwifery skills when she went into labour. Meanwhile I had changed my mind and had convinced myself that the vasectomy hadn't worked so I was getting quite excited about becoming a dad again. I had under Jenny's instructions transformed the room that I slept in into a nursery. We'd bought a crib, lots of cuddly toys and I'd drawn and painted animal cartoons on the walls. A kindly neighbour arrived one day with some tiny bootees she'd knitted and we'd stocked up with nappies, rattles and baby powders.

Jenny's eating habits changed dramatically. All at once she developed a craving for oily fish and rare almost raw steaks. Then there was chewing gum and dark chocolate. Weirdest of all, when I returned home one evening after delivering my drawing in London I found her spooning dog food from a can into her mouth while Puta sat at her feet drooling with an indignant expression on his face.

"Yuk," I said. "That looks disgusting."

"Taste's great," she answered, tossing the empty can into the coal bucket.

I went to retrieve it. "Have you fed Puta?"

She shook her head. "Don't worry about him. He'll be fine."

"He's got to eat," I said, carrying the empty can into the kitchen.

"He's just a fucking dog," I heard her mutter.

I opened the rubbish bin and threw the can inside. There was the clatter of tin on tin. Something wasn't right. I opened the bin again. It was chock full of empty dog food cans, I'd emptied the bin only that afternoon. Surely Jen couldn't have eaten that amount of Puta's food in only a few hours?

I glanced back into the living room. She was lying like a beached whale on the settee scrolling unperturbed through the programmes on TV. She had something in her hand which she was licking and I assumed it was an iced lolly which had become another of her cravings.

"There's no food left for Puta," I said.

"Well, get some more. He's driving me mad with his constant whining."

Mrs McSweeney was about to close shop when I arrived.

"Goodness me," she exclaimed when I told her what I'd come for.

"How many dogs are ye feeding? Didn't I sell you a box only two days ago?"

"Just stocking up," I lied. "We had a friend who turned up with her dog so we had to feed it too."

"Anything else?"

"Yes. I'll have some chocolate and a few packs of chewing gum."

"Ah. The new bairn, eh? Causin' all that craving."

I nodded.

"Y'know your wife's asked me to help with the birth?"

"Yes. I hope you will."

"She's a stubborn one, that. I've told her she should be seeing a doctor on a regular basis to check everythin's alright. Ye canna be too careful."

"What can I do, Mrs McSweeney? She won't budge."

She shook her head. "Well, I suppose I'll just have to do my best without a doctor ... she's a very big girl now, are ye sure it's not twins ... even triplets?"

"Oh, God. Now you're scaring me. How would I know?"

"By getting her to see a doctor."

"The only way I could do that is by marching her at gunpoint to the surgery with handcuffs on."

She shuffled off to the back of the shop and returned with a large box of dog food and a small plastic bag containing chocolate and chewing gum. "I know who wears the trousers in your house," she said.

Puta never got to eat that food. When I got back to the cottage I found him lying beside the gate. His head had been smashed to a pulp and his tiny body was covered with blood. I knelt beside him barely able to believe that our beloved little pet was dead. I assumed he must have followed me out of the house and got hit by a car, I felt a tear run down my cheek and I swore at myself for not checking the gate when I left. I put the shopping on the doorstep then carried the small corpse carefully round to the back of the cottage where I laid him gently behind a bush hidden until I could bury him the next morning, then I braced myself to break the news to Jenny. She didn't look up when I entered the living room.

"Jenny, darling," I said. "Something terrible has happened."

"Oh?" she replied, her eyes fixed on the TV screen.

"Puta's been killed," I said in a whisper.

She didn't respond.

"Did you hear that, Jen? Puta's been killed. Must've followed me out and got hit by a car ... Sweetheart, I'm so sorry."

She turned to face me and with a shock I saw small black flakes on her lips and a trickle of blood running down her chin.

"That's terrible," she said.

I moved to her side. "I'm so sorry," I said and put a hand gently on her shoulder. She reached up and brushed my hand away. "These things happen," she muttered and turned to face the screen again.

I stepped back from the settee in disbelief. "Is that all you can say?"

"What do you want me to say?"

"Jenny. Puta is dead. Out little pet that both of us have loved so much has gone and all you can say is 'these things happen'. What's happened to you?"

"Oh, for God's sake, Gus," she snapped. "Don't be so bloody soft. He's not your mother or father, he's a bloody dog. Always whining for walks or food, always getting in the way tripping me up, being a fucking pest. Stop being such a bloody wimp. Man up!" She turned away and faced the TV again.

"I can't believe what I'm hearing," I said. "What's got into you? Where's that loving compassionate girl I married? This pregnancy has changed you utterly. I don't know you anymore."

The next morning I discovered that what Jenny had been licking the night before was not an iced lolly. It was the small glass jar I'd found in Eliza's hiding place which I had thought was an inkwell was now completely empty and licked clean. Then later when I went into the garden to bury little Puta I saw that the spade which was normally kept in the lean-to shed was now propped against the wall outside. The blade was covered in dried blood.

****

"Eating dog food is unusual but not surprising," Charles said. "I've heard of pregnant women chewing on coal, liquorice, bits of leather, or all manner of things. Nobody knows for sure why but don't worry about it. It's quite normal.

I'd panicked, left Puta unburied and cycled into the village to phone Charles from a telephone box. I badly needed some advice, someone to confide in and who might possibly explain my wife's behaviour. "So much for your phantom pregnancy diagnosis," I groaned.

"Okay, sorry about that," he said. "But remember I wasn't allowed to examine her. I would've known for sure then."

"But I think she killed our dog." I said. "She loved him more than she did me. That's not normal."

"I know, I know. This is a bit extreme. Are you sure it was blood on the spade?"

"Well I didn't perform a chemical analysis. It certainly looked like blood to me."

He was quiet for a few moments then said "Look, Gus. I have to be at my surgery in the morning. I'll drive up to see her this afternoon."

"No, don't do that. She'll be furious that I've asked you to come against her will."

"Okay. How about this? I'll say I was just passing so thought I'd pop in to see you both. She might change her mind about an examination when she sees me."

"I somehow doubt it. You'll notice a big difference in her."

"Agreed?"

I was desperate. I would have agreed to anything. "Thanks, Charles," I said. "See you this afternoon."

I cycled home again and set about the task of burying Puta. He was laid to rest under an apple tree at the far end of the garden. A place where he liked to lie in the shade on hot summer days. I made a small headstone with a tile that I'd removed from the kitchen wall when I was working on the renovations and painted his name on it. Then when it was finished spent some time just staring down at the small grave and remembering the fun times we'd all enjoyed together. "Cheerio, my little friend," I said.

For the rest of the day I was extremely apprehensive about Charles' visit but somehow I managed to get some work done, driving into town, delivering my drawing and back again in time for his arrival. Jenny it seemed had spent most of the day watching day time TV and I noticed that two cans of dog meat had been taken from the box I'd bought home the previous night. I made us both a cup of tea and tried to engage her in light conversation but an old Walt Disney film was much more interesting than anything I had to say so I left her to it. At around four thirty in the afternoon there came the expected rat tat on the door and I rushed to open it.

"Charles!" I said in mock surprise.

"Hi, Gus," he replied. "Don't look so shocked. I was just passing by and thought I'd say hello."

"Fantastic," I said, probably in too loud a voice. "Come on in. Hey Jenny. Look who's here."

I ushered him into the kitchen. "Lovely to see you. What're you doing in this neck of the woods?"

"A medical forum in town. I was on my way home. Couldn't pass so close to your place without scrounging a cup of tea, could I?" As he spoke Jenny walked in from the lounge.

"Jenny!" Charles cried and I could see the astonishment on his face when he took in her size. "Wow. You look blooming. How are you?" He walked forward to give her a hug but she warded him off with a hand on his chest.

"Charles," she frowned. "What are you doing here?"

"I was just passing by. Thought I'd get a cup of tea."

"Great," I chimed in. I'll put the kettle on,"

"Wait!" Jenny ordered. "You're here to check up on me, aren't you?"

"No," Charles spluttered. "I was just pass …"

"I don't believe you," she yelled. Her face had turned red with anger. She turned to me. "I told you I don't want a fucking doctor!"

"Now calm down, Jenny love," Charles said holding both hands up in a kind of supplication. "I was just …"

"Rubbish," she screamed. "The pair of you have planned this." She turned to me again. "You're a conniving fucking bastard. Get him out of here!"

"Jenny," I pleaded. "This is Charles. One of my oldest friends. What are you …?"

She stepped forward and pushed Charles hard on the chest. "Fuck off!" she screamed, even louder than before. Charles had staggered backwards and crashed his back against the wall. "Go on!" she bellowed. "OUT!" She swung the door open and pointed her finger at the street. "… and don't come back, you smug fuck. OUT!"

He hurried out of the door, a look of pure shock on his face. Eyes wide he glanced over at me and whispered, "Give me a call," then climbed into his car.

Jenny slammed the door behind him. "You stupid prick!" she snarled at me. "Don't try that again!" then waddled heavily back to her seat in front of the TV.

I followed her in. "You ungrateful bitch!" I yelled at her back. "He was trying to help you, for God's sake. He's a friend. Have you gone completely fucking mad? You don't need a mid-wife, you need a psychiatrist!"

She leaned forward and turned up the volume.

That did it. I lost it completely. Shaking with anger I rounded her chair and kicked the TV on to its back on the floor. "Listen to me, you stupid cow. Why have you turned into such a shit?" I roared. She stayed silent. I leaned forward and screamed into her ear, "ANSWER ME!" For a moment or two she didn't move, then slowly she stood up and turned to face me. Her eyes were filled with hate and her lips were curled in an angry grimace. She walked silently into the kitchen and returned with a long carving knife. I backed up against the wall as she advanced menacingly towards me. "Hey, don't do this," I choked. "What are you thinking?" She stopped inches from me then waggled the knife in front of my face and said almost in a whisper, "If you interfere once more with this birth I'll kill you. I'll cut your fucking throat. Do you hear me? You've done your bit, the next part is up to me ... my way. Got it? MY WAY."

She flicked the tip of the blade against my cheek and I felt a rivulet of blood run down my face then reaching up with her other hand she put her finger on the cut. Staring straight into my eyes she slowly put the bloody finger to her mouth and licked it.

"Do you understand?" she asked.

I was too shocked to speak. I could only nod.

The scowl turned into a smile. "Good boy," she whispered then turned away and righted the TV.

*****

At five forty five I walked into the snug bar of my local pub. I didn't know where else to go. I just had to get out of the house. Get away and give myself time to think. My head was spinning and I was trying unsuccessfully to control the shudders which had set my whole body trembling. It felt like an earthquake was about to erupt in the pit of my stomach.

Nan, the landlady, looked surprised to see me and I could see she was about to tell me that the pub didn't open till six, but instead she stared at me for a second or two, dropped the cloth she'd been cleaning glasses with and asked anxiously, "Are you alright, Gus?"

I nodded. My teeth were chattering so violently I couldn't speak. She rushed over and took me by the arm. "You look terrible. Have you got a fever or summat?"

I shook my head and she sat me down on a bench at the side of the bar. "Shall I call your wife?"

"No!" I blurted, "No, please don't."

"Look," she said, "We're not open yet an' I'm not supposed to but would you like a drink?"

I nodded again and mumbled, "Thanks, Nan. A scotch please."

Seconds later when she handed me the glass she said, "Do you want to talk about it?"

I took a large gulp of the whisky and felt the soothing almost magical effect it had on the turbulence in my gut.

"Thanks Nan. You're an angel. Sorry to be a pest barging in here so early. Had a bit of a shock, that's all. My little dog got run over and I'm behaving like a baby. I was very fond of him." She patted me on the shoulder.

"Aw, poor little bugger. He was adorable. No wonder you're so upset. I'm really sorry. I know how I felt when we lost our dog. We 'ad him sixteen years." She bustled back behind the bar. "I'll leave you alone. I expect you'll be glad of that and I must get on. Give us a yell if you want another."

She was right. I did want to be alone. I stared into my glass and allowed myself to wallow for a while in self-pity. Why had the fates turned my life upside down so completely? How could the all-consuming love I had for my wife evaporate so quickly? I realised that my feelings for her now bordered on hate. A change that only a few weeks ago I would not have believed possible. Jenny was mentally ill. I knew that for certain. She needed help but had rejected all attempts to give her any. Meanwhile over the past few weeks my health had been suffering too. I think I was on the verge of a nervous breakdown. Each nerve in my body was stretched tight like piano wire. I was continually tense and unable to sleep properly and was prone to sudden bouts of tears. I had lost interest in food and was drinking too much. Consequently no matter how hard I tried to apply myself to work I couldn't and was well aware that I was turning out mediocre crap. It was the slippery slope and I was staring into the abyss.

A few customers had arrived and I could hear their merry chatter in the bar next door. I hoped no one would come into the snug. I didn't want company, I just needed to wallow for a bit longer.

I ordered another whisky plus a pint of beer to wash it down with and asked Nan for change to use the pub's public telephone.

"Well that was a bit of a shock," Charles said as soon as he picked up.

"I'm sorry Charlie," I said. "I didn't expect Jen to react like she did. It was a shock for me too."

"She's ill," he said matter of factly. "I'm afraid the pregnancy has made her mentally unstable."

"Yes, I think you're right. Have you ever known that to happen before?"

He paused to think about it, then said, "Afraid not. Well nowhere near as bad. pregnant women undergo many changes during their confinement which sometimes includes severe depression, rejection of their condition or extreme irritability but your Jennifer … well … it's beyond anything I've ever experienced before."

I sighed. What can I do?"

"She needs treatment."

"Treatment?"

"Yes. I think she should have some tests. Here at the clinic, but not until after she gives birth. She might be more rational then and agree to having some help."

"Right now it seems unlikely she'd agree to anything," I said.

"Wait and see, Gus. Don't give up. I'm hoping that after the baby arrives she'll be more like her old self again." He paused then said, "I don't envy you, you poor bugger. It must be hard to live with. How are you feeling?"

"I feel like shit."

"Sleeping alright?"

"Nope."

"I'll pop a few pills through your door next time I'm up. I won't come in if you don't mind."

"God, no!" I said. "I couldn't put you through all that again."

"Keep your chin up, my old pal," he said before ending the call. "It'll be all over soon. Let me know when she goes into labour." I glanced at my watch. It was only eight thirty. Perhaps I should go home now? The muscles of my stomach tightened at the thought. Oh God! Had it come to this? I was terrified of my wife and scared to go home. I decided to wait till I was sure Jennifer would be in bed.

Half an hour later I was pleased to see Ted McSweeney enter the bar. After my wallowing it was a relief to buy him a few drinks and to engage in small talk right up until the pub closed. When I staggered into the cottage Jenny, thank the Lord, was fast asleep upstairs.

A few days later there came a call from the newspaper that I had been dreading. Howard Kirby wanted to see me. This was no surprise. I'd been expecting the summons and was pretty sure I knew what it was he wanted to discuss.

I prepared some food for Jenny, told her I'd be home as soon as possible then drove through heavy rain to London. The interview went exactly as I had predicted. Howard waved me to a chair and said, "This is going to be difficult for me, Gus."

I nodded. "For me too, I guess." I said.

"There was a time when readers bought the paper just to see your cartoon." He shrugged his shoulders and lifted his hands in a despairing gesture. "It's not happening any more."

"I'm sorry."

"What the hell happened to you? You used to win awards. There was nobody else who could compete."

I shook my head. "I've had a pretty rough time recently. It's been hard to concentrate."

He stared at me for a while, those famous eyebrows drawn into a deep frown. "You've lost weight. Are you ill?

"No, I'm okay. Just stressed out."

"D'you want to talk about it?"

I would have liked to unload right then, to tell him the whole sorry saga but he was a hardened Fleet Street editor who was used to dealing with facts, not tales of ghosts assaulting women in their beds. He would have thought I'd gone mad. I shook my head again and told him the marriage was going through a bad time.

He grunted and walked to the door. "Carla, would you bring in two cups of coffee please." She glanced up from her hand mirror and nodded. He came back into the room then bellowed over his shoulder "... and some biscuits." Then to me: "I'm sorry to hear that Gus. I always got the impression you were as happy as a pig in shit."

"We were. These things happen I suppose. I'm really sorry my work hasn't been up to scratch. I've tried hard but I can't get my mind off all the other things."

"Why don't you take a break? Take her away somewhere and mend broken fences." He spun a large globe of the world standing on one side of his desk. "Big world out there."

"There's a baby on the way. Due anytime soon. Maybe I could take a few days off when it arrives."

There was a knock on the door and Carla came in carrying a tray with the coffee and biscuits. She placed it on Howard's desk, gave me a sympathetic smile and left.

"Close the door!" Howard shouted then when she had done that muttered "Nosey woman. Always leaves my bloody door open so she can snoop. I daren't even fart sometimes." He pushed a mug of coffee towards me then took a long time stirring sugar into his drink and putting biscuits on a separate plate. He didn't look at me when he spoke again, just stared fixedly down at his plate. "I wasn't thinking about just a few days, Gus."

I knew what was coming so waited for him to finish. "The board want to replace you." He waited for me to speak, then when I didn't respond continued, "I'm really sorry. You have been a huge asset to the paper for years but it's a tough old business we're in and I'm afraid that if you don't come up with the goods you're shown the door and that applies to everyone."

"I think I saw this coming," I said at last. "Who's the new boy?"

"Dave Spark. He's coming over from the Express."

"Good choice. I like his work."

"Aw shit," he said. "I hate doing this to you, Gus. Especially as you've got a kid on the way. I truly hope you'll be able to sort things out with your wife but heck, we've given you a chance, we waited hoping things would improve but … well, we're not a marriage guidance organisation, we have a paper to run. It wasn't my decision. I hope you'll understand."

I nodded. "I've got the drift."

"Listen. You have a year's contract and I've organised a generous severance pay deal. That should give you a chance to sort yourself out." He took a bite from his biscuit then stood up and held his hand out. End of interview … end of career. I shook his hand then he led me to the door. "Good luck," he said, and "Congratulations on the baby news."

I left his office in a daze. Even though I'd expected the chop it still came as a bit of a shock. All at once I felt stripped of all stature. I'd been dumped like a lazy office boy. From being on top of my game for thirty years to being a forgotten non-entity in the space of only a few weeks. Normally journalists who'd been in the profession a long time would have news of their imminent departure broken to them over a nice lunch. I'd sunk so low all I got was coffee and biscuits. Once again I was engulfed with self-pity and depression. Life was so unfair. How could so much shit pile up on my doorstep? It was just one stinking thing after another. There seemed no end to it.

Twelve thirty. Time for a consoling drink. Down the street a few yards from the office was a favourite watering hole for journalists "The Mucky Duck", a cosy Blackfriars pub that's real name was "The White Swan". It hadn't had a lick of paint for several years and so had been re-christened with its new title by some long forgotten hack – and it had stuck. I ordered a large whisky with ice and took it to a far corner wondering what the fates had next in store for me to push me further into the mire. There were quite a few people in the bar, none of which I

179

knew. Mostly up and coming eager young men and women with one foot on the ladder eager for the climb ahead. I sat on my bottom rung and watched them gloomily, remembering when I was the new boy on the block and the excitement of facing the challenges ahead.

I walked to the bar for another whisky and was about or order when I felt a tap on my shoulder and voice said, "I thought I'd find you here." I swung round. Carla, the editor's secretary was staring anxiously at me with those big black Dusty Springfield eyes. It was like looking at the negative photograph of a panda. Everything was in reverse. "Gus," she whispered, "You've got to go home." Oh God I thought, what now? "Why? What's happened?" I said in alarm.

"A Mrs McSweeney has just phoned the office. Your wife had gone into labour."

The traffic leaving London at that time of day was intense. Nothing was moving faster than at a snail's pace, sometimes stopping for agonising minutes before creeping forward again. I found myself screaming obscenities and thumping the steering wheel in frustration. It turned out that an oil tanker had overturned on the A20 and the road had been completely closed because of the danger from spilt petroleum. Vehicles were eventually diverted from a village near Foots Cray through Orpington and then onto the motorway going south east. At last we were moving. I didn't care about the speed limits. I was in a state of panic, overtaking when I could, taking risks that I shouldn't and in general driving like a maniac. This was my undoing. More shit in the life of Fergus Munroe.

Trying to overtake a lorry which had been lumbering up a hill at an agonisingly slow pace I realised too late that I wasn't going to make it. A sports car appeared at the top of the slope and was hurtling towards me at great speed. I braked hard and tried to get back in time but clipped another car and very nearly pushed it off the road. Amidst a clamour of tooting horns and swerving vehicles both cars managed to pull out onto the hard shoulder. As luck would have it the other driver was a huge West Indian man, not only huge but very angry. He stormed up to my car. "What the fuck you doin' man?" he roared as I wound down my window.

"I'm really sorry …" I began.

"Get out of the car!" he screamed.

I got out and he grabbed the front of my jacket with one big fist pushing me back against the door. "You nearly fucking killed me an' my family you clown. Who the fuck do you think you are, Stirling fucking Moss?"

"I really am sorry …" I spluttered again.

181

He dragged me across to his car. I could see a frightened woman and a small child sitting in the back. "Look what you done to my motor," he yelled.

The front wing of his car was completely stove in, the metal almost resting on the tyre and the headlight on that side was shattered. A long line of rubber and broken glass led from the main carriageway to where he was parked. I stared dismally down at the wreckage. "My wife has just gone into labour and I was panicking to get home in time," I said.

"Your wife, your fucking baby. What about mine?" he screamed, his face inches from mine. I smelt garlic on his breath, but he must have smelt the whisky on mine. Still holding my jacket he moved back and held me at arms' length. "You've been drinkin'," he snarled.

"Only the one," I stammered. "I'm not drunk."

"Don't give me that crap, man," he said, his voice rising in pitch. "You've had a skinful!" There was no use arguing with him, he just kept shouting me down.

"You stupid bastard. I'm gonna call the police."

When at last he allowed me to get a word in I said, "Look, what happened was entirely my fault. I was driving badly and I accept full responsibility. I'm very sorry. Let's exchange insurance details. You'll get full recompense."

He went quiet for a moment or two then said, "Nah, man. I want cash."

"Don't be ridiculous. I don't carry that amount of money on me."

"How much have you got?"

"Not enough."

"How much."

He was shuffling his feet and glancing up and down the road nervously.

Then I understood. "You don't have any insurance do you?" I said.

"How much cash you got?" he persisted.

I checked my wallet. "I've only got fifty pounds."

"That'll do." He held out his hand.

"But that isn't going to …."

"Hand it over, man, or I'll throw you in that fucking ditch."

I gave him the money. I was desperate to get back on the road again. I needed to be home with my wife when she gave birth to our child but before I could get away he insisted that I help him get his car roadworthy. He produced a heavy metal jemmy from the boot and together we levered the metal wing away from the tyre. Then he climbed in, switched on and moved the car forward and back to see if anything else was catching on the wheel. Eventually he drove off with a final "You're a fucking wanker!" and I climbed into my car with a sigh of relief.

By now it was getting dark. I kept to the speed limit for the rest of the way. The last thing I needed was another hold up. So by the time I turned off the main Plaxtol road and into the lane that led to my cottage the light was gone completely and I had the headlights on full.

Here the vengeful fates intervened again. About twenty yards from the cottage the road had been cordoned off. One of those blue and yellow police tapes had been strung from one side of the lane to the other and I could see a small knot of people huddled in front of it. Caught in the glare of my lights one of them turned and pointed, "There he is," he shouted. "They all moved away from the police tape and crowded round my car. I climbed out, fear rising in my chest. What the hell was going on?

"Thank God you're back," said a woman I vaguely recognised. "What's happenin' in your house?"

"Yeah," said a man next to her. "Why've they closed up the road? I need to get through."

I pushed my way through them wanting to know the answer to their questions too. I got to the tape and was about to duck under it to get to my front gate when a young policewoman barred my way. "Where d'you think you're going?" she barked.

"This is where I live," I said. "What's going on?"

"Fergus Munroe?"

"That's me."

She put her hand up and said, "Wait there please, sir," then walked quickly into the cottage. She reappeared a few seconds later accompanied by a man wearing a grey suit under a thick navy overcoat. He had a very red face polished and shiny like a ripe apple and a comb over hair style covering only a small strip of his bald head. "Mr Munroe?" he asked.

"Yes. What the hell's going on? Why are you in my house? Is my wife okay?"

He lifted the police tape. "This way if you don't mind, sir." I followed him into the kitchen. I could feel my heart pounding painfully in my chest and an ominous creeping dread in my brain making my limbs seize up   It felt as though at any moment my legs would collapse and I'd topple onto the floor.

Two men in white boiler suits and wearing surgical masks brushed past and went outside. I wanted to speak but no words came out. Then I saw Ted. Ted McSweeney sitting hunched at my kitchen table. He had his head in his hands, his shoulders were shaking and I saw that he was crying into a grubby handkerchief. I looked at the man with the shiny face who had stopped in front of the living room door and was staring at me with a quizzical expression. "Has something happened to my wife?" I managed to say through chattering teeth.

He nodded. "I'm afraid so."

I waited for him to continue but he just carried on staring at me with that same penetrating gaze.

"Well, come on," I screamed. "Tell me."

His eyes moved away and concentrated on my left shoulder. "I'm sorry, Mr Munroe. Your wife is dead."

"Wha …?"

"I'm afraid so. Something awful has happened here."

He looked me in the face again. "The work of a maniac. Your wife has been brutally murdered and so has this gentleman's wife who was with her at the time." He nodded in the direction of Ted. At that Ted let out a squeal of anguish and buried his head deeper into his handkerchief.

"I am Detective Inspector Peter Vaughan, Mr Munroe. Can I ask where you have been all afternoon?"

I shook my head. "Never mind where I've been for Christ's sake. Where is she? Can I see my wife?"

He looked at me for some time then nodded. "Alright. It's a sight you might regret seeing. It's carnage in there. It's your right, your decision. Do you want to go ahead?"

"Come on, come on! I want to see her," I screamed.

"This way," he said. "Please put on some plastic overshoes and don't touch anything. This is a crime scene and must not be disturbed in any way until the forensic team has finished their work. Last of all," he said as he turned towards the door, "I can only allow you to stand on the threshold. Please do not enter the room."

He tapped on the door and a woman dressed in a white boiler suit and mask opened it a crack. He turned to me. "Are you ready?"

I pulled on the plastic overshoes that I'd been handed and gave him another nod. The door was opened wide. The first thing I saw was the blood. It was everywhere. It seemed that the whole room was painted red. The floor was awash. There were smears on the walls and splashes across the furniture. It was hard to comprehend that this was for real. That I hadn't somehow wandered onto the set of a horror film. Mrs McSweeney lay on her back, one leg propped up on a coffee table that had been toppled on its side. A gigantic bloody gouge was where the front of her throat used to be and her eyes stared sightlessly at the ceiling.

I turned my gaze to the settee and my heart almost stopped. Jenny, my Jenny, the love of my life was sprawled in a scatter of cushions. This was the source of most of the blood. She was lying in a sea of it, naked apart from her nightdress which was rolled up above her breasts and tucked under her armpits. From her sternum to below the waist was a long ragged hole as though the baby had been ripped from her stomach or had burst from it. Her eyes too were open wide in an expression of sheer terror and her mouth was gaping and slack. Suddenly I couldn't breathe. I felt bile surging up to my throat and my whole body began to tremble violently. The room started to spin and I tried to steady myself against the door frame but my flailing arms couldn't find it. I felt my knees crumple then I was falling. Before I hit the floor everything had changed from red to black.

*****

I was arrested on suspicion of killing Jenny and Mrs McSweeney, driven to the main police station in Tonbridge and locked into a cell for the night. I was in a daze throughout it all. So numbed by the events I couldn't protest or even speak my first name. I just complied with every instruction I was given, nodding without comprehension like a zombie whose brain has ceased to function. It was only later in the solitude of my cell that it came to life again and I spent a sleepless night churning over the events of the past few months and especially the last few hours. Guilt and sorrow took it in turns to twist the knife in my stomach. Guilt about things that were now too late to mend. Should I have been more patient? Did I do something to trigger the change in Jenny? Was it all my fault? Could I have been kinder? Then the sorrow would butt in when I remembered the good times, the laughter we shared, the intimate moments. Small endearing things like watching her in her beloved garden, her passion for Elvis Presley, how she'd stand in tippy toes when she got excited. Her lovely face swam before my eyes and I wept for the loss of those wonderful times, the loss of our love and the loss of her. After a meagre breakfast of porridge and lukewarm tea I was taken to a large windowless room a few corridors away from my cell. It was exactly like all the television detective dramas I'd watched over the years, completely bare save for a rectangular bench surrounded by four chairs. There was a large screen on one wall behind which there had to be a senior policeman watching through the one way glass. On the table was a lamp and a recording machine. I was asked to sit down and wait by a young constable who looked as though he hadn't started shaving yet. We both waited, me in my chair and he guarding the door.

After about five minutes Detective Inspector Vaughan walked in clutching a file of papers. He was accompanied by another man about the same age with thick grey hair flattened on top like a manicured hedge above his angular face. He was introduced as Detective Constable Glover before sitting down opposite me. Vaughan went through the preliminaries, switching the recorder on, naming all those present, opening his file and giving me a hostile look.

"We're not charging you with anything, Mr Munroe. We just want to eliminate you from our enquiries," he said. "Let's start with how you spent yesterday. Tell us about it."

This was easy. The whole of yesterday was engraved for ever in my memory. I told them about driving to London, getting sacked from my job, having a drink in the pub afterwards, the panic when I got the news that my wife had gone into labour, the delays on the motorway, the accident with the West Indian man's car and lastly, the shock of finding what had happened in my absence.

"You took an excessively long time to drive home," Vaughan said.

"Yes. I just told you. There were traffic jams and I spent a lot of wasted time sorting out the accident."

He took a sheet of paper from the file. "Yes. You gave us details of the accident last night. There's a small problem."

"What problem?"

"According to our enquiries with the DVLA, the registration number of the car that you say you hit is from a Volkswagen beetle, yet you told me the vehicle you collided with was an old Citroen."

"It was an old Citroen. Dark racing green. It had had quite a few bumps and scrapes before."

"Yes, weird isn't it." He folded his arms on the table and gave me a hard stare. "How do you explain one car transforming itself into another one?"

I couldn't. I sat for a long time, my mind racing, trying to recall the scene on the motorway. I had no doubts about the make of car. I could picture it straight away. A battered old wreck. No wonder the aggressive West Indian had accepted my fifty pounds. It was more than the car was worth.

"It must have been a stolen car," I said. "… and a stolen number plate. One theft to cover the other. He didn't have any insurance. I gave him fifty pounds. He took it and left hot foot. I thought he looked very edgy. Kept looking up and down the road. I expect he was scared that one of your boys would turn up and he'd be nabbed."

The Detective Sergeant spoke for the first time. "There could be another explanation," he said.

I waited.

"That you did see an old car, made a note of the number and used it to concoct this story of why it took you so long to get home. Are you sure you hadn't already been home, killed your wife and Mrs McSweeney then driven off again to return later as the innocent husband?"

I was so shocked by the accusation I couldn't speak. I just stared at him with my mouth open. At last I managed to splutter, "Are you accusing me of their slaughter? For God's sake man. I couldn't do that. She was my wife. I loved her!"

"So you say," grunted Vaughan. He glanced again at his notes. "We've had a chat with Mr. McSweeney, the husband of the other victim and he told us that it was not all harmony between you and your wife. Is it true she packed her bags and left you for several days recently?"

"Recently?" I shouted. "That was months ago. Besides which she didn't leave to get away from me … it was …" I hesitated then added, "… our ghost."

They both looked at each other then back at me.

"Your ghost?"

"Yes. I know it sounds crazy but the cottage is haunted. Ask around the village. They all know we have a ghost. The previous owners were well aware of it too. My wife was so scared by it she needed a break. That's why she went to live with her parents for a while."

They both continued to stare at me saying nothing so I told them about Peter's exorcism and how it had seemed to work as we hadn't been troubled by Gordon for quite a while. When I'd finished Vaughan turned to his colleague.

"We must get him in for questioning, Sergeant. Gordon, the ghost, wanted for scaring poor innocent women out of their homes."

"I tell you it's true!" I said angrily. "I'm not the only one who's heard it."

Glover abruptly changed the subject. "What have you done with the baby?" he snapped.

"I'd like to know that too. Where is my baby?"

"Your baby?" Glover asked. He leant back in his chair. "Your medical records show that you've had a vasectomy. How could it have been your baby, Mr Munroe?"

I felt my anger rising. I wanted time to grieve but instead was being harangued by relentless questions.

"These things happen. Sometimes vasectomies go wrong. What other explanation could there be?" I said.

They glanced at each other again before Vaughan answered sarcastically, "Another explanation might be she'd had an affair with another man." Glover followed up with "If that happened to me I might be so jealous I might hate that baby and its mother. Why I might even consider violence."

They both stared at me waiting for me to respond. I felt an uneasy feeling creeping up my spine. Never for one moment did I think I'd be considered as a suspect ... not until now. I shook my head again and said, "Jenny denied she'd had an affair. I did ask her but she was emphatic, said it was definitely my child she was bearing. I had to take her word for it."

Another glance at the notes, another change of subject. "Mr Munroe," Detective Inspector Vaughan said, "A garden spade has been found in your shed with traces of human blood on the blade. Perhaps you could explain that."

"It's not human blood. It's dog's blood. My terrier was run over recently. I used the spade to bury him."

"Right. We'll be verifying that at the labs."

"Please do."

"Was your wife in a normal state of mind before she was killed?"

"Sadly, no. She'd become extremely irritable and intolerant, swearing a lot and not letting me near her. She wasn't like her old self at all. I confided in a doctor friend who knew her well and he thought the pregnancy had affected the balance of her mind."

I gave them Charles' full name and address knowing that he'd vouch for my story.

The questioning went on for what seemed an eternity before I was taken back to my cell where I had to sit staring at the wall for two more days.

Then at last after confiscating my passport they let me go. Apparently my story had been verified by my editor, the Reverend Reilly and Charles my doctor. Not a trace of the West Indian had been found but the old green Citroen had. It had been dumped in a lay-by thirty miles away from where we collided. Even better news was that the police forensic team had identified the blood on the garden spade to be that of a dog. Anyone might think that these little fragments of good news would have cleared me but they didn't. I felt suicidal. My whole world had been torn apart. I'd lost the love of my life, my job and my self-esteem. I hated what fate was dishing out for me and dreaded what calamities were still to come.

All I wanted was to go home, curl up in a corner and die.

This was not to be. Sitting in the waiting room of the police station were my two children, Andrew and Karen. They rushed over to me. "Dad," Karen said putting her arms around me. "Are you alright? We've been so worried about you." Yeah, what happened?" Andrew chimed in.

"Later, later," I said. "I'll tell you all about it when we get home."

"You can't go home," Karen said. "It's still cordoned off. Still a crime scene. You'll have to stay with me for a while."

"You're all over the papers," Andrew said.
"Oh God. Am I?"

"Yeah," he said grabbing my arm. "C'mon. Get ready for the onslaught."

"Eh?"

We walked out into a clamour of photographers and journalists all jostling and pushing around us, shouting questions and waving notebooks. A TV camera perched on the shoulder of a BBC man almost butted me in the face. The noise was deafening. Andy and Karen took an arm each and hauled me through the throng and almost threw me into the back of her car. We moved slowly forward. Reporters were hammering on the windows still yelling their questions, several in front of the car trying to block our way to the gate but Karen pushed onwards relentlessly and eventually we were free and on our way to her flat on the south coast.

I'd managed to miss a barrage of questions from the press but couldn't avoid them from my children. As we drove I told them all that I knew and afterwards they brought me up to date with all they knew. They'd been interrogated by the police and hounded by the newspapers offering money for stories about their upbringing and what kind of father I'd been. It seemed they'd had a pretty stressful time. "Not easy," Karen said, "when your dad is suspected of being a vicious killer."

Andy tossed some newspapers onto the back seat. I groaned. The headlines were all about the two murders. One read: 'PREGNANT WOMAN MURDERED FOR HER BABY', another: 'WELL KNOWN CARTOONIST SUSPECTED OF DOUBLE KILLING' and another: 'BABY MISSING AFTER BLOODBATH IN KENT'. There were photographs of me getting out of the car, Mr and Mrs McSweeney outside their shop and an early snap of Jen and I at an awards ceremony. These were alongside lurid columns speculating about the state of our marriage and of my mind. My own newspaper had reprinted a few of my old cartoons together with an article stating that although I'd been a very fine cartoonist who had won many awards I had always been a bit of a loner keeping myself at a distance from my colleagues and known as a mystery man. Who knows what dark secrets I kept hidden? I groaned. 'Thanks a lot, Howard Kirby!'

We didn't go to Karen's place after all. A squad of reporters had been camped outside her door for two days so instead she drove us to a small guest house on the outskirts of Tunbridge Wells. I was to be there for four weeks trying my best to avoid the other guests and only popping out occasionally to buy provisions from the local shop with a thick scarf covering half of my face.

The owner of the shop was an Iranian whose grasp of the English language was not good and I doubt if he had ever picked up a newspaper so trying to hide my identity was probably unnecessary.

Andrew and Karen kept me up to date with what was going on. Jen's beloved garden had been dug up by the police. The bloodied furniture and carpets were now stacked outside the cottage waiting to be taken to the dump and some kind soul had painted the word 'MURDERER' on the side of my car in big black letters.

During that month I tried several times to phone Ted McSweeney. I wanted desperately for him to believe that I had not killed his wife but on each occasion he hung up as soon as he heard my voice. So it was with great trepidation that after the month was up I got my son, Andrew, to drive me home.

The following weeks were the bleakest of my life. I replaced my ruined furniture with stuff from a charity store. I was treated like a pariah by my neighbours. Old friends crossed the street if they saw me coming and the newspapers continued to write scurrilous articles about me. Worst of all were the notes that were constantly being pushed through my letter box, most often badly spelt and asking where I'd buried the baby, or to threaten my life.

The police hadn't given up on me either. Detective Inspector Vaughan visited several times to repeat his questions, no doubt hoping to catch me out with any small change to the answers I'd given before.

However, I learned who my real friends were. Charles called often and the Reverend Peter Reilly popped round to see me regularly. From the word go he be believed my story. It was he who after one of my long periods of depression persuaded me to pull myself together and out of the pathetic self-pitying state I was in, encouraged me to stop my continuous isolation and be defiant, come out of my shell and face my detractors head on. To hell with the gossip mongers, and the hate merchants. If they didn't like it, Sod 'em! (His words, not mine) and so I did. Slowly at first then boldly. Old acquaintances scurrying by avoiding eye contact were greeted by, "Hello, nice to see your happy smiling face on this beautiful morning," or "Hi, long time, no see." I started going to the pub again, ignoring the hostile silence when I walked in. Mostly though I'd be on my own, sipping a pint in the big space created by customers keeping their distance as though I had some terrible infectious disease, but often I'd be joined by Charles, one of my children or Peter Reilly who never needed much persuasion to go out for a drink.

Having decided to face the world again there was however still one more thing that was top of my list to confront. I needed to talk to Ted McSweeney. I'd heard that to avoid me he'd started to go to a different pub some way from the village, so not wanting to embarrass him by marching into his new watering hole I decided to take the bull by the horns and go to his home.

I set off down the lane one morning feeling extremely nervous about what kind of reception I'd get when I got to his door. It had started to rain and by the time I reached Ted's house it was hammering down on my umbrella. Ted was obviously not a keen gardener. The horse trough so lovingly attended to by his wife was now full of weeds and the small front garden once neatly trimmed was overgrown and cluttered with old planks and soggy cardboard boxes.

I took a deep breath and knocked on the door. There was no response. I looked at my watch and wondered if he was next door in the shop in which case I'd leave it till another day. It was important to me that I saw him alone. I knocked again and was about to turn away when I heard his gruff voice from within shouting, "All right, all right. No need to knock the door down. I'm comin'."

There was the sound of locks being drawn back then the door opened and Ted's astonished face was looking up at me. He was dressed in baggy trousers and a rather grubby white vest. I'd obviously caught him in the middle of shaving for a white soapy foam covered half of his chin.

"You've got a bloody nerve," he grunted angrily and started to close the door. I put out my hand to stop him. "Wait Ted," I pleaded. "Hear me out."

"You can bugger off," he shouted. "Why would I want to talk to you?"

"Because we've both lost women we loved," I said. "I didn't kill your wife and I certainly didn't kill mine. I could never do a thing like that. I need to set things straight. Please can we talk?"

He stared at me for a long time then turned and picked up something that was to one side of the door. It was a double-barrelled shot gun. I stepped back in alarm.

"Right now," he growled, "I'd like to blow your fucking brains out with this." He pointed the gun at my face. "You tell me why I shouldn't."

"Because you'd be killing an innocent man," I said as calmly as I could. "Let me talk to you then you can blow my brains out."

He took some time to digest this, his eyes exploring my face then he lowered the gun and moved to one side. "You'd best come in and whatever you say had better be good." He gestured with the rifle for me to go ahead of him down the hallway then we entered a small cosy sitting room with beams so low that I had to duck. The room was very warm. It felt as though I'd entered a war museum for on every wall there were photographs of men in uniform, large shell cases propped the door open and a pair of criss-crossed rifles were fixed on the wall over a large inglenook fireplace. Ted stood like a sentry by the door as I surveyed the room. Facing the TV were two floral patterned armchairs and on one of them was a pile of old newspapers and magazines. He pushed them to the floor with the end of his shotgun and said "Take that coat off an' sit down. The umbrella was taken from me and was propped up beside the fireplace then he threw my wet coat across a small wooden chair and moved it on to the flagstones in front of the blazing fire, all the time clutching his rifle under one arm. I sat down. "There's no need for the gun," I said. "I'm not going to attack you. All I want to do is talk." "Yeah," he said and sat on the other chair with the weapon on his lap. He lifted a corner of his vest to his face and wiped away the shaving lather. "Get on with it," he said.

I let it all tumble out. I described how idyllic my relationship had been with Jennifer. How happy we'd been. How my doctor friend Charles had assured me that her weird behaviour during her pregnancy was extreme but not completely unusual and that throughout I had continued to love her. I went through my every movement on the day of the murders and put a theory to him that both women could have been killed by a female who was infertile and driven mad by her desperation for a child. Or perhaps her partner had done the deed for her. That it was my hope that the baby was alive and was being cared for and that the police were following that line of investigation. I finished by saying, "Ted, please believe me. I loved my wife and liked your wife very much. I would never have harmed either of them. I'm alone now as you are and miss her every minute of every day."

He stared at me for a long time then the frown dropped from his face and he said with a sigh, "Yeah. Takes a bit of gettin' used to, bein' alone. She was a wonderful woman was my wife. Couldn't have kids together but we was happy. That young girl what works in the shop now we adopted when she was only a year old. Thank the Lord I've got her. Been a blessing she has. She's the one what took the phone call."

"Phone call?"

"Yeah. From your missus to say she was in labour and could my wife come and help."

"I'm sorry."

"She'd 'elp anybody, would my missus."
He shook his head sadly. "I miss 'er a lot. Feel a bit lost without 'er. Don't know what to do with meself half the time."

"I know the feeling."

He glanced up a me, his eyes brimming with tears. "'Aven't even got the bloody dog now."

"What?"

"Nobby. My little dog. A fox 'ad him."

"Oh no!" I said, remembering the scruffy rug he was so attached to. "What happened?"

"Found him in the wood back yonder. Poor little bugger 'ad been torn to shreds. "Fuckin' foxes. I'd shoot the bloody lot of 'em."

He stood up and put the gun on the floor. "You want a cup of coffee?" he said. "I normally 'ave one this time of day."

I nodded. This was obviously a peace offering. "Thanks. That would be nice. No sugar."

He shuffled out into the kitchen and returned a couple of minutes later carrying two very chipped mugs of extremely milky coffee and a plate of digestive biscuits. He handed me a mug and said, "I'm glad now that you came. It's sorted a lot out in my mind. I'm prepared to believe you though part of me still thinks that I shouldn't. If you're lying you're bloody good at it. So let's go along with your story for the time being and 'ope the police will come up with summat." We talked for quite a long time about the murders and the awful effect it had had on both our lives but later the conversation drifted on to much lighter matters. I learned that Ted had been born in Edinburgh but moved with his parents at the age of four to live on the outskirts of Birmingham where his father had found work.

"It weren't a nice time for me," he said. "I hated school from the word go. Mother sent me to school on my first day wearing a kilt. Thought it was normal. Of course all the other kids took the piss out of this new lad wearing a kilt and talking with a funny accent. I very quickly became a Brummy."

"No sign of a Brummy accent now," I said.

"Right. I'm posh now. A man of Kent. It's Moira who took over takin' the piss."

"Moira?"

"My missus. Told me I was a wee Sassenach." He smiled to himself. "Best thing that ever 'appened to me. We met at a dance. She was the most beautiful woman I ever clapped eyes on. A real bobby dazzler. We was married within six weeks of meetin' an' set up home here in Kent. Been here ever since. Happy as Larry we were … Till what 'appened."

He stood up and took a framed photograph from the wall. It was of a very young Ted in uniform wearing a beret that looked far too big for him with his arm around the extremely slim waist of a pretty dark haired girl.

"That's my Moira," he said.

We sat quietly for a while, he lost in reminiscences staring at the photograph and me trying hard to associate the round ball of a woman in our local shop with the bobby dazzler in the picture. I failed.

Ted seemed near to tears again so I changed the subject.

"How long were you in the army, Ted?" I said, pointing at all the military memorabilia which seemed to take up every inch of spare space in the room. He brightened immediately. "Five years. Would've been longer but I got injured. Broke my heart 'aving to leave. I loved the army."

"What happened?"

"I was serving in Korea nineteen fifty six. Bomb disposal. Missed one bugger an' the thing went off. Was in 'ospital for weeks."

"Did you tread on it?"

"No. I saw the bloody thing an' was going to defuse it but before I got near the platoon commander comes chargin' round the corner in a Jeep. I screamed at him but he didn't hear.

Would've killed him and his driver so I jumped on it, backpack first. Next thing I knew I was in the 'ospital tent with a Korean nurse bendin' over me. They thought I was a goner but I pulled through. Lost one of my kidneys an' still have terrible trouble with me back."

"Bloody hell, Ted," I said. "That was brave. You're lucky to be alive."

He nodded. "Yeah. Got a guardian angel, I 'ave." He picked up a small padded box from a shelf beside his chair and opened it. "Got this too for my troubles," he said proudly,

I stared at it in awe. It was a Victoria Cross medal. "Wow!" I breathed. "You're a hero!"

He smiled. "Yeah. An' I met the Queen. She was the one what pinned it on. It's a nice thing to 'ave I suppose but I'd much rather 'ave my kidney back."

"Ted McSweeney," I said. "I'm full of admiration. I've never met a hero before and insist on buying you a pint … but in the Bugler. They've missed you. You've been away too long."

"I'll be there tonight," he said.

I walked home that afternoon feeling much relieved. At last someone in the village believed my story and was willing to accept that I was not a killer. I decided that Ted was a very nice man and wanted him as a friend.

So I stayed on. The village changed, people died, others moved. Newcomers came here to live who had no idea of past events and very slowly I became more acceptable even though I knew that tittle tattle about the murders and my missing child still persisted. It was a relief that neighbours no longer snubbed me completely. Held me at arm's length would be a better description.

I got back to work, changed my style, used a different name and started contributing to a well known greetings card firm. Birthdays, weddings, mother's day, Christmases and Valentines day cards. It was slow at first but after a while I started to become quite successful. The money was good but more importantly I needed something to occupy myself. Then at the end of October 1992 I joined the twentieth century by acquiring a mobile phone. It was a present from Karen and Andy. Up till then I'd resisted having to lug something about the size of a house brick around that needed a car battery to charge it so that I could make unnecessary calls to tell someone I was on the train. The truth was I wasn't even excited by owning a more modern version. However, I thanked both my children profusely and faked interest as they spent hours explaining to their non-tech father how to use it. I promised to keep the damned thing charged up and not to chuck it in a drawer but to use it if I ever felt at a low ebb and needed a chat.

Life moved on. Gordon the ghost seemed to have packed and gone. For fifteen years all was harmony in our little Kent village. My daughter Karen got married to an architect called Geoffrey and went to live in one of his designs down on the South Coast, a year later my son phoned from Australia to tell me he had married a beautiful physiotherapist called Julie and I got myself a new dog from Battersea Dog's Home. An odd little mutt with a fringe of yellow hair hanging over its eyes, one ear black, the other brown, a little brush of a tail and the most appealing eyes which had stared at me through the bars of the cage and seemed to be saying 'please take me home'. So I did and called him Heinz (fifty seven varieties). He'd been knocked about a bit in his short life so we had a lot in common.

All was well with the world.

Then the killings started.

The body of a twenty eight year old Swedish woman who had been back-packing in the area was found partially clothed in a ditch on the border between the woods and Morgan's Meadow. She was horrifically scarred and one of her arms was almost completely severed. Of course the whole village was in shock over such a brutal murder but inevitably my door was the first one to be knocked on by the police. Fortunately for me I had been down on the south coast to celebrate my daughter's birthday and at least twenty of her friends could vouch for the fact that I was with them when the incident took place.

Two weeks later a middle aged couple were found dead in the bedroom of their house. Again both were badly scarred and had been sexually assaulted. It is thought that the intruder entered the building after scaling a wall at the back of the premises before smashing through an upstairs window.

These murders took place only fifty yards from my cottage so again I was the first to be questioned but once more I was able to prove I was nowhere near the village at the time. Nevertheless I noticed that an unmarked car with two occupants had taken to parking a few yards from my front door and was there both day and night. So I knew that I was being watched. When the fourth murder happened the story hit all the major headlines. "SADISTIC KILLER TARGETS SMALL VILLAGE" screamed one, and "THE VILLAGE OF THE DAMNED" another. Both papers were unable to resist mentioning that I who was once a suspect in a double murder was a resident.

This latest killing was a particularly brutal one. Two young boys, both about fourteen years old, had been playing hide and seek in the woods adjacent to Morgan's Meadow. One of the boys had gone off to hide and then after an hour of searching and calling the other lad gave up and went home. There followed an intensive house to house police search. Teams clad in high viz jackets combed the surrounding woods and fields. Everyone in the village was questioned but without success. The parents of the child made desperate pleas for his return on television but to no avail until sadly three days later the boy's pitiful remains were discovered in the hollow of a tree by a couple walking their dog. Again the body had been horribly mutilated but this time there was evidence of bite marks and large portions of flesh were missing. Strangely inside the same hollow were the remains of cats, squirrels and other small animals. One of the forensic squad was quoted as saying that it was rather like a primitive pantry.

All at once the whole area was crawling with police and teams from the media. Reporters were hammering on every door, especially mine, for interviews so I was glad of the mysterious car parked nearby. I knew it was the police and consequently they would also know I hadn't been anywhere near the scene of the recent attacks.

There was a frantic rush to buy new locks and heavy bolts for front and back doors.

Companies that sold security alarms were busier than they'd ever been before and the village streets were deserted as soon as it got dark.

One night, however, eager for some company I phoned Peter Reilly and arranged to meet him at our local pub, the Kentish Bugler.

As it turned out later on I made a stupid mistake by avoiding my two police watchers in the car outside. I left the light on in the living room and left through the back door with Heinz on his lead then made my way round the side of the house and in the shadow of a large hedge walked the few yards to the pub. My reason for this was I knew they would follow me and I just wanted a private chat with my friend without being scrutinised by two plods only a few feet away.

It was a cold crisp night. The whole village was bathed in light from a full moon and a glittering frost was already forming on the hedges and surrounding fields. It was eerily quiet. The only sound that of my footsteps on the gravelly path but just as I was crossing the pub car park a sound from somewhere a fair distance behind me shattered the silence. It was a high pitched cackling sound. A long warbling howl followed by a witch like exultant laugh. I turned and looked back down the lane. There was nothing to see. I waited for a while but the sound didn't come again so I went into the pub.

As I entered the bar I saw Peter deep in conversation with a reporter from my old paper. This was Eddie Thompson, a man of about forty five with a wispy moustache and a bald head. From time to time I'd illustrated a few of his articles and until my sacking we had been good friends. Also standing in the group and staring forlornly into an empty glass was Ted McSweeney.

"Ah, Fergus," Thompson said as soon as I walked into the bar. "Long time no see. Let me get you a drink." I must have glared at Peter because he immediately held his hand up and said, "Before you say a thing, I did not invite the press along."

"Nope," Thompson said, "I was already here before the Reverend turned up, talking to this gentleman." He put his hand on Ted McSweeney's shoulder.

"... So relax and let me buy my old colleague a drink."

He shook my hand. "Nice to see you again."

"Ditto," I said. "Okay, I'll have a pint of bitter."

"And you Reverend?" he asked.

"Same for me, please," Peter replied.

"… and you sir?" He took Ted's empty glass from him.

"Oh, that's very kind," Ted answered with a relieved smile. "Just to be sociable."

Thompson went to order the drinks. "Well," said Peter. "This is a pretty kettle of fish is it not?" He gestured at the empty room. "Everyone scared to go out. Look at the place. Deserted. Who would've thought it?"

"There's a maniac loose," Ted growled. "I don't go nowhere without my gun nowadays. Let the bastard try breakin' into my place!"

"You be careful with that weapon," Peter said.

Thompson joined us with a tray of drinks. He handed them around then said to me, "What's your theory, Fergus? You were involved in the first of all these murders."

I smiled and held out my hand, palm uppermost.

"What?" he said.

"The phone."

"Aw, alright," he groaned and put his hand in his pocket and handed me his mobile phone. "I'm a journalist, for heaven's sake."

I switched the phone off and handed it back to him.

"Well, you crafty bugger!" Ted said rounding on him. "Were you recording everythin' I said earlier?"

Thompson shrugged. "Don't worry. You didn't say anything incriminating."

"I don't know nothing incriminating," Ted snarled.

"Okay, okay," I said. "Calm down. Let's have your theory first, Eddie."

Eddie leant over in a conspiratorial hunch and talked in such a low whisper we had to crowd around him in order to hear. "Right," he said. "Here's what a lot of us journos think. This guy … it has to be a guy, is a fantasist. Probably into Superheroes. We think he probably dresses up before he ventures out to kill and rape. I'll bet he even wears a mask. Each of his victims had appalling gouges and tears in the skin which suggests he wears gloves with claws fixed to them or he carries some kind of sharp instrument in his hand like a small garden tool."

"Not the only tool he uses," Ted said.

"Yeah. This fella has one hell of a libido. He'll shag anything with a hole." He hesitated then turned to face Peter. "Sorry vicar."

"Ah, don't be worrying about me," Peter smiled. "I'm not easily shocked."

"D'you think this is the same bastard who murdered my wife?" Ted asked, then added, "… and Fergus's missus?"

"It's possible."

"He's kept very quiet for the past fifteen years."

Thompson nodded. "Yeah. That is a puzzle. Anyway it's only a theory. So far the police haven't a clue so why or what is anybody's guess?" He turned to me. "What're your thoughts, Gus?"

"I'm like the police," I mumbled. "Haven't got a clue."

This was not entirely true. Over the past few years little bits of the jigsaw had been slowly joining together in my head and forming a picture so preposterous that if I was to voice them people would think I'd gone off my head.

"So you think a psychotic Batman figure is roaming around the area do you, Eddie?" I asked. "I reckon it's you who's being the fantasist."

"Alright, give me another scenario," he retorted.

"I think it's some kind of animal."

"Bollocks!" he said. "Animals do not go around raping human beings."

"Well whatever it is, it's very clever at hiding its tracks. The police are getting nowhere."

"They searched my house. Made a right mess they did," Ted groaned. "… and the shop, 'ad to close for a whole day."

I told them about the police car outside my cottage. "I'm still high on the suspect list," I said. "Probably hoping to apprehend me sneaking out in my Batman's outfit."

"Scoff away, Munroe," Eddie said. "But if I'm right I want a full apology from you, you cynical bastard."

"Deal," I nodded.

Peter who had been rather quiet suddenly announced that he'd been to the police station that very morning.

"Blimey," Eddie snorted. "Surely the local vicar isn't a suspect?"

"No, no, nothing like that," Peter said indignantly. "I've been very worried about one of my little dogs. He's been missing for over three days."

"Little?" I said. "Do you mean one of your Great Danes?"

He nodded.

I patted his arm. "Don't worry. There's probably a bitch on heat somewhere nearby.

He'll come home soon with a big smile on his face,"

He managed a small smile, sighed and said, "I hope you're right. Anyone for another drink?"

Ted quickly drained his glass. "Oh, go on then," he said.

Later when I arrived home I tapped on the window of the surveillance police car still parked a few yards from my door. Both occupants looked stunned when they wound the window down and saw it was me.

"Fancy a cup of tea?" I asked.

I went into the cottage, smiling to myself over the shocked expressions the plods wore when they realised they'd been rumbled.

It was too early for bed so I poured myself a small whisky and switched on the television just in time for the news. There were several shots of the cordoned off area in the wood where the boy's body had been found, men in white forensic boiler suits prowling around in the trees and later a young woman talking into camera in front of a background picture of Morgan's Meadow. I was about to switch off and go to bed when the phone rang. It was Peter Reilly. "Hi Peter," I said. "What's up?"

"Fergus. Have you by any chance seen my sister Rosemary?" he asked.

"No, why?"

"I got back and she was not at home. I wondered if you'd seen her when you went back to your place."

"What would she be going out for at this time of night?" I asked.

"No, it was earlier," he answered. "Rosemary left home long before I went to meet you at the pub. She was looking for our dog, so she was. Remember I told you he was missing? Well now they're both missing. I tell you what Fergus. I'm more than a little worried. I warned her to get home before dark."

"Quite right too."

"Normally I wouldn't be so concerned, but with all these shenanigans going on, poor innocents being murdered and all … well, you'll understand."

"Of course," I said. "Have you called the police?"

"I have. Did it straight away. They promised to look for her as soon as it gets light. Oh sweet Jesus. I don't think I can wait that long."

"Get over here now, Peter," I said. "We'll have a look together."

It took him only ten minutes to get to my cottage in his old car. I meanwhile had taken a small torch and a high powered lamp from the shed outside and as soon as he arrived we set off down the lane. He with his other Great Dane and me with little Heinz. We climbed over the stile and into Morgan's Meadow. It was pitch dark and I gave a silent thank you prayer to Peter's boss that I'd remembered to bring two torches along with us. Morgan's Meadow is a vast area and over the next couple of hours we must have covered most of it calling Rosemary's name and that of Satan which turned out to be the name of the missing dog. Serious as the situation was and worried as we both were I couldn't quite suppress a smile as I listened to the vicar of our parish wandering around the park in the early hours of the morning calling for Satan. The search was fruitless. We had decided that we wouldn't go into the wood with its myriad of paths but to delay that until daylight, so we walked back to my cottage, both of us fearing the worst. I don't think Peter got much sleep in what was left of the night but I was in dreamland as soon as my head hit the pillow. It was not a long sleep. At seven in the morning the police were hammering at my door. There were three of them, all of whom I recognised. Detective Inspector Peter Vaughan, my old adversary from a decade and a half ago who surely now must be on the verge of retirement, accompanied by the two men who'd been parked outside the cottage for the past few days. In my mind I had christened them

Tweedledum and Tweedledee. I let them in. Suddenly my living room seemed smaller as they squeezed their vast bulks on to the settee and an armchair. When they were settled I asked in true English fashion if they would like a coffee or a cup of tea.

"Yeah, we'll have that one you offered us last night," said Tweedledee, glaring at me with hostile eyes.

"No time for that," grunted Vaughan, turning to me. "Might I ask where you were last night, Mr Munroe?"

"Yes. I was in the Bugler's pub up the road. Why?"

"We'll come to that. Did you meet anyone? Someone who might vouch for you being there?"

"I arranged to meet our local vicar, the Reverend Peter Reilly. He was there when I arrived talking to a journalist named Eddie Thompson and the owner of the shop down the lane, Ted McSweeney."

"What time would that be?"

"About eight o'clock."

"I see." He gestured at his colleagues. "So why did you choose to leave by the back door and sneak past the surveillance team that you knew were parked outside. Bit furtive wasn't it?"

I shrugged. "It was just a game I was having with them. Testing their spying abilities. They didn't pass the exam. I give them two out of ten marks and a 'could do better' comment."

"Fuckin' comedian, aren't you?" Tweedledum snorted.

I ignored him. "D'you mind telling me what all this is about inspector?"

He glanced at a small notebook. "You were out when your wife and Mrs McSweeney were both murdered over fifteen years ago and the child your wife was expecting disappeared."

I winced and nodded, the memory of that horrendous evening still painful.

"Well you seem to be making a habit of it, Mr Munroe. Last night while you were out and about the Reverend Peter Reilly's sister, Rosemary, was brutally slaughtered." He paused and then added, "… and savagely raped. The manner of her death was very similar to that of the two killings in this house all those years ago!

"Oh no! Oh my God!" Three faces were glaring at me. "That's terrible news," I spluttered "… but I was out with Peter for hours last night searching for her."

"Yes. He has testified to that, but what were you doing in the hours before meeting him in the pub?"

I tried hard to think. What the hell was I doing before I left to meet Peter? I couldn't remember. I stared blankly at them and shook my head.

"She was eighty nine years old," Vaughan said accusingly, "… a helpless old lady."

"Oh, for God sake!" I shouted. "I couldn't do a thing like that. Jesus Christ. I would never harm an old lady."

"Then what about a young lady like the unfortunate back-packer who died recently?" Vaughan asked.

"Or the middle-aged couple just across the road from here," added Tweedledee.

"You know damned well I was away from here on both occasions. You've questioned me about those already. The facts are still the same. Nothing's changed."

Vaughan scribbled something into his notebook. I stood up and pointed out of the window. "That poor child found in the hollow of a tree. Parts of him had been eaten. There were bits of other animals in there too. D'you think I did that? Have you bothered to investigate why so many household pets have gone missing recently? No, I bet you haven't. You're too stuck in a rut, convincing yourselves that it's a human being you're after. I'm sure there's a wild animal on the loose out there."

Vaughan looked up from his notes. "Animals aren't known to prowl around raping old ladies."

"So you just shut your eyes to the possibility?"

He nodded. Tweedledee and Tweedledum nudged each other and grinned.

"Okay, Inspector," I said, "if you're here to arrest me for cannibalism, rape and murder, before you do, I'd like all the cats and squirrels I have eaten taken into consideration."

There was a glimmer of a smile, then: "Not right now, Mr Munroe, but we may want to question you again later." He stood up. "Till then, take my advice. When you leave the house don't go sneaking out the back way and through the garden. It makes people like me ask the question – why?"

As soon as they had gone I rang the vicarage. I needed desperately to talk to Peter to console him and to convince him that I had nothing to do with his sister's murder. There was no answer from his mobile so I tried his main line. After an interminable wait an official sounding voice answered which I guessed was from a police woman. "The Reverend Reilly is not taking any calls today," she barked. "Who is this?"

"A friend."

"I'll inform him you rang – name?"

"Fergus Munroe."

There was a pause then she said in clipped tones, "Right now, Mr Munroe, I think you'd be the last person he'd want to talk to." Then she hung up.

I shouted abuse at her down the empty line, considered driving straight away to the vicarage then decided it would be better to wait till I'd cooled down. Perhaps next time I called, Lucretia Borgia would have changed shifts. I looked down at Heinz who was wagging his tail and had a hopeful expression in his face. "Okay, Heinz," I said. "Let's go for a walk."

It was a beautiful chilly morning and although still covered in frost the trees had begun to show signs of life with small green buds poking their enquiring heads from the tips of seemingly dead brown branches but despite the weather, the pretty surroundings and Heinz bounding happily ahead of me giving little yelps of excitement, I couldn't lift the feeling of gloom that the news of Peter's sister had left me with and to be the main suspect made my mood even worse.

When Heinz and I left the cottage I noticed that Tweedledee and Tweedledum's car was no longer parked in its usual place but I knew they'd be lurking somewhere keeping an eye on me. More people than usual were strolling along the many woodland paths and it was an even bet a couple of new plods would be amongst them and if so they were in danger of obtaining severe leg injuries from Heinz who loved to carry a log in his mouth several times longer than himself sweeping away whoever was in his path.

After a while however he was forced to drop his chunk of tree as we headed down a smaller track with thick undergrowth on either side. Quite soon we came across a small clearing with a pond at its centre. A flock of startled pigeons rose up with a thrum of wings and settled high in the trees above our heads. I remembered the place. Jenny and I used to come here because it was such an attractive spot but now I saw that some environmentally ignorant moron had dumped an old fridge in the water. The corner of an unwanted mattress was poking out from the weeds and several lumpy black plastic bags had been thrown in for good measure.

Further ahead we came across an even more sad and depressing sight. Our path was blocked off by long lines of blue and white police tape stretching from tree to tree closing an area of about half an acre. This would be the place where the body of the young boy had been found. I stood for a while staring into the almost impenetrable area of scrub thinking about the tragic loss of such a young life and wondering how his poor parents were coping. I thought how lucky I was that both my children were alive and well and how devastated I would have felt had the victim been one of them.

These thoughts were interrupted by some excited barking coming from beyond the rubbish filled pool. I retraced my steps and followed the sound down the overgrown path until I came to another clearing. I recognised the place immediately. We must have walked in a large circle because here we were at the badger's sett.

There was a musty odour in the air which I thought at first was that of a fox but this was more rank and acrid, like the smell of rotten meat.

Heinz was on the other side of the sett growling and tossing something that looked like a black ball around in his teeth. When he saw me he trotted over, tail wagging happily and proudly dropped the thing at my feet then started to bark excitedly. I think he wanted me to throw it so he could chase after it. I rolled the object over with my foot and my whole body froze. It was the head of a young dog and unmistakably that of a Great Dane.

*****

That afternoon I left Heinz at home and drove to the vicarage. A uniformed police woman was standing at the gate. She obviously thought I was one of Peter's parishioners. "Sorry," she said, holding out her hand to stop me going through. "The vicar is not receiving any callers today." I recognised her voice. It was Lucretia Borgia.

"I'm a close friend of his," I said. "I'm here to comfort him if I can. I'm sure he'd like a friend at a time like this."

"Name?" she demanded.

"Fergus Munroe."

She looked shocked. "Oh, it's you again," she groaned. "I told you earlier. I don't think he'd want to see you Mr Munroe.

"Why don't you let him make that choice?"

She hesitated then said, "Wait here." She walked away to talk briefly with another woman in plain clothes at the front door. Then she waited with her back to the house staring across the driveway at me with ill-concealed hostility. After a couple of minutes the other woman appeared at the doorway again and there was another whispered conversation. Lucretia walked back to the gate.

"He'll see you." She stood to one side, then added "He's in rather an emotional state and is very fragile. Tread carefully."

Peter was sitting in one of the overstuffed armchairs when I entered the big living room. He was still wearing his pyjamas under a blue dressing gown and there was a thick blanket draped across his shoulders.

The plain clothes woman who had accompanied me showed me into the room then discreetly left. "Peter, I'm so sorry," I said.

He nodded and gestured to a chair. "Sit yourself down," he said, almost in a whisper. I sat. He didn't speak for a long time then said huskily, "Y'know, Gus. Sometimes my faith is sorely tested and I wonder if I've been wasting my time, that God doesn't exist at all and if he does why does he allow such terrible things to happen to so many innocent people."

I had to strain to hear what he was saying. It was as if he was voicing his thoughts to himself. "Poor Rosemary," he continued. "She'd never have hurt a fly. What am I going to do without her?"

I didn't have an answer to that so I just patted him on the shoulder.

"Eighty nine years old and they found her poor body naked under a hedge in somebody's front garden. Who could have done such a thing?"

"It's hard to comprehend," I said.

He looked up at me, his cheeks wet with tears. "She'd been raped and her poor head almost ripped from her body." He started to sob quietly. "Oh, if only she hadn't gone out looking for the dog."

I sat listening to him feeling dumb and inadequate, unable to find any suitable words of consolation. Is there anything I can do, Peter? Anything at all?" I asked. He shook his head. "No, no thanks. Just sit there while I let it all out. Thanks for coming over. I needed someone to talk to."

He stared into the empty fireplace for a long time then he said angrily, "Ironical, isn't it. I've been preaching the words of the Lord for years. Turn the other cheek, He says. Turn the other bloody cheek! I tell you if I found the bastard who did what he did to my sister I'd fucking kill him."

He glanced up at me. "Sorry," he said. "Sorry, ignore that … I'm not myself."

"Peter. I felt exactly like you when my wife was murdered, so say what you like. I'm with you all the way. I'd help you kill the bastard."

He nodded and said, "Y'know, there is something you can do. It's a wee bit early but there's a bottle of Bushmills in the cupboard over there." He pointed to the far side of the room. "I don't bloody care what time it is right now. I need a pick-me-up."

I found the whisky and two glasses. It was only four thirty in the afternoon but if there was a time to break the unwritten sobriety rules about waiting for suns to go over the yardarms, this was it.

I poured two generous tots and handed him a glass. He took a long sip, sighed and sank back in his chair, holding the glass up to the light. "Look at that," he said, "… Awesome amber. An enemy to some, a comfort to others. It has the power of healing and if ye have enough of it, it blots out all the bad things." He thought about what he'd just said, then added, "Trouble is the bad things return later and you feel like shit."

I smiled. "Very true. I've had that feeling many a time."

"I've been sitting here for hours," he said wistfully. "Thinking things over and I still can't get my head around it … asking myself over and over … why? Why my lovely sister who was the nicest and kindest of human beings? I can't bear the thought of what pain she must have gone through. For eighty nine years a blameless life and then this. It's hard to comprehend."

"I'm sorry to tell you the police have me down as their main suspect," I said.

"Ach, nonsense," he exclaimed angrily. "I believe you to be a good man. You haven't got it in you to go around killing innocent folks."

"You don't know what a relief it is to hear you say that."

He waved his hand dismissively. "She was battling with cancer," he said sadly.

"Oh, I didn't know that."

"A lump in the breast. Had it removed a few years back but it was knocking at her door for a return visit. He leaned forward and topped up his glass. "Ach," he growled again. "I should've done what my da wanted me to do. So I should. Gone into the family business."

"What was that?"

"He ran a very successful plumbing business in Dublin."

"Somehow I can't see you under a sink mending broken pipes," I said.

He smiled. "At least I'd be working for a boss that was real. Right now I'm not sure about the boss I've devoted my whole life to."

He was becoming increasingly morose so I decided to change the subject.

"Y'know Peter," I said, "I have a theory about all these dreadful killings. I don't know if this is a bad time to tell it to you but as soon as you're able I'd like your thoughts on it."

"There is no time like the present, Fergus. I've got nothing else to do apart from getting drunk. So to avoid that you can put that bottle out of sight and fire away with your theory. I'm interested to hear it."

"You might think I'm crazy."

"I'll let you know at the end of it."

I walked across the room and put the whisky back in its cupboard. "Okay," I said, "make yourself comfy. This may take some time." I sat down again. "You'll remember coming to my cottage to do an exorcism?" He nodded.

"Well, I think the spirit you tried to get rid of was a hybrid created by two German scientists way back in the eighteen forties. A monster that terrorised this area after escaping from P T Barnam's freak show." I told him how I'd found Eliza's notebook and her detailed description of this half human/part animal creature, then about the night I'd been thrown out of bed, my horror of seeing my wife apparently in a trance having intercourse with something unseen, her subsequent pregnancy and my suspicion that she might have been unfaithful. "Later I convinced myself that my vasectomy hadn't worked," I said, "... and I was indeed going to be a father again, but Jenny changed. Slowly she transformed herself from the sweet loving woman that I married to a foul mouthed, bad tempered and violent stranger."

Peter held his hand up to interrupt. "Wait, are you telling me that your wife became pregnant by this creature?"

"I am convinced of it."

"But to impregnate a woman a certain ingredient is necessary. Sperm. How could an invisible entity with no substance produce an actual living cell?"

"I did warn you it would sound crazy."

"Go on," he said.

"Well here it gets even more unbelievable. I think that during the period of Jenny's pregnancy she was harbouring a parasite. A malignant, vile abomination that was not born in the normal way but clawed and burst its way out of her womb like a bird pecking its way out of its shell, then unlike a helpless human being was instantly to its feet like many animals do when born to avoid predators. Jenny must have died after enduring agonising pain."

"And the other woman, Mrs McSweeney?"

"Slaughtered by the parasite."

Peter shook his head. "Fergus. This is an awful lot to swallow. The child of a ghost let loose on the world to rape and murder?"

"That's what I believe. It is probably just as described in Eliza's notebook. Hideously formed and possessing immense strength."

"Well, really Fergus ..." Peter began.

"How else can you explain the strange disappearance of the baby? For nearly two decades there's not been a sign of it apart from the fact that peoples' pets start to go missing. This thing has to eat. Remember the police found a stash of animal parts in the hollow of the tree along with the remains of a poor child. It was a pantry. A place where it stocked its next meal."

Peter groaned but I carried on. "And now this thing has grown. It is mature. It has sexual urges. So suddenly the rapes begin. It doesn't care who or what its victim is. It rapes and it kills then it eats. The police are looking for a human but what they should be hunting down is an animal. A very vicious and dangerous hybrid."

He stared at me. I think I had convinced him that I was crazy after all.

"Are you suggesting that my sister Rosemary was a victim of this … this thing?"

I nodded.

"Oh, sweet Jesus," he muttered. "I have to tell you Fergus that the rational part of me thinks that you have gone completely do-lally … and I feel sure if you were to tell the police your story you'd be in a padded cell in no time at all."

"It also killed your dog," I said.

His head jerked around to face me. "My Great Dane? How d'you know?"

I told him how Heinz had found the skull of his dog. He gave a cry of pain and covered his face with his hands.

"Where was this?" he moaned.

"Besides the badger's sett in the wood."

There was a tiny dribble of whisky left in Peter's glass. He gulped it down and stared at the empty glass sadly. After a while he turned to me and said in a tired voice, "It's been quite a day, Fergus. Not the happiest of days I'm afraid. Would you mind very much if I asked you to leave now? I have a lot to think about and I'd like to be alone for a while."

"Of course. I quite understand. I'll let myself out."

"Thanks for coming," he said.

****

It was getting dark by the time I got back to the cottage where I found a crowd of journalists waiting for me at the gate. They turned excitedly when they saw me approach.

"Have you any comment to make about this recent murder, Mr Munroe?" one of them asked. Another man caught me by the arm. "I believe you know the dead woman. Was she a friend, Mr Munroe?" I held up my hand to quieten them then asked "Why are you asking me? I just happen to live nearby. I don't know any more than you do."

"Your wife was the first of the murders in the village, Mr Munroe. Do you think it's the same killer?"

"Yes," said the first one. "Still no news about your missing baby."

I pushed my way past them, closed the gate and turned to face them. "I wish I knew the answers to all your questions but I don't. I'm sure if the police come up with something, they'll tell you, so till then give me a break, will you." I let myself into the house to cut out the barrage of questions feeling completely gutted. It's hard to describe the loneliness of being prime suspect of multiple murders and once again to be trailed by plain clothes police officers and having the ever present feeling of being the odd one out in a crowd, the person other people point at and whisper about. I felt then as people with the plague must have felt in mediaeval times when they were forced to carry a placard hung around their necks proclaiming that they were 'unclean'.

I set about making myself something to eat. The only thing I'd put in my stomach for hours was the Reverend Reilly's whisky so as well as being hungry I was a little light-headed. TV's coverage of the murder of Peter's sister was getting saturation coverage. There were interviews with frightened residents, statements by high ranking policemen, long shots of the police tent in the garden where a body had been found and views from the air of the whole area which had now been dubbed 'The murder capital of England'.

I had just settled down with a tray on my lap, about to eat a heated-up pepperoni pizza when my mobile phone buzzed. It was Detective Inspector Vaughan. "Mind if I pop round?" he asked. "I've got some news for you."

I sighed. "Who have I murdered this time?"

"Half an hour?"

At least he'd given me time to eat my meal. He arrived almost exactly thirty minutes later as I was stacking the dishwasher. His face seemed even redder and shinier since we last met and the comb over had thinned a great deal. I offered him a chair but he refused anything to drink.

"I have good news for you," he said. "First let me apologise that it has taken this long but the science is still in its infancy."

"Science?"

"Yes, Mr Munroe. Science. You know of course about DNA?"

I nodded.

"Well, DNA samples have been collected from all the murder victims in the vicinity. Sperm samples mainly and none of them match yours."

"I haven't given any sperm samples," I said.

"That's not necessary. Hair from your hairbrush would do the trick. Same DNA apparently. Also you were an occasional blood donor some time ago. All goes down on your records.

This was true. I had donated blood a couple of times long before I'd met Jenny.

"Well, I'm pleased you've been nicking my hair," I said, "if it's helped to eliminate me but have you got a match for anyone else?"

He shook his head. "Like I said. Things are a bit slow in the laboratories but they seem to be even slower with this one. The samples taken are of a kind they've never come across before and are still under analysis."

"Have you considered it might be an animal?"

"I think we've been through this before," he retorted. "Animals don't go around raping human beings."

"Look," I said angrily at his blunt refusal to even consider the possibility. "I've just returned from the vicarage after trying to console Peter Reilly on the loss of his sister."

"Yes, yes, we know all that."

"… and during our conversation I broke more bad news to him. That I had found the head of his missing dog in Morgan's Wood beside a badger's sett. That wasn't the work of a human, it must have been an animal." Vaughan tried to respond but I carried on. "Your own forensic people found a hoard of animal parts plus some human remains in the hollow of a tree. For God's sake, surely that's worth investigating."

"Investigations are under way," he said.

"And what about spoor. Have you found any? This creature has to have a shit now and again."

He looked heavenwards and raised his arms in a despairing gesture. "Mr Munroe, have you any idea how much pressure my officers are under? We're all working our socks off night and day trying to find this maniac. Morgan's Wood covers a huge area. Do you seriously think I'm going to make them search every inch of it looking for a few animal turds?"

"Yes, I do," I said. "Five people have died. How many more before you do something about it?"

He stood up. His face had gone from red to crimson. "Like I said. Investigations are under way."

"Good. Then don't just dismiss my theory."

"I won't. So in return don't dismiss all the hard work my colleagues are doing either. You don't show it but I assume that you're glad that you're no longer a suspect." He paused, then added, "… but I must warn you that even after all this time we have not closed the case on your late wife, Mrs McSweeney and your missing child."

With that veiled threat, he walked to the door.

"So are you giving your surveillance team something more important to do other than hang around outside my house?" I asked.

"They will be given other assignments," he snapped. "Good night Mr Munroe."

He walked off into the night but two days later was back on the phone to tell that a squad of policemen had dug up the deserted badger's sett and discovered nothing other than what would normally be found in a badger's dwelling, so would I please not waste any more of his hard working men's time with my fanciful notions.

There were very few people at Rosemary's funeral. A blanket of misty rain fell on the proceedings and a chill wind blew across the cemetery as the coffin was lowered into the ground. Peter Reilly conducted the service himself and it was obvious to all what an effort it was for him. He spoke in a hushed whisper, his voice often cracking with emotion and when the first handful of earth was thrown on to the casket, he couldn't hold back the tears any longer and sobbed openly. I put my arm across his shoulders and walked with him back into the church. The drinks and cucumber sandwiches usually dispensed after a funeral had not been offered so the only other mourners, an ancient female cousin of Peter's and two friends had gone back to their homes. We sat on a pew at the back of the church.

For at least half an hour neither of us spoke. Peter sat with his head in his hands and I could do nothing but wait till he had composed himself. Eventually, he sat up with a great sigh, told me it was his intention to retire, that his faith had been badly shaken and he no longer had the heart for it. I tried to persuade him to wait till his emotions had calmed down then perhaps he would see clearly the path to take but he insisted that now was the time and he had already started writing his letter of resignation to the Bishop.

"There is evil pervading our community," he groaned. "… and I am too old and right now too unsure of my God to fight against it."

As if to justify his decision only twenty-four hours later another body was discovered. Again, it was close to Morgan's Meadow, and only yards from the children' play area. Zarek Muckbar, or Zak as he was affectionately known, was our local postman. A keen body builder and keep fit enthusiast he was a cheerful and friendly individual, very powerfully built, over six foot tall and much loved by all the village residents. Zak had left his home on the previous evening for his regular run which normally took only about forty five minutes, so when he had not returned after two and a half hours his wife had called the police. By this time it was dark and there was little the police could do apart from send out a patrol car to retrace the route of his run. However, next morning before a proper search party could be organised the mutilated body of our beloved postman had been discovered by a couple of keen bird watchers new to the area who were staying with friends. Apparently, they had been walking through the meadow then thought they'd heard the cackling call of an Australian Kookaburra, a bird that had never been seen in the UK before. Excitedly they had gone to investigate then made their gruesome discovery.

I remember thinking at the time that probably they were right. I thought I had heard a Kookaburra on the night I met Eddie Thomson and Peter at the pub. Was it possible a bird native to Australia could have been blown off its course such a distance? Or perhaps someone living nearby kept one as a pet. Zak's injuries were identical to all the other victims. His throat had been torn out and there were multiple lacerations to the body. He had been raped and there were deep bite marks on his neck and shoulders.

Once again, within days the population of the village had doubled. Two thirds of the newcomers were police and one third media. Television crews, cameramen and journalists prowled the streets banging on doors, peering through windows, desperate to get a new slant on the growing story. Residents locked themselves away too scared to venture far from their homes, only daring to open their doors for deliveries of food. Some with water-tight alibis were allowed to leave to stay with distant friends or relatives and several even put their properties up for sale. The place was like a war zone.

There were only two beneficiaries in the panicked community. The pub which was crammed each evening with media folk and Ted McSweeney's shop which had to take on more staff to cope with the demand for food and supplies.

In the middle of all this chaos and panic I got a surprise visitor. My daughter, Karen, who like most of her age group assumed that parents never went anywhere, were always at home and had no personal engagements, just turned up on my doorstep. Suitcase in hand. "Hi Fathery thing," she said. "Surprise, surprise!" I put my arms around her. "Not only a surprise, one hell of a shock," I said. "Welcome. Why didn't you let me know you were coming?"

"Is it okay?"

"Not just okay. I'm thrilled. Come on in." I picked up her suitcase and led her into the living room. She slipped off her shoes and parked herself on the settee. "Well, here I am in the village of the damned ... scary or what?"

"What made you come here, been missing your dad?"

"I've been worried about you. Aren't you glad to see me?"

She picked up Heinz who had been trying to wag his tail off and placed him on her lap. "Heinz looks more pleased than you do."

"Of course I'm pleased. I'm delighted. Where's Geoff?"

"Got himself a big juicy contract and has flown to France so I thought I'd come and see you."

"Good thinking."

She grabbed my hand. "I've been so worried about you. All these murders are headlines on TV and all the papers. Is there a suspect?"

"Well, they've decided it's not me, thank God."

"Aren't you scared?"

I pointed at the bars I'd fitted on the windows. "Lots of folk living here have had these fitted. They're made by a local blacksmith. He's making a mint. I got steel doors while I was at it."

"Lummee. Must be like living in prison."

I nodded. "It is a bit. You've put yourself in a danger zone, I'm afraid."

She gave a little laugh.

"I'm serious, Karen. You can stay as long as you like but I insist that you don't go anywhere on your own. You go everywhere with me or you stay in the house."

"No get out of jail free cards?"

"Nope."

"I might dig a tunnel."

"Don't even joke about it."

She laughed. "Okay. Serious stuff now. I have some news for you."

"Go on."

"You are going to be a grandad."

My mouth must have dropped open. I stared at her in shock.

"You're kidding!"

"It was confirmed two days ago."

"Karen, that's wonderful." I bent down and kissed her forehead. "What fantastic news. My daughter is a very clever woman."

"I'm not the first, dad. Women have had babies before y'know."

"We must celebrate. Let's have some champagne!"

"Woa," she said. "I'm not allowed alcohol."

I went into the kitchen and took some bubbly from the fridge, went back to the living room and handed her half a glass. "Here. A little taste won't hurt you."

We clinked glasses. "Here's to the first of many."

"Steady on, Father."

"I want a full football team!"

It was a special treat for me to have someone else sharing the house. I'd been living on my own for such a long time so having my daughter there to talk to, cook with and care for reminded me of the good times I'd shared with Jenny. We went for long walks together steering well clear of the woods or deserted areas. We played Scrabble in the evenings or watched TV. Like her brother, Karen was a much more adventurous cook than I was and conjured up some truly delicious meals, so for a short while I was able to forget the traumas taking place in the village. One afternoon we decided to take a picnic lunch on our walk so that we could explore a little further than usual. I packed sandwiches, a thermos flask of tea, a couple of beers and a few dog biscuits into a haversack, slung it over my shoulder and we set off down the lane with Heinz trotting happily ahead of us. On the way we stopped at the village shop and I introduced Karen to Ted McSweeney. "Can't be your child," he said. "She's far too good looking."

"I'm told my mum had a very handsome plumber working for her before I was born," Karen said.

"Well there you go then," he laughed. "Mystery solved,"

I glanced around his tiny shop it was crammed with customers. "You're a busy boy these days."

"Yeah, but I'd rather not be for the reasons I am. Much rather have the old days back before all these murders."

We bought some peppermints and resumed our walk. It was an ideal day to be out and about. Bright and sunny with a crisp chill wind blowing in our faces as we marched through the meadow. The children's play area was busy with shrieking toddlers and anxious looking parents. Two or three armed policemen lingered nearby and a man with a camera was taking long shots of the scene. After half an hour we got to the edge of the meadow and sat down on a bench where I unpacked the haversack. This was a particularly pretty part of the area with lots of different shrubs and high trees under which thousands of daffodils formed a long yellow line stretching as far as the eye could see. The air was pungent with the smell of newly mown grass and we spotted two or three baby rabbits playing nearby.

I poured Karen a mug of tea and unwrapped the sandwiches. Heinz immediately went into food mode. I gave him a biscuit.

"That man," Karen said, "was he the person whose wife died at the same time as Jenny?"

"Yes, that's him. For a long time he thought I had killed them both."

"He obviously doesn't still think that."

"No, I managed to convince him otherwise. He's quite matey now. He's a good man."

"Thank God for that."

She chewed reflectively on her sandwich. "How can you bear to still live here, Dad, after all that's happened?"

"I love it here," I said, "well I did until all this shit happened. If I scuttled off to pastures new now there would be a few people start to think why. Is he escaping something? Perhaps he's got something to do with the murders after all."

She patted my hand. "I suppose you're right."

"Besides," I continued, "the cottage is where I was at my happiest. It still holds so many memories of Jen and how good we were together."

"Yeah, you were a great team."

I put the remains of our picnic into a nearby bin and we followed the line of daffodils round the perimeter of the meadow until eventually we came to a bumpy and muddy tract leading out of the park. In the distance I could see houses so assumed it would be safe to explore further. Here was an avenue of mature oak trees towering above the thick undergrowth. Fly tippers had been at work again and we had to clamber over a pile of dismembered kitchen cabinets which blocked the path. Soon we came to the houses I'd seen. It turned out to be an abandoned building site. The beginnings of three houses stood in a line facing the path we'd walked along. Each had a concrete drive leading on to what I supposed would one day become a tarmacked road. There was a muddy ditch running along the length of the site and a long concrete pipe was laid to allow water to flow unimpeded underneath the driveways. The buildings had hardly been started. The footings had been laid as had the flooring above which was now covered in old sheets of corrugated iron, solidified cement bags and old galvanised buckets. The few walls that had been built were only two or three foot high with gaps left for the doors and windows. From the path the site looked like a huge mouth with lots of missing teeth.

A battered sign was propped crookedly against a wall of the middle house informing us that this site was protected by a 'private security company' and as such is under constant CCTV surveillance.

"Blimey," Karen said. "What happened here?"

I shook my head. "Looks like the builders went bust or maybe there's been a dispute."

"Doesn't look like much building has been done for quite a while," she said.

"Nice spot for a house."

"Yeah, but it's a bit pongy. Is there a sewage plant nearby?"

"Yes, I noticed it too. I don't think it's sewage. Smells more like rotten meat to me."

Just then I heard a pitiful whining sound and looked around for Heinz. He was nowhere to be seen so I walked back to the muddy path. He was standing about thirty yards away. His ears were down and he was trembling.

"Heinz, what's the matter, boy? Come here," I called. He gave a short sharp bark but didn't move.

"C'mon Heinz," Karen shouted. He gave another bark but still didn't budge. "Something's spooked him," she said.

I was standing directly over the open end of the large pipe leading under the driveways. The smell here was at its most powerful and it was obvious that this was there the foul odour was coming from. I jumped into the ditch and peered into the yard wide drain. A small trickle of water seeped from the opening into the mud of the ditch. It was too dark inside to see anything but just as I was about to turn away I heard a sound. A scraping and shuffling noise echoing from deep within the pipe, then a soft gravelly cooing almost exactly like the cooing sound of a pigeon. A chill went up my spine. I was suddenly afraid. What the hell was I thinking about bringing my daughter to a deserted woodland area when there was a pandemic of murders going on all around?

I scrambled out of the ditch and walked quickly over to where Karen stood holding Heinz in her arms.

"Let's go," I said.

"What's up, Dad? You look worried."

"No, no. Just want to get back now. Come on." I linked my arm in hers and pulled her along the lane.

"Dad, you're frightening me. What's the matter?"

"I just think I've been stupid bringing you to a deserted spot like this with all that's been going on. Sorry love."

We arrived at the pile of dumped kitchen furniture and as I was helping Karen over it I had to stifle a cry of horror. Standing out clearly on the white surface of an old cupboard door was a large muddy footprint. No human foot could have made that print. It was massive with long toes, a huge bent thumb and muddy dots made by the tips of sharp claws. Karen hadn't seen it, thank God, but I fairly yanked her off the pile and down the lane until with a sigh of relief we reached the open space of the meadow.

"You saw something, didn't you." Karen said.

We slowed down so that she could catch her breath.

"What did you see?"

"Honestly, I didn't see anything. I just had the scary feeling that I might do. Now come on, let's hurry."

I yanked her along again, my heart beating fast and I kept looking over my shoulder to check that we were not being pursued, then at last after what seemed an eternity, we arrived back at the children's play area. Never in my whole life had I been more glad to see an armed policeman. They were still where they'd been earlier only looking slightly more bored. Karen was puffing hard. "For God's sake, dad," she panted. "Can we relax now? I wasn't expecting to run a flipping marathon! … and it's not the wisest thing to do when you're pregnant."

I couldn't answer straight away. My heart was still racing and I was blowing hard. "Sorry, sweetheart," I wheezed. "You have a very stupid father. We shouldn't have wandered into the wood. I had to get you safe."

We got back to the cottage and I immediately set about locking all the doors and windows, then I put the kettle on to make some tea. Karen took her cup to her room saying she wanted to give her husband, Geoff, a call, so while she was doing that I got on the phone to DI Vaughan to tell him about the footprint I'd seen. I dialled the number he'd given me earlier. A woman's voice answered.

"Hello, DI Vaughan's phone."

"Can I speak to him?"

"Depends who you are."

"I'm Fergus Munroe. Who am I speaking to?"

"This is his wife. Does he know you?"

"Yes. He knows me well. Can I have a word with him please?"

"If it's about police matters, no! He's having a well earned rest here with his family."

I sighed. "It's quite urgent. I think he'll want to hear what I have to say."

"They're all urgent. Have you got a pen?"

"I have."

"Write this number down." She rattled off a series of numbers which I had only just time to scribble down on the back of an old envelope. "That's his deputy's number. It's about time he did something instead of leaving everything to my husband."

"What's his na …? I started but she'd already put the phone down.

So much for the long arm of the law, I thought. It's handcuffed to its wife.

I dialled the number she'd given me and asked if I could speak to DI Vaughan's deputy and after only a few seconds a very deep baritone voice came on the line.

"Hello. Detective Sergeant Redmond. What can I do for you?"

"This is Fergus Munroe. It's about the murders around Morgan's Meadow."

"Ah," the voice said. "Fergus Munroe. DI Vaughan has told me all about you. What have you got?"

I told him about the walk with Karen and what we'd seen at the building site.

"So you smelt a bad smell. Might that not be just sewage?"

"There's something living in that pipe," I said, "… and I think it's the killer you are looking for."

There was a long pause then Redmond said in a world weary tone, "It's not long ago that you had us digging up a badger's sett. Isn't that right, Mr Munroe?"

"Yes. I think it lived there for a while and now it's in that pipe."

"Packed up all its furniture and moved house. Did it use Pickfords?"

I wanted to scream at him but instead took a deep breath and said in as calm a voice as I could, "I'm just a citizen trying my best to help. Remember I am more involved than most people living here. My wife was the first to be murdered."

He said nothing for a while then in a quieter tone he apologised. "I'm sorry, Mr Munroe. It was wrong of me and very rude. Look, tell me exactly where this building site is and we'll check it out in the morning."

I started to describe the route to the site and was about to mention the footprint I'd seen when he interrupted with "Oops, sorry Mr Munroe. I'll have to put you on hold. I'll be back in a sec."

His voice was replaced by loud pop music which after a deafening five minutes stopped and the line went dead.

I groaned and put the receiver down. It was obvious from Redmond's condescending tone that he like his boss thought that I was an interfering busybody, a bit of a nutter and a time consumer. It seemed that the police had given up on me.

I stood for a long time staring out at the gathering dusk through the metal bars in the window, clutching my mug of cold tea and wondering what I should do next. Karen must have let Heinz out. He was lying on the lawn chewing happily on one of those disgusting leathery dog strips which was almost as long as he was.

It seemed to me doubtful that Redmond would keep his promise to investigate the building site but I was certain that I was right. There was something living in that drain pipe. I needed someone to talk to but not my daughter. I didn't want to scare her more than I had done already. Perhaps I should give Peter Reilly a call or maybe my friend Charles. Or should I march straight to the police station and demand that they investigate my suspicion. I would go with them, lead the way, show them the footprint I'd seen.

I had been totally preoccupied by these thoughts when suddenly and abruptly I was jolted into focus by a terrifying howl from outside. A long piercing shriek of pain which almost made my heart stop. The mug of tea fell with a clatter to the ground and I lurched forwards both hands flat against the glass of the window. There, in the middle of the lawn, was the creature that had brought terror to the whole of the surrounding district. A nightmarish, hideous deformity with long powerful arms sticking out from a small stumpy body. It was ripping my beloved dog to shreds in front of my eyes with such ferocity that blood flew from its poor little body in great spouts which ran in rivulets down the creature's chest. I heard Karen call from upstairs. "Dad, what was that noise?"

I couldn't move, couldn't speak, my whole body was frozen in horror. I just stared at the carnage taking place outside, watched as this abomination stuffed parts of my pet into the slit of a mouth and threw partly chewed limbs to the ground. Suddenly it leant back on its haunches, threw back its tiny head and gave a long almost triumphant high pitched cackling laugh. The sound I'd heard before, like that of a Kookaburra bird. Then it turned and using its long hairy arms as crutches to swing its dwarf like legs forward it disappeared with remarkable speed into the bushes at the back of the garden. This had happened so quickly, so unexpectedly. I was paralyzed with shock and could hardly take a breath. I just stood staring blankly at the now empty lawn strewn with bits of fur and blood.

Karen brought me out of my stupor. She appeared beside me. "Dad, speak to me. What was that noise?"

I turned and grasped her by the shoulders. "I've got to go out. Lock the doors after me and don't let anyone else in but me. D'you hear?"

"But what's going on?"

I grabbed my coat, opened the back door and said, "I'll explain later. Lock the door!"

"But…"

"Do it!" I yelled and ran to the shed in the garden then armed with a spade I followed the direction the creature had taken through the bushes. It was getting dark. I climbed over the small wooden fence behind the shrubbery then headed along the hedgerow which led towards the meadow, holding the spade like a baseball bat ready to strike at anything that moved.

It was difficult to progress quickly. The ground was very uneven and soft from some recent rain. I stumbled frequently, my breath was coming out in great sobs and I swore silently to myself for not bringing a knife.

After about ten minutes I'd travelled maybe only two hundred yards so decided to climb through the hedge and on to the road so that I could move faster. Some instinct made me look back towards the cottage. The building stood like a silhouette against the fading light. Something was moving on the roof. I stopped, cupped my hands around my eyes and tried to focus on the shape, then it appeared clearly on the apex and headed towards the chimney. Long arms reaching upwards from a squat and misshapen torso. I screamed, "Oh no … no … no." The shock and fear numbing my whole body again. The beast must have circled back. I had thought the bars on the windows and the steel doors were security enough but I'd forgotten the inglenook fireplace with its wide chimney.

I rushed as fast as my panic filled body was able along the pot holed lane. My legs seemed to be working in slow motion and I had an agonising pain in my chest but at last I stumbled back into my garden where I had to stand for precious seconds clutching the wall and gasping for breath.

I knew that Karen would have obeyed my instructions to lock the doors so there was only one way in. I wrenched open the shed door, grabbed the small step ladder I kept in there and in seconds was standing on the shed roof, wobbling precariously towards the thick ivy that clad one wall of the building. I had to discard the spade in order to climb and I think it was sheer panic that gave me the strength to haul myself up on to the tiles above but I managed it, clawing myself up the incline and seconds later was staring down the black hole of the chimney leading into my living room twenty five feet below. Once again I caught the rancid smell of rotten meat. There was no time to climb down. I just threw myself into the black hole, crashing into the ancient rusty sweep's rungs as I fell and landing painfully on the pile of logs I always kept stacked in the hearth. The stench was appalling. I staggered forwards in a cloud of soot and dust on to the fireside rug. There were sheets and items of clothing scattered around the room and my ironing board lay on its side. Three yards away the creature stood over my daughter. Her eyes were closed and she seemed to be unconscious. One gigantic claw was pinning her to the ground while the beast's other hand was tearing at her dress. I saw a line of deep scratches oozing blood from the lower part of her neck and more blood flowed from a gash on her side.

The creature was making excited snuffling noises and that strange chittering sound I'd heard before like a roosting bird. It was so intent on its business that it completely ignored me or was unaware of my presence. Sticking out from its lower abdomen like a Nazi salute was an enormous horse sized penis, bloated, ugly and ready for action.

I turned and picked up the heavy poker that lay in the fireplace. For the first time the vile thing must have sensed danger for it suddenly swung one arm in a great arc and the back of its massive paw hit me hard on the side of my head, sending me sprawling across the room. It was as if it was swatting an irritating fly.

The beast hadn't taken its eyes off what it was doing. I got up groggily and approached from behind. The two hairy stubs of legs were apart and its testicles hung down between them like a sackful of melons almost touching the floor. I swung the poker like a golf club and smashed it as hard as I could into its balls. There was an ear splitting roar of agony and the thing turned to face me, arms flailing like windmills and only missing me by inches. Between the massive shoulders was a small lump of a head with angry tortoise like eyes on each side and a slit of a mouth turned down in a grimace of pain. I lunged forward again with the poker, but this time it could see me and was quick to react. It grabbed the poker on its downward arc, tore it from my grasp, bent it in two and threw it to the other side of the room. Then using those great long arms as crutches it swung its way towards me with its mouth open wide, revealing sharp pointed teeth and making loud AAAK! AAAK! AAAK! noises like a wounded hyena. I backed up against the wall but my legs had turned to jelly and I felt the strength draining out of me. I had no fight left and was sure that this was the end. One giant claw shot forward and clamped me by the throat then lifted me off my feet and threw me like a bundle of rags against the far wall. I crashed to the ground completely winded and gasping for breath then without having to move from the spot the creature reached forward, picked me up again and tossed me effortlessly over the settee and into a bookcase behind. I lay still, completely defeated. Blood was running down my forehead and into my eye and the whole room was spinning crazily.

Through a liquid curtain of blood I saw that my attacker had scrambled over a pile of fallen books and was now standing astride my body. I didn't care any more. I'd given up and wanted it over with. Every part of me was in pain and my right hand throbbed and burned as though I'd just shoved it into a furnace. I turned my head slightly and saw that the back of that hand was resting on a still plugged in iron which was quietly burning a hole through the carpet. Up above the creature had turned its tortoise like head and was scrutinising me with one bulbous eye. It was snorting and grunting and a long sliver of drool fell from its chin and landed on my chest, then it seemed to make a decision and raised one huge claw high in the air ready to strike.

I snatched up the iron and pressed it hard again the vile hairy belly which wobbled only inches from my face. The injured brute screamed and reared back clutching its smoking stomach. Scrambling painfully to my feet, I jammed the iron against its chest. Another scream. It flailed its arms desperately trying to hit me but I ducked under them, pulling the plug from its socket and whacking the iron hard against the now flaccid genitals. The deafening howl of pain and anguish that was let loose just then must have echoed around the whole village and continued as the agitated beast hopped around the room frantically looking for a means of escape from the hot iron until it eventually found the inglenook again and scrambled in a welter of plaster, dust and soot up the chimney to freedom.

I hobbled over to where Karen lay. She was deathly white but thank God still breathing. I lifted her up and laid her gently onto the settee, whispering reassurances so that everything was alright now and that she was no longer in danger. It must have been the mixture of overwhelming relief that we'd both survived and guilt about leaving Karen on her own that brought on a huge surge of emotion because I remember howling and sobbing like a baby as I cradled my daughter's head in my arms screaming at myself for leaving her on her own. I waited, then at last, after what seemed a very long time, her eyelids began to flutter and she groaned loudly. I stood quickly and covered her nearly naked body with one of the larger garments littering the floor. She opened her eyes and stared up at me. "Dad," she whispered, a big smile on her face before realisation dawned and she sat up, the smile changing to a look of terror. "Dad!" she screamed. "The thing is in the house ... the animal ... it hit me!" I held her by the shoulders. "It's alright, my darling. It's gone now. You're safe."

She glanced nervously around the room. "It ... it came up behind me ... I was ironing ... I didn't see it. How did it get in? ... Dad ... Oh my God, Dad ... has it gone?" I held her close, her whole body was trembling violently. "It's okay, darling. It's okay. I'm with you now," I whispered.

"But it's in the house ... It's here in the house!" she screamed. "Please don't let it get me."

"No, no. It's gone now. It can't harm you any more."

She turned her frightened eyes to me. "It was the thing wasn't it? ... The thing that's been murdering all those people."

I nodded. "Yes, sweetheart. I'm afraid it was."

"Oh God, I was so scared. Where were you? Don't leave me again. Please stay with ... is the thing dead?"

"Not yet."

Karen burst into tears. "I hate this place. I want to go home." She sobbed.

"Now Dad. I want to go home now!" She was on the verge of hysteria.

I patted her arm. "Okay, sweetheart. I'll give Geoff a call. He'll come and get you."

She clutched my hand and said in a trembling whisper, "Do you think I'll lose the baby?"

*****

I made two calls. The police got to the cottage first, the ambulance minutes later. Detective Sergeant Redmond was about six and half foot, an extremely handsome man who obviously spent quite a lot of spare time in the gym. Muscles bulged under the confines of his grey suit as though he'd poured himself into it then forced in a bit more. He moved like a panther almost floating across the room to shake my hand. I guessed he was in his early forties and learned later that he was from Nigeria.

He stared in astonishment at the carnage in my living room but before he could ask any questions the ambulance arrived. Karen was now wearing one of my old dressing gowns and looked very small and frail. There were still traces of blood on her face and a reaction to the ordeal she'd been through had set in. She was shivering and her teeth were chattering uncontrollably. The medics wrapped her in silver foil, took her blood pressure and did a couple of other checks before loading her into the ambulance and whisking her off for tests in the hospital five miles away. Before she went she pleaded with me. "Don't forget to phone Geoff."

I promised then went back indoors.

"You look as though you should be in hospital too," Redmond said as I walked in. He had a slight American accent. I nodded, made my way into the kitchen and held my head under the cold tap for a few seconds. Then I swallowed a couple of Paracetamol tablets. Redmond followed me in and filled up the kettle. "Where do you keep the tea?" he asked.

I pointed to the caddy on the work surface and watched as he prepared two mugs. He handed me one. "Here," he said with a smile. "This might help."

The two young policewomen he'd arrived with must have looked a bit peeved that they were excluded so Redmond said, "Tea's in there girls, help yourselves."

He turned to me. "Do you mind?"

I shook my head and we sat down. "Right," he said, taking out his notebook. "What happened here?"

I described as best I could how the creature had unexpectedly appeared on my lawn and killed my little dog, how I'd stupidly tried to follow the thing armed only with a spade and how fortunate it was that I'd happened to look back and seen the beast climbing on to the roof of the cottage. If I hadn't then my daughter would surely be dead.

"Quite a fight you put up," Redmond said.

"Thank God my daughter had been ironing."

"Yeah. You sure took the creases out of it's wedding tackle." He tapped his note book with his pen then asked, "What d'you think this thing is?"

I tried to explain my theory of how the creature came to exist but I could see that I'd lost him when I started to talk about hauntings from the past.

"So you think this thing that's been going around killing and raping is a hybrid, half man, half animal. Is that scientifically possible?" He looked at me with a 'come on, you must be joking' look.

"What other explanation could there be?"

He sat for a while stroking his chin then took out his phone.

"S'cuse me a moment," he said, then, "where did you say that building site was?"

After I'd described how to get there he gave instructions for a squad of armed police to investigate the site immediately and to shoot anything that moved in the vicinity of the drain under the driveways.

"I don't know for sure that's where the thing is living," I said when he'd finished his call. "Your boys may find nothing. But I did hear something and the smell there was the same that you can smell now, here in this room. I opened all the windows earlier but you can still smell the stinking thing."

He smiled. "Yep. He could sure do with a good deodorant."

There were a few more questions but I was glad when at last he stood to go. I was desperately tired and keen to take off my smelly clothes. Uppermost in my mind was to wallow in a hot bath and perhaps ease all the aches and pains away.

"I owe you an apology," Redmond said at the door. "We thought you were a bit of a crackpot but now you've been proved right. Sorry."

"Good luck," I said. "I hope you kill the bastard."

A policewoman opened the car door for him and as he squeezed his massive frame inside he said, "I'm afraid we'll have to question your daughter ... but not straightaway of course. Maybe tomorrow."

The car started to move, then stopped. The window wound down and he said, "And get that chimney blocked up!"

They drove off. I got on the phone to Karen's husband Geoff then ran myself a hot bath.

It was at this point I decided to write this version of events. I wanted to get it down on paper before anything happened to me. I'd seen the creature full on and was sure it would remember me, so I was scared, really scared. It knew where I lived and most certainly would want revenge for the burns I'd inflicted. This caused me to be apprehensive, nervous and extremely jumpy for twenty four hours of every day.

There had been persistent doubts about my innocence throughout the dreadful catalogue of deaths and mayhem that tore our once peaceful village apart and I wanted to set the record straight by telling my story right from the beginning, so now I'm up to date.

Karen was kept under observation at the hospital for nearly a week. Meanwhile Geoff moved in with me and helped me clean up the damage in the living room. He was not his usual placid self. Now he was tense and nervous, continually peering up and down, never able to relax for long and when he did sit it was on the edge of his chair, one leg twitching and pumping up and down as thought he'd left some internal engine running.

He complained about the heat in the cottage and scoffed when I explained that as a precaution I kept the fire going in the inglenook until I could get some bars fitted to the top of the chimney. It was impossible to convince him that what had attacked his wife and me was anything other than human. He was having none of it. "I think you've been at the magic mushrooms" he'd say, or "You're kidding yourself. It's a bloke or an animal. Can't be both."

Together we visited the hospital every day. Geoff eagerly striding quickly along the corridors yards ahead of me as I hobbled along clutching a walking stick. The bruises that covered almost my entire body were now of so many different hues I could have won the Turner prize and my right hip felt as though it had been torn from its socket.

Karen was still quite tearful but obviously very pleased to be reunited with her husband. She told us she hadn't been sleeping well and had been having repeated nightmares about the creature breaking into the hospital in search of her. She also gave us the good news that the baby apparently was unharmed by the recent trauma and that she could expect a normal confinement.

"Have you been interviewed by the police yet?" I asked.

"Tomorrow," she replied. "… and I'm not looking forward to it."

"Tell them no!" Geoff said. "You don't want to go through all that again.

"It'll be fine. It has to be done."

He sat forward on his chair, his leg bouncing. "Are the boys in blue buying all that stuff about a monster, half man, half animal?"

"They'll have to because it's true," Karen said angrily.

"But you didn't see it."

"It came up behind me. I felt it though and I believe Dad's description. It's a foul, unnatural thing and it could have killed me."

He shook his head. "It'll be a bloke, you'll see. A nutter dressed in scary gear pretending to be Dracula."

"You're being a complete prick, Geoffrey," she snapped. "What attacked me was not human."

Two days later Karen was discharged from hospital and straight away came back to the cottage, packed her belongings then the pair of them scuttled back to their home in Brighton. I was not surprised. Who would want to spend another minute in a place where they'd narrowly missed being ripped to pieces?

Apparently Karen's interview with the police had not been as bad as she had expected. Detective Sergeant Redmond had questioned her gently and with great respect. Her description of events tallied exactly with mine, so at long last my story had been accepted by the law. I left vindicated and extremely relieved.

The next day two friendly Polish builders arrived and proceeded to fix a heavy metal grill to the top of my chimney. At once I felt a huge surge of relief. I'd been terrified that the creature would return to seek revenge for the burns I'd inflicted. In the early evening I received a phone call from a very disappointed Redmond to say his team of armed police had gone to the site with sniffer dogs and had found nothing. He said that there were signs something had been living in the drain, excrement and the bones of so far unidentified small animals but nothing resembling the creature I'd described. None the less during day light hours a policeman had been stationed at the site in case the thing returned.

"I hope he's armed," I said.

"You bet," came the reply "... and he's a crack shot. We'll keep him there for a couple of days then I reckon we'll have to re-think."

"Sorry you've wasted your time."

"No matter. We'll get there in the end." He paused then continued, "I hope you don't mind, Mr Munroe. But for the time being we'd like to keep quiet about your recent attack. I reckon if the news got out that this thing has been seen in your garden and that it tried to kill you and your daughter there'd be a widespread panic. Things are bad enough now. What do you think?"

"Suits me fine," I said. "I'd be swamped by journalists again. I've had enough of that."

"Great. I hoped you'd say that."

When the call finished, I swore loudly. I'd felt certain that we were near the end of the affair, that the police would find the vile creature, kill it and we could all live without fear once again. Now it seemed we were back to square one. The beast seemed to be constantly one step ahead of everyone. Where the hell was it hiding now?

I needed something to lift my depression so I rang Peter Reilly and asked him if he'd like to join me for a pint at the pub. There was a two second hesitation before he agreed.

I got there first and bagged a small table in the snug bar. It was early and at that time of night there were only a few customers but I knew it would get very crowded later on. I ordered a couple of pints and had just sat down again when Peter arrived.

"Ah," he said, parking himself on the chair opposite and looking longingly at his glass. "There's a sight to warm the heart. How are you, Fergus?"

"I'm fine," I said. "It's been a while."

"It surely has. God save us. What a time we're all going through."

"What have you been up to?"

"Ah, not a lot," he said. "Keeping myself to myself mostly. I'm still missing Rosemary. She's left a big gap."

"Of course."

"But it's nice to see you again Fergus. Have you been in a fight by any chance?"

I laughed and touched the big yellow and blue bruise on my cheek. "You should see the other fellow."

"Whoever it is. He's a scoundrel, rearranging your features like he has. What happened?"

I remembered the promise I'd given to DS Redmond but felt sure I could trust a friend like Peter not to tell anyone else my story. After all he was a man of God.

"The police think I'll start a mass panic if I tell you about it." I said.

"Okay. That's fine. None of my business." He lifted his glass. "Cheers."

I clinked my glass against his. "But it is precisely why I asked you to meet me here. I need to talk about it," I said.

"Ah. Then you have a dilemma, so you have. I have to admit I'm intrigued and all ears too." I smiled. His face was a mask of cherubic innocence.

"Okay," I said. "Are you sitting comfortably?"

I recounted the whole story beginning with the horror I felt when I was at the building site with Karen and how sure I'd been that there was something living in the drainpipe. I told him about seeing my little dog being slaughtered and ended by describing my terrifying fight to save my daughter.

When I'd finished he sat for a long time, a look of pure astonishment on his face, then "So you were right all along?"

"It seems so."

"The same creature you read about in that old notebook you found?"

"Almost identical."

He shook his head. "This is the strangest story I have ever heard. Your poor wife was carrying in her womb a malignant thing … a parasite. Oh God. The devil's child!"

I patted his arm. "No, Peter. The devil had nothing to do with it. This was a man made creature. The produce of two mad German scientists tampering with nature."

He put his chin in his hands and stared at me. "I still can't understand how a spirit, a ghost if you like, of some long dead hybrid could impregnate your lady. It's … it's something without substance producing substance. Not possible surely?"

I nodded. "I don't get that part of it either, but scientists would have us believe their big bang theory. How the earth and the whole universe were created from nothing but gases. Bit hard to get one's head around that one too."

Peter thought about that for a while, then pointed at my empty glass. "Talking of which," he said. "I see a massive void … an area of complete nothingness ... a vast empty space. Shall I give it some substance?"

I laughed. "Go ahead, Einstein."

He got up and ordered two fresh pints.

"Tell me more about this building site," he said as he sat down again.

"I'm sure there was something in that drainpipe. I could feel its presence. I have to admit I was scared stiff. I had to get my daughter out of there. Shouldn't have taken her to such a deserted spot in the first place. So stupid of me."

"Thank heavens you did get her away ... this thing, this hybrid. It moves about a bit doesn't it?"

"Yes. It has intelligence. I think it deliberately keeps moving house to avoid being caught."

"And where is this place? I certainly don't know of it."

I told him about the unmade track leading from Morgan's Meadow. "We just stumbled upon it. I think the builder gave up on the project years ago."

"How strange when there's a housing shortage in the area. What went wrong I wonder."

I shrugged. "Not sure. Boggy ground possibly. Water table too high. But I got the weirdest feeling of menace when we were there and when I saw that muddy footprint I was convinced I'd found the hiding place.

"What did the police say about the footprint?"

"Sadly it rained before they got there and it had washed off."

"That's a bummer." Peter sighed. He pulled a small diary from his inside pocket and thumbed through the pages.

"I have to see a parishioner in the morning but afterwards I'm free all day. You've aroused my Irish nosiness. Why don't we go together and have another look at this building site. See if you feel the same way on a second visit."

Even though I'd been scared witless the first time this suggestion appealed to me a lot. To go again without the responsibility of my daughter's safety would maybe satisfy the overwhelming curiosity I'd been feeling for the past few days.

"Okay," I said. "Maybe you'll get the same vibes as I did. What time shall we go?"

"What about just after lunch … say two o'clock?"

"Are you sure now, Peter. It could be dangerous."

He polished off the rest of his drink. "If the police found nothing then I expect we will too. Besides I'm fed up being on my own and just staring at the wall in the vicarage. It'll be an adventure."

I picked up the empty glasses. "Fancy another?" I asked.

"Stupid question."

I went back to the bar. The pub was filling up and I could see through the glass screen which separated the snug from the saloon Ted McSweeney in conversation with a couple of other locals. This gave me food for thought.

"I think we should take precautions," I said when I returned to the table.

"Precautions?"

"Yes. Just in case. Remember this creature is a killer. I've seen the vile thing. I know how strong it is. We wouldn't stand a chance if it suddenly appeared."

"What kind of precaution then?"

"A gun. I know someone who owns a gun. If we could borrow it I'd feel a lot safer."

"Who?"

I got up. "Hang on a minute, he's next door."

I asked the barman to tell McSweeney there was a pint waiting for him in the snug if he could spare a moment. Within minutes Ted had joined us at our table. "What's going on?" he asked, clutching his new pint. We told him what we intended to do and I asked if could borrow his shotgun.

He laughed. "That ain't allowed. Against the law. You've got to 'ave a licence. Besides which 'ave you ever fired a gun?"

I shook my head. "Can't be that difficult can it? You just point it and pull the trigger."

He winced and turned to Peter who said, "I don't really need a gun when I'm in the pulpit."

"Well then," Ted said. "Looks as if I'll 'ave to go along with you. I'm not lendin' any weapons to a couple of oiks like you two. Probably blow your own foot off."

"He's right," Peter said, looking at me. "What do you think?"

Ted held up his hand before I could answer and said, "Look. All three of us 'as lost someone dear to that bloody thing what the coppers can't catch an' if I could shoot the bastard I'd die an 'appy man."

"We may not find anything," I said. We're only going to have a look."

"Nothin' gained, nothin' lost," he growled.

With that we drank up and went our separate ways. I came straight here to my study to do what I always do each evening … record the events of the day. It's not just a diary, for me it's an obsession. If I don't get it down on paper straight away little details or sometimes whole conversations get forgotten. So here I am thinking about Ted McSweeney. The little man with his flat cap and scruffy wellington boots. A bit of a scrounger right enough but a stalwart of the village, a forgiving, warm-hearted man and now a good friend. I'm glad that he's joining Peter and I on our trip to the building site. When I agreed to go it was with a good deal of trepidation remembering the fear I'd felt on my first visit, but now that Ted is coming along with his trusty shotgun I feel a lot braver. We arranged to meet here at the cottage tomorrow afternoon. The three musketeers are on the case.

PUBLISHERS NOTE

It was at this point Fergus Munroe's log came to an abrupt end. These unfinished hand written pages were found in his study by his daughter, Karen Philips. It seems obvious that the author intended to complete his bizarre story but sadly due to further events was unable to do so.

However, much later Karen visited the Reverend Peter Reilly and persuaded him to write his version of what happened on that fateful afternoon.

There follows his account of events which concur exactly with the statements he and Mr McSweeney gave to the police immediately after the tragedy.

THE REVEREND PETER REILLY'S ACCOUNT OF EVENTS

When I arrived at Fergus's cottage that afternoon he had prepared some sandwiches and was packing them along with three bottles of water into a haversack.

"Ah, so it's a picnic we're going on," I remarked.

"Y'never know. Later on we might appreciate a bite to eat. Be prepared. That's my motto," he said.

"Where's McSweeney?" I asked.

"We're picking him up on the way," Fergus answered. "He rang earlier. Said he was preparing something."

"Oh? Maybe he's doing a picnic too."

"I don't know what frightens me more," Fergus said. "The creature or the thought of eating sandwiches prepared by Ted."

We left the cottage, locked the door and set off down the lane. It was a cold afternoon and the sky a leaden grey with dark threatening clouds building up behind us as we walked. Fergus was clutching a walking stick and wearing a short green Barbour raincoat and a black woollen bobble hat and I was glad of my scarf and the two jumpers I had underneath my leather jacket.

We got to McSweeney's shop where his daughter told us he'd be down in a minute, so we perched ourselves on the edge of the old stone horse trough outside and waited. It would be another ten minutes before Ted finally put in an appearance. He was accompanied by an older man with a florid face and small grey moustache who stood tall and straight backed carrying a silver handled walking stick under one arm. He didn't need to be wearing uniform. Ex army was stamped all over him.

"Sorry to keep you waiting," Ted said with a wide smile. "This is an old army colleague of mine. Captain Oxenford."

"Nice to meet you, Captain," we chimed, shaking the proffered hand.

"Ditto," he said, not asking our names. Instead he turned back to Ted.

"Be careful, Ted, and remember not a word. There'll be hell to pay if this gets out."

"Don't worry. It'll probably be unused," Ted responded, "… and thanks. I'll be in touch."

Oxenford shook his hand and then turned to us. "Gentlemen," he said with a nod before walking briskly towards an old Jaguar saloon parked a few yards from the shop.

"What was all that about?" Fergus asked.

"I'll let you know later," Ted replied. "Depends," he added mysteriously.

Oxenford's car drove past us with a brief toot and the three of us set off down the lane.

"You're up to something," Fergus said, trying to keep up with Ted's pace, "... and if the army's involved probably something dangerous."

"And illegal by the sound of it," I said.

Ted flapped his hands. "Don't worry. It's all under control. Let's just say if there's summat in that drainpipe you told me about, it'll be sorry."

"We're only going to have a look," I said. "I'm hoping we won't find anything. I'm not much good at running nowadays."

Fergus nodded. "Yeah. Nor me, if we do see something we'll let the police deal with it."

"Police?" Ted snorted. "They're bloomin' useless. If they ever catch this bloody animal they'll probably only charge it with loitering. I've been to a lot of trouble before comin' out here. I thought you'd be pleased."

"How can we be pleased if we don't know what you're up to?" We quickened our pace and soon arrived at the entrance to Morgan's Meadow, Ted grumbling all the while about not being appreciated. The meadow seemed to be completely deserted. A light drizzle had started to fall and the grass was wet and slippery, while up ahead more dark threatening clouds were gathering. Ted stopped and leant heavily against a tree. He was breathing heavily. "Sorry," he wheezed, "goin' a bit too fast. Gettin' old."

To tell the truth I was glad of a rest myself. "Shall I carry the rifle?" I volunteered.

"No, no. Wait on. Just a quick breather."

We waited silently until he recovered then at a much slower pace made our way through the puddles until we reached the far side of the common. A line of daffodils drooping from the rain stretched along the perimeter and we followed them until we reached an overgrown track leading off into thick woodland. "This is the place," Fergus said in a whisper. "Mind how you go. There's all kinds of rubbish to climb over."

Ted removed the gun from his shoulder and slid two cartridges into its chambers then tucked it under his arm. We entered the track nervously, glancing from side to side and only talking in whispers. As Fergus had warned it was rough going. There were deep rain filled potholes to wade through, branches and fallen trees to clamber over, low hanging branches to duck under and just to make it a proper obstacle course some kind soul had blocked the whole path by dumping a pile of unwanted kitchen units on it. Old doors and flattened drawers, some whole but mostly in bits were stacked like a wall in front of us and strewn on either side beneath the trees and bushes.

Fergus immediately started grabbing bits of kitchen and lobbing them off the path and into the trees on either side. "Just in case we have to make a quick getaway," he explained.

"Oh thanks for those reassuring words," I said, suddenly feeling even more nervous than before. I gestured to Ted and soon all three of us had the path cleared.

After a couple of hundred yards we reached the building site. It was exactly as Fergus had described. A few bits of wall standing on slabs of concrete, strewn with rubble, planks and rusty sheets of corrugated iron. Somebody must have spent a lot of money before their dream collapsed. We approached the drain under the driveways warily. Ted had the shotgun balanced in his hands, cocked and ready to fire as we crouched by the entrance to the pipe and listened. There was nothing, not a sound. Neither was the smell that Fergus had experienced apparent. Just a very unremarkable drain. My heart had been pumping hard. I think I expected something to pounce out and slaughter us all but the very ordinariness of the place calmed me. We walked over to the first building and stood on the footings hoping to find footprints or maybe spoor that would indicate recent occupation but found nothing.

Fergus said, "I think the police must've given up on this place. They told me there would be somebody here during the day."

"Poor bugger's probably gone home," Ted said. "Can't say I blame him."

We strolled through the debris to the middle house. Again there was not much to see but then we heard a call from the track behind us. We all jumped.

It was a woman holding an umbrella in one hand, a dog's lead in the other. On the end of the lead was a rather chubby Norfolk terrier. She was about seventy years old, quite short with black hair and wearing a bright red headscarf tied around her neck.

"You won't by buying one of them, love," she shouted. "They'll never be finished. Builder went bust." We walked over to her. "We're not here to buy," Fergus said, "just being nosey. What happened here?"

"Well," she said taking a deep breath as if she was at her garden fence and about to have a good gossip with a neighbour, "whoever it was what did the plans for this place must've been bonkers. Who'd want to live out here in the first place, cut off from everything? Not me for sure even if I could've afforded it."

"Were they going to be rather grand?" I asked.

"Ooh, very. I think it was an American bloke. The houses were going to be real luxury. Four bedrooms each with its own bath and loo and it was going to be American style too. You know, big basement for the utilities and a games room. Very posh."

"So what happened?"

"The whole thing was a mess. God knows how he got planning permission. If he'd bothered to check with the council they would've told him this is a flood plain. He'd only just got the basements in and in no time they'd filled up with water. The concrete cracked with the pressure. Water nearly pushed them out of the ground like boats."

"Typical Yank," grunted Ted.

She nodded. "I walk past here nearly every day and sometimes the pong is terrible. At first I thought it was a sewage problem but it can't be can it? There ain't no sewage 'an never has been. Weird or what?"

"What happened to the Yank," Ted asked.

"I'm told he scarpered back to America leaving a lot of debts." She glanced down at Ted's shotgun. "What's the gun for?" she asked. "You shooting rabbits?"

"No, it's for protection," I told her. "Surely you've heard about a creature that's been roaming these parts. It's pretty dangerous. You really shouldn't be out walking on your own."

"Oh yeah, I've heard. The panther thing. It doesn't bother me. Besides …" she pointed at her little dog. "I'm not on my own. I've got Cyril. He'll see it off."

As if to acknowledge this the dog gave a couple of barks and tugged at its lead.

"Must go," the woman said, "it's past his supper time."

"Nice to meet you," we all chorused.

When she'd gone Fergus turned excitedly to face us.

"Are you thinking what I'm thinking?" he asked.

"Basements!" Ted and I said together.

We walked quickly back to the first house. Now we knew what we were looking for it was quite easy to find. Partly hidden by the rubble and litter strewn across the footings were two sheets of corrugated iron held down by breeze blocks at each corner. Ted held his gun at the ready while Fergus and I picked up one of the sheets and moved it to one side. A gaping hole was revealed with rough concrete steps leading down to a lake of greenish water below. Bits of plastic and old bottles floated in the mire and a small furry rodent swam hurriedly away from the sudden bright light. Fergus gestured to Ted to be ready with the gun and walked slowly and warily down till he was standing on the last slab above the waterline.

"Jeepers," he said, his voice echoing off the walls. "It's vast. You could fit my whole house in here."

"What d'you see?" Ted called.

"Not much. Just a great big empty space. The water's about a foot deep. It's very cold down here." He climbed back up to join us. "What a place," he said. "Shame it's not finished. It would've been a real palace."

I looked down at the water below and tried to imagine what it could have been like. Wooden bannisters leading down the carpeted stairs to a place where a family could eat, play games, do their laundry, have parties, watch television. A film star or maybe a famous footballer would entertain here.

We pushed the corrugated iron sheets back into place and walked across to the middle house. It was identical to the first. The hole in the floor in exactly the same place. We moved the cover away. This time it was my turn to go down. I turned the light of my mobile phone on and crept nervously down the steps. "Why didn't I think of that?" Fergus whispered.

It was quite eerie down there in that vast cavern and as Fergus had found, very cold. The walls were covered in green slime which indicated that the water here was at times much deeper. There were lots of pipes running up the walls on one side and in one corner I could see the top of a small door just visible above the waterline. I climbed back, happy to be out.

"It's a bit like visiting the remains of the Titanic," I said. "What a colossal waste of money."

"Tell you what," Fergus said, "let's have a gander at the last house then we'll have a sandwich and go home. You've got to admit it's been interesting.

"Good idea," Ted said. "Lead on McDuff."

It was as we crossed from the middle house to the last one in the line that we became aware of the smell. Faint at first, then getting more powerful as we approached. A sour, acrid odour of sewage but tinged with a sharper scent like ammonia which made the eyes sting. I felt the hairs on the back of my neck rise and a nervous fear gripped my insides. Ted was now pointing the gun at the corrugated iron sheets just ahead of us. We had slowed to a snail's pace and I heard Fergus whisper, "One of the covers has been moved!" Sure enough one corrugated sheet had been shifted to one side and there was now a gap about six feet wide leading down to the third basement. Ted crept forward, finger on trigger and squinted down the hole, then turned to me and gestured for my mobile phone. I switched the torch on and handed it to him. He knelt down and pointed the light into the recess, moving from side to side then suddenly he screamed and reared back on his knees, his eyes wide with shock. "Oh, Christ almighty," he gasped.

We rushed forward. The basement was exactly the same as the previous two. Full of slimy water with all manner of debris floating on the surface but on the bottom step half in and half out of the water was a human arm. It wore the remnants of a sleeve and attached to the sleeve by a few threads floated the ripped remains of a blue uniform bearing the word 'Police'.

As one we moved as fast as we could away from the hole. Ted was muttering, "Oh my God, oh my God!" and Fergus was walking around in circles his head clasped in his hands, retching and gasping as though he'd been punched in the stomach. As for me, my body had begun to shake uncontrollably, my teeth were chattering and I couldn't stop whimpering. It was difficult to put one foot in front of the other and I couldn't breathe. All I wanted to do was to get out of there.

At last Fergus stopped pacing and pulled out his phone. He punched in a number and after a few seconds someone must have answered because he was yelling in a high pitched, almost hysterical voices, "Redmond, we're at the building site. You've got to get over here fast. Your officer has been killed. Hurry, for God's sake, hurry!"

"Let's go, let's go," I croaked, trying desperately to get my numbed body to move.

"Yeah, let's get out of here!" Ted screamed but Fergus was holding up his hand to silence us. He pointed towards the hole. We stood stock still and listened. For a few seconds I heard nothing then the noise came. A splashing sound echoed up from the chamber below as though something was wading through water then came a loud deep throated cooing like a much amplified pigeon. Suddenly one of the corrugated metal sheets that had been partially covering the entrance to the basement flew high into the air and crashed noisily to the ground yards away. Out of the black pit a long hairy arm appeared, a huge clawed hand grasped the edge of the top step and the creature that Fergus had so accurately described hauled itself up on to the flat concrete base. It was the most vile and repulsive thing I have ever seen. A very small body with immensely long arms and a tiny head. It stood staring at us for a moment or two, water cascading from its limbs, the head moving from side to side. The bulbous eyes on each side seemed to be summing us up while we stared back unable to move, like rabbits caught in the headlights of a car. Then, with incredible speed, it shot towards us propelling itself along using the long hairy arms like crutches to swing the grotesque body forwards. It headed straight for Fergus. Indeed, it seemed to recognise him and was screeching, its mouth open and snarling with anger. "AAAK. AAAK, AAAK!" One massive claw was reaching out but before it connected with Fergus's throat a shot rang out. It turned. Ted stood barely one yard away from the beast, smoke coming from the barrel of the shotgun in his hands. Incredibly, even from that range, he had missed. He attempted to raise the gun again but it was too late. The thing was upon him wrenching the weapon from his hands and tossing it to one side. Then in almost the same movement it swung its arm around and slashed poor Ted across the throat. He screamed, a spurt of blood flew from the wound before he was lifted from the ground and thrown across the open space to land in a crumpled heap on the concrete. Something fell from his pocket and rolled across the concrete with a metallic clatter.

To my eternal shame I was in such a state of terror that instead of rushing to help my friends I had thrown myself over one of the half built walls and only saw what happened next through a gap between some breeze blocks.

Fergus was scrambling on his hands and knees towards the shotgun which lay two or three yards away from his outstretched hands. I saw him pick up the round object which had fallen from Ted's pocket but he didn't have a chance of reaching the rifle. He too was picked up as though he weighed nothing then thrown viciously to the ground. The sound of a human body hitting the hard concrete with such force was sickening but then my poor friend was scooped up once more and swung by the ankles in a great arc before being hurled through the air like a sack of potatoes to land with a horrific crunch hard against the wall behind which I was hiding. Chunks of breeze block and a cloud of cement dust fell down on my face and chest.

The creature pulled itself forward and stood looking down at Fergus's broken body. I had flattened myself to the wet ground, face upwards, not daring to breathe but certain that this repulsive deformity must be able to hear the frantic beating of my heart.

For a long time it stood directly above me moving its head slowly from side to side as it surveyed the carnage then it arched its back, raised those huge arms high and let out a long cackling squawk like a laughing hyena. It was a cry of triumph.

I waited, eyes screwed shut in terror, expecting at any moment to be snatched up and thrown across the concrete like my friends but then I heard the scrape of its claws moving away. I waited a while then raised myself up and peered through the gap in the wall.

The beast was gone and so was Fergus. All I could see was the crumpled body of Ted McSweeney a few paces away. I rushed over. He was lying face down in a puddle of water which was rapidly turning red from blood seeping from a deep wound on his neck.

I turned him over on to his back. His face and forehead were grazed badly but I was relieved to see that he was still breathing. I took off my scarf and held it hard against his bleeding neck. Fortunately for Ted, I saw he had buttoned his mackintosh high up under his chin which must have taken the full force of the blow, otherwise I'm sure he would be dead.

After a few moments, his eyes flickered then opened. He stared up at me then said in a tired whisper, "Oh God. A vicar. I must be in heaven."

I forced a smile. "Still got your sense of humour then?"

"You okay?" he croaked. I nodded.

"Fergus?"

I shook my head.

He winced and screwed his eyes tight shut. "Oh shit!" He groaned then a second later his eyes opened in fear and in a panicky croak asked, "Where's that bloody thing now? Has it gone?"

Just then came the noise of something moving across the gravelly ground behind us. I whirled around, my heart back in my throat then I let my breath out with a sigh of relief. A very large African man was creeping slowly towards us. He was holding a pistol in one hand and waving the other at us. To his left were three armed policemen. He got up beside us and knelt on one knee. "Don't worry fellers, you'll be okay now," he whispered.

"Merciful heavens," said Ted. "The Cavalry!"

"Right. Where is it?" the man asked again in a whisper. "This thing that attacked you."

I pointed at the opening to the basement. He waved his arm at his three colleagues and they quickly moved to surround the hole pointing their weapons down into the darkness.

The big man reached forward and lifted the bloodied scarf from Ted's neck and gave a low whistle when he saw the open wound. "Stay calm, old feller. I'm going to call the medics."

"I think I've got a broken arm," Ted said "… and less of the old fellah."

The officer ignored him and spoke into a gadget he took from his pocket. "Redmond," he said. "We're gonna need a medic. Pronto. Got that?" He received an affirmative then turned to me.

"Where's Munroe?"

"The creature took him. I think he must be dead," I said.

Redmond cursed and shook his head. "Damn! What the hell were you old guys thinking about coming here in the first place?" He didn't wait for an answer, just stood up and said to me, "Stay with him, will you? The medics are on the way." He walked over and joined the other policemen. One of them produced a large torch which Redmond took and pointed it into the basement then got down on his hands and knees and shouted, "Munroe. Are you okay? … Munroe, can you hear me?"

Of course there was no reply. He walked down a few steps then reappeared a few seconds later. The four men then walked away from the hole and stood in a huddle, no doubt discussing what to do next.

By this time it was getting quite dark and also a lot colder. Ted had started to shiver violently so I covered him with my leather jacket and while we waited for the medical team to arrive I tried to keep his mind off the great pain he must have been in by chatting about anything that came into my head. Looking back he must have been relieved when they got to us if only to get a little peace.

At last they arrived. Ted was lifted gently on to a stretcher and I followed on foot till we got to the waiting ambulance at the end of the lane.

It turned out that poor Ted had not only got a broken arm. To add to his miseries he had also got two cracked ribs and a fractured collar bone. The wound to his neck had only been centimetres from his jugular. He'd been lucky. If this brave old man hadn't been buttoned up to the neck he would certainly not have survived.

I was only treated for shock so was released early. When the ambulance dropped me off at the vicarage. I went straight to my living room, poured myself a very large whisky and promptly burst into tears. Thinking about it as I write this I suppose it was a release. The past few hours had been the most traumatic in all my life. My head was filled with turbulent emotions. Relief that I'd survived, sadness because I felt sure that I'd lost a very dear friend and guilt that I'd chosen to hide rather than help my companions.

There wasn't much sleep that night. Where was that nasty vile freak now? Had it got Fergus? Was it still alive? Would there be any more deaths? On and on these questions tumbled through my head until at about six o'clock next morning I fell asleep through sheer exhaustion. However, my slumber didn't last long. I was woken at nine thirty by a loud hammering on my front door. Two large policemen were standing on the doorstep. One of them I recognised as Detective Sergeant Redmond and the other an individual with a very red face and shiny bald head who was introduced as Detective Inspector Nigel Vaughan.

"Sorry to bother you so early," Vaughan said glancing at my dressing gown and slippers with just a hint of sarcasm. "We need to talk to you about the events of yesterday afternoon."

"We could come back later if this is inconvenient," Redmond added.

"No, come on in," I said. "You'll have to excuse me. I haven't had a good night."

They entered and I showed them into the living room. "Sit yourselves down. I'll just move this whisky bottle. I had a wee nip before I went to bed."

"Can't say I blame you after all you went through," Redmond smiled.

"Can I get you anything … tea, coffee?"

"Thanks, no," Vaughan answered for them both. "You are not the only one who's had a bad night, Vicar. After you left my officers set up arc lights around the site and a team of frogmen searched the flooded basements thoroughly."

"Frogmen? The water was only a foot or two deep."

Vaughan sighed and said, "My men have to scrabble around on their bellies in the freezing cold water searching for clues, discarded food, bones, even bodies. It's not the easiest of occupations."

"I'm sorry. Did they find anything?" He shook his head. "There were signs that something had lived there recently. We found animal fur, probably rabbit of squirrel and a few bones which have been sent for examination but not a trace of the creature your friend Munroe described to DS Redmond here."

"What of Fergus?"

"Nothing, I'm afraid. He seems to have vanished into thin air."

"Well that gives me hope."

Redmond fished a notebook from his pocket, leaned forward in his chair and said,

"Reverend Reilly. It would help us a lot if you would describe as well as you can the events of yesterday. From the time you three gentlemen assembled together and set off on your walk right to the end, filling in as many details that you can remember."

I stood up. "I'm happy to help in any way I can," I said, "but I'll be much more lucid with an injection of caffeine. So you'll have to be patient while I make a brew. Are you sure you won't join me?"

DI Vaughan shook his head.

"Right then," I said when I returned with a steaming mug of Gold Blend flavoured by just a hint of whisky. "Are you sitting comfortably? Then I'll begin."

I went through the whole of yesterday, telling them what time the three of us had met, our walk along the lane and across Morgan's Meadow, the track leading to the building site and our meeting with the lady and her dog. When I got to the part where we were attacked and described the weird creature that attacked us DI Vaughan looked incredulous, rolling his eyes up to the ceiling and giving a little shake of his head. Perhaps I shouldn't have mentioned Fergus's theory about how the creature came into being because he screwed up his face in disbelief and looked on the verge of shouting 'Rubbish'. That part of it was completely beyond his comprehension.

"This thing," he smirked, "long hairy arms, you say, small body, stumpy legs? It sounds like the bogeyman from a children's story."

Redmond turned to him. "Can't fault it, Sir. That's exactly how McSweeney described the thing. Fergus Munroe too. Every detail the same, even down to the smell."

Vaughan shook his shiny dome. "It's beyond me. I really have to see this thing to believe it."

"If you ever do meet it you'll need clean underpants after," I said.

Redmond laughed but his superior ignored my little attempt at humour. "I'd be grateful, Vicar, if you would keep your description of the thing that attacked you to yourself. It would cause mass panic in the community if people were aware of the kind of creature we're hunting. I've asked McSweeney for his discretion on the matter too."

And with that parting shot they left.

EMAIL FROM PETER REILLY TO MRS KAREN PHILIPS (SENT FROM HIS IPHONE)

Hello, Karen. Just to let you know I've finished (as promised) my account of what happened before your dad disappeared. It's hand written as I'm the world's slowest typist. Are you at the cottage? If so shall I bring it there? When would it be convenient?

RETURN EMAIL FROM KAREN PHILIPS

Hi Peter. Wow, I'm shocked. You've actually charged up your phone at last. Welcome to the 21st century! I've been trying to call you for ages. Yes, I'm at the cottage sorting some of my dad's things. Been here a week. So pleased you've written down what happened. I'm looking forward to reading it. Are you free this afternoon? Karen x

KAREN PHILIPS'S STORY
(Written after her meeting with Reverend Reilly)

My favourite vicar in the whole world turned up promptly at 2 o'clock. He's such a gentle soul and possessed with enough charm to raise the Titanic. He arrived clutching a sheaf of papers and a bottle of Pinot Noir.

"Peter," I scolded. "I'm pregnant and not supposed to drink alcohol."

"Ah, so you are. Stupid of me. Save it for another time. Is there a beer in the house?"

After I'd settled him down in an armchair with a beer he said, "You've been here a week now. How does it feel to be back? Do you get scared? It must be difficult for you."

I'm still having nightmares about what happened here but I'm okay. Dad got the place looking like Fort Knox. Locks, bolts, grills are everywhere. It would have a heck of a job getting back in here again."

"True."

"D'you think he's dead, Peter?"

He shook his head and put his hand on mine. "I honestly don't know," he said.

"Why did you all go there? What made you do it?"

He shrugged. "Ted had a gun. We thought we'd be safer as there were three of us. Remember, we'd all lost someone dear to us. We needed to feel involved."

"Yes, and look where it got you! You should've left it to the police. You're all too old to be taking risks like that."

"I'm sorry, and you are right," Peter said. "We were stupid and far too old to do what we did. Ted was very slow with his gun. Have you told your brother?"

I nodded. "I left a message with his wife. He's away for a few days in a cabin they own a few miles from their house in Sydney. Apparently it's impossible to get a signal there."

Peter fell silent so I asked if I could read what he'd written. He handed me the sheaf of papers. "You're going to find it hard reading," he warned. "I didn't hold back!" I waved his warning away and started to read. He had lovely flowing handwriting. Bold and easy to read with very few crossings out. He sat quietly nursing his beer and waited for me to finish.

Peter was right. It was hard reading. When I reached the part where my poor father was being hurled around like a rag doll and thrown against the walls, I broke down and couldn't continue reading for some time. Peter brought me a glass of water and some tissues.

309

"You don't have to read any more," he said. I shook my head. "I have to know it all." So I finished his story and afterwards we both sat for several minutes not saying anything. I was imagining the scene, living the horror of what my poor dad had endured and clinging to the hope that somehow he was alive and was trapped somewhere.

"Where do you think he is?" I asked.

"If only I knew," he answered. "Please don't raise your hopes too much. That creature has no pity or scruples. It's a wild animal."

I thought about that. "Yes," I said. "You know when this is all over and someone finally kills this horrible thing, the press will be told to put it all down to an escaped animal, a panther or a wolf. Anything but what it is. The government and the police won't want the world to think scientists have created a monster. It'll all be hushed up, you'll see."

"I don't doubt you're right."

Well I think the story should be published. Why shouldn't the truth be told? I'm going to add your story to my dad's story and I'm going to take it to a publisher."

"Wouldn't it be better to wait till the creature has been found and disposed of?" Peter asked.

"My father would be pleased if I do it. Publish and be damned, he'd say."

Just as I said that there was a pinging noise.

"What the hell was that?" Peter said.

"I think it's your phone," I said. "Sounds like you've got a message."

He took his phone from his pocket and stared at it.

"Oh," he said. "I have four voice mails. I'll listen to them when I get home."

"Don't mind me," I said, "hope they're not urgent."

He dithered for a moment or two then said, "Alright. Excuse me. I can't resist a wee peek." He very ponderously jabbed at some buttons and I heard a very squeaky message being relayed. "Ah that's one of your calls that I missed," Peter muttered. "Don't need it now you're here ... Delete."

The next two messages were from me again and also got deleted. When the last and oldest message came through Peter suddenly reared back in his chair with a scream as if the phone was red hot. It fell to the floor with his empty beer bottle.

I jumped up and knelt beside him, quite sure he was having a fit. "What's the matter?"

"It's Fergus!" Peter yelled hysterically. "It's a message from your dad!"

We both scrambled on the floor for the phone. It had switched itself off. Peter keyed in his code and went straight to voicemail then turned up the volume. The line was extremely faint with lots of interference, crackles and gaps between the words but the voice was unmistakably my father's. He spoke slowly as though he was in considerable pain.

"Peter … It's me … Bloody thing's got me …
thinks I'm dead … hope you and Ted are okay
…
this is it for me, Peter … can't feel my legs …
something wrong with one arm …

(Here there were lots of words we couldn't understand under the crackling and interference) …

don't know where the beast is … I'm down some
kind of …….. hole … like a cave … don't
know where … I woke up in here …
roots of a tree hanging down on me …

(He stops to take a deep breath)

… battery low … hope you get this …
probably no reception

(He's breathing hard, almost panting)

… got a feeling this is one of its larders and I'm
on the menu … hope I choke the bugger … listen,
Peter … tell my kids … I love them … tell them

sorry … story in cottage … read it please

(He is interrupted by a screeching noise)

AAAK! AAAK! AAAK! … oh shit … here it comes … I can hear the bastard

(He starts shouting)

"GOT A SURPRISE FOR YOU, SHITFACE … YEAH, A PRESENT FROM TED …
(Panting for breath now)
COME ON, COME ON!

(More screeching coming closer)

… OH DAMN, THE PIN'S STUCK … OUCH … THAT HURT! … YOU UGLY PIECE OF SHIT! … AH, GOT IT. YES COME CLOSER YOU FUCKER …

COME TO DADDY … COME ON FUCKER! CLOSER …"

He was cut off by a dull thud, a brief crackling noise and then the phone went dead. I stared at it in horror. Numbed with shock. I'd just heard the moment of my father's death. Peter gripped my hand. I was too stunned to cry.

"Wh … what happened?" I said.

"I think your dad was carrying a hand grenade."

"What?"

"A grenade. I saw it fall out of Ted's pocket when he was attacked. Fergus picked it up."

"How would Ted get one of those?"

313

"Army contacts, I guess. I met one of them before we went to Morgan's Meadow. My thinking is they did a deal." Peter put his head in his hands and started to weep.

"Oh God, oh God," he mumbled. "Why didn't I pick up my phone? Poor Fergus ... dear, dear Fergus."

Now we were both crying. We clung to each other sobbing bitterly, both of us knowing the terrible ordeal my father had faced with such bravery, until there were no more tears to shed.

Eventually Peter stood up and went into the kitchen and when he returned with two mugs of tea he sat down beside me and said, "Your dad must have phoned soon after the attack, so he can't have been all that far away from where we were. My mobile was in my shirt pocket but I was wearing two jumpers over it and there was so much mayhem going on I didn't hear it ring. I'm so sorry. If I had we might have saved him."

I put my arm round his shoulder. "Even he didn't know where he was. How could he have been found in the dark?"

He sat thinking about this for a while then said, "I suppose you're right. My, my. What your dad did took some courage. He was very brave. I think one of the bravest and nicest men I've ever met."

He started jabbing numbers into his phone.

"Who are you calling?"

"The police," he said.

*****

The following day I found this article in the Mail.

Today the residents of Plaxtol and surrounding villages in Kent are heralding the bravery of one of their number, Mr Fergus Munroe. The community had been living in fear after a spate of brutal killings in the area. For months dozens of police have been searching for the perpetrator of these horrific attacks but without success. In total,eight people died including Mr Munroe's wife,Jennifer, earning the small hamlet of Monk's Green the sobriquet: "The village of the damned" after the science fiction novel by John Wyndham.

Now the local residents can breathe more easily, unlock their homes once again and feel safe to go outdoors.

The killer has been found and is dead.

The officer in charge of the investigation, Detective Inspector Nigel

Vaughan, gave us a brief statement which said that he had suspected all along that this was the work of a large animal, an escapee from a zoo or a travelling circus perhaps and so it has been proved. It seems that Mr Munroe was its last victim.

He had been snatched by the beast and taken to its lair near a deserted badger's sett in the massive woodland adjoining a park called Morgan's Meadow. Mr Munroe had somehow armed himself with a lethal explosive device which he detonated in the lair killing himself and the fearsome carnivore immediately.

The remains have been examined by scientists at police headquarters in Tonbridge who say they are one hundred percent sure that they are that of a black panther.

The police are making further enquiries with circus owners and local zoos.

Mr Munroe was a successful, award-winning cartoonist who worked on this paper for many years under the pen name "Gus". We salute his bravery. He will be greatly missed and leaves a son, Andrew, and a daughter, Karen.

*****

A huge crowd turned up for dad's cremation. Mostly grateful neighbours and other villagers from Monk's Green but also relatives of the people who died, colleagues from the Mail, a few policemen and of course the family. My brother Andrew flew over from Australia with his wife, Julie, and our mum Maureen drove down from London. A few distant cousins, some of whom I had never met, turned up unexpectedly too and all present hailed dad as a true hero who had given his life in order to save other possible victims. Of course there were tears all round, but mine were not only of sorrow but immense pride. My father was not only a hero, he was a very kind and generous man much loved by everyone who knew him closely.

It must have been difficult for Peter Reilly who conducted the service. I could see that he too was close to tears but he managed to struggle on and gave a very moving eulogy, carefully avoiding any reference to black panther's which both he and I knew to be utter tosh.

Dear, sweet Ted McSweeney. sitting in a wheelchair beside the lectern with one arm in a sling, read a poem by Christina Rosseti then later as we left the church my cousin, Finlay, played 'Scotland the Brave' on the bagpipes.

Somehow half the congregation of that huge church managed to squeeze themselves into dad's tiny home where we all raised a glass or two to say goodbye. Much later, when the four of us were sitting in the living room sharing a huge pizza and reminiscing about dad, brother Andy asked me more about the night I was attacked.

"I don't really know much about it," I said. "All I do know is the thing came up behind me, everything went black and the next thing I woke up and dad had got me in his arms."

"It can't have been a panther."

"That's for sure. Dad and his two friends have told me what it looked like. It wasn't an animal."

"A police cover up?" Julie asked.

"Yep, they don't want to panic the public with tales of man-made monsters wandering around the countryside."

"I still think it was a bloke," Geoff chimed in.

"The thing I don't understand," Andrew said, "... is how the police lab boys sorted it all out."

"What d'you mean?"

"Well, dad and this creature are in the confines of this hole, presumably right up close to each other. Dad detonates the grenade. Surely they would both be blown to bits. All their parts intermingled. How did they sort the two out?"

"DNA I suppose."

He was quiet for a moment or two then shook his head. "I dunno," he said, "I have a horrible suspicion we've just cremated bits of them both."

"Oh God, Andy! Why did you put that thought in my head?"

Over the next few weeks there was much to do. Andrew, Julie, Geoff and I stayed on to sort out dad's affairs. We arranged for a local builder to remove all the bars and grills from the windows and chimney then we put the cottage up for sale, having agreed earlier that half the proceeds from the sale should be shared by the families who had lost a loved one during the spate of killings. It seemed only fair. The house didn't take long to sell. The market had picked up considerably and so within a very short time we got and accepted a really good offer.

Nick and Tess Corbette were a delightful young couple who were about to take over the running of his parents' restaurant in nearby Plaxtol. They were a handsome couple, very bookish and wearing thick black framed glasses and looking more like librarians than restaurateurs. I liked them immediately and they had fallen in love with the cottage as soon as they saw it. Everything went smoothly. All was settled. The sale seemed done and dusted so we left the rest of the transaction in the hands of the agents. And that was it. Time to go home. Only one last thing to be done. On the day before Andrew and Julie flew back to Australia all four of us together with Peter Reilly and Ted McSweeney gathered in the cottage garden. Peter said a last prayer and we scattered dad's ashes between the shrubs and rose bushes.

Geoff and I stayed on for another week to sort out a few details with a solicitor and obtain death certificates then packed our bags ready for the return trip to our home on the south coast.

Our first stop, however, was at the vicarage. Peter's hallway was full of packing cases.

"Ah. It's time I was leaving," he explained. "The Bishop has accepted my resignation and I'm off to pastures new."

"The villagers will miss you," I said.

"Pah! Half of them don't know of my existence," he laughed. "I don't think they know what a church is. What's that big building with the pointy bit? I expect they say. I counted three people at my last service and two of them were asleep."

"Surely it's not as bad as that."

"I'm afraid it is," Peter sighed, "... besides which my heart's not in it any more. You'll no doubt have heard that saying 'The Lord giveth and the Lord taketh away'. Well as far as I'm concerned over the past few months I'm afraid he hath taketh away much more than he hath giveth. So I'm off."

We both laughed then Geoff asked, "Where will you go?"

"To my sister Rosemary's house. She had a wee place nearby before she moved in with me. There's been a tenant there for years but now by a stroke of good luck he's decided to leave. So I'm moving in." He waved his hand at all the heavy old furniture practically filling the whole room. "... and all this is going to the dump or the Red Cross and good riddance to it!"

Next up was a visit to Ted McSweeney's house who gave us a very warm welcome. He had dispensed with the wheelchair and was now hobbling around with the aid of a walking stick. He too had decided to retire and leave the running of the shop to his adopted daughter. "From now on," he proclaimed, "half my life will be spent getting the garden back to how it was when my dear wife was alive."

"And the other half?"

"Will be in the pub with a very dear friend who has recently retired from the clergy."

****

Two months later at a hospital near our home near Brighton I gave birth to a beautiful seven pound six ounce baby boy. He had a tuft of black hair and a pair of lungs like Luciano Pavarotti. We decided to call him Fergus. So after the mayhem and sadness of the past two years, life slowly returned to normal. The story of Monk's Green and of all the horrific deaths that happened there gradually faded from the newspapers and we were no longer pestered by reporters to tell our side of the affair.

I collected all my father's writings together with Peter Reilly's contribution and my own recollections and started contacting publishers. After the fabricated black panther account by the police it was important to me that the true story be told and made public. I got three immediate replies, so I emailed the manuscript then printed copies, parcelled them up and headed for the Post Office. It was when I was in the queue at the counter that I got a call on my mobile which made be scurry home again to add one last addition to the story.

"Hello?"

"Oh, hi. Is that Mrs Philips? This is Nick Corbette. My wife and I bought your lovely cottage."

"Yes, I remember. Is there anything wrong?"

"Well, no. Nothing wrong. Just mysterious."

"Go on."

"Did you ever live in the cottage, Mrs Philips?"

"I stayed there from time to time. It was my father's home. Why?"

"Oh, I expect we're being stupid and worrying about something trivial."

"I'm intrigued."

"Well, it's just that sometimes at night when we're sitting downstairs we hear a strange noise from the corridor above … like slow dragging footsteps."

THE END

Pressman
House

Printed in Great Britain
by Amazon

35019359R00183